Restaurant to Another World 2

"Welcome!"

WRITTEN BY

unpei Inuzuka

ILLUSTRATED BY

Katsumi Enami

The young lady dressed in a strange uniform greeted the newcomer.

"I'm Aletta, and I'm a waitress here at Western Cuisine Nekoya!"

"On the second floor of the Nekoya Building was a bar named 'Leonhart.'"

The master spent his early years as a salesman at a trading company before starting this little adult space some twenty years ago.

"Aye, Here's your katsudon!"

Yamagata, the previous master, gently lifted the lid.

A sweet, appetizing aroma filled the area surrounding the bowl.

This...
Why, it's
magnificent.

Shia took a bite of
the cookie. What
surprised her the
most was its texture.
By stacking multiple
thin layers atop one
another and baking
them, the cookie had
a softness to it that
made it remarkably
easy to bite into.

"Mm, I knew it! Natto pairs super well with rice!"

Fardania looked like a small child happily enjoying her food. Seeing this, Christian picked up his own fork and started to mix his food. After stirring in just the right amount of dashi soy sauce, green herbs, and yellow stuff, he added it all to the rice.

The young lady's hands were trembling. Perhaps she was unused to dealing with royalty like Tiana, or maybe the cautious group of faeries were making her nervous. Either way, she set down the plate on top of the table. In front of the small creatures of legend was a cloth-like object with light yellow and brown patches all over it. This cloth wrapped itself around some kind of white, soft-looking stuff and a host of colorful fruits. It almost looked like a bouquet of flowers.

"S-sorry for the wait. Here's your **fruit crepe!**"

洋食のねこや

In another world, once every
seven days appears a door with a
mysterious cat illustration on it.
Where it shows itself is entirely
random: it might appear in
the forest, some old ruins, a
desert, or perhaps even a town.
Just beyond this door and its
ringing bells lies...

*Western Cuisine
Nekoya*

Restaurant to Another World

VOLUME 2

WRITTEN BY

Junpei Inuzuka

ILLUSTRATED BY

Katsumi Enami

Seven Seas

Seven Seas Entertainment

ISEKAI SHOKUDO 2
© Junpei Inuzuka 2015

Originally published in Japan by Shufunotomo Co., Ltd.
Translation rights arranged with Shufunotomo Co., Ltd.
through Tohan Corporation Japan.

Seven Seas press and purchase enquiries can be sent to
Marketing Manager Lianne Sentar at press@gomanga.com.
Information requiring the distribution and purchase of
digital editions is available from Digital Manager CK Russell
at digital@gomanga.com.

Follow Seven Seas Entertainment online at
sevenseasentertainment.com.

TRANSLATION: Elliot Ryouga
ADAPTATION: Nino Cipri
COVER DESIGN: KC Fabellon
INTERIOR LAYOUT & DESIGN: Clay Gardner
PROOFREADER: Jade Gardner, Kris Swanson
LIGHT NOVEL EDITOR: Nibedita Sen
MANAGING EDITOR: Julie Davis
EDITOR-IN-CHIEF: Adam Arnold
PUBLISHER: Jason DeAngelis

ISBN: 978-1-64275-684-5
Printed in Canada
First Printing: September 2019
10 9 8 7 6 5 4 3 2 1

Restaurant to Another World

VOLUME 2

Nekoya's Menu

Special Business Days

M Y SHOP CAN BE FOUND in the basement of a building just around the entrance of the shopping arcade near the office district, only a five-minute walk from the train station of this small town.

Its name is "Western Cuisine Nekoya." My gramps started this place up some fifty odd years ago. We've been going ever since!

I know it says "western cuisine" in the name and all, but Gramps could be pretty *whatever* when it came to names. Our restaurant is well known for serving all sorts of dishes, western or otherwise.

Lunchtime is typically from 11 AM to 3 PM, with dinnertime being from 5 to 9 PM at night. The only day we're not open is Saturday, when the office district is fast asleep.

The most expensive item on the menu is 1,000 yen, and we offer free refills on rice, bread, and soup. See? We're not so different from most other joints out there.

...Well, except for one kinda strange thing that's unique to Nekoya.

I guess...

Every Saturday is a "special business day" here at the restaurant.

"Didn't you just say you were closed on Saturdays?" you ask? Well, yeah. That's why it's special.

Saturdays are when we get customers from the "other side."

All I really know is that Gramps started doing this thirty years ago. The only thing that matters to me is that there are folks over there who look forward to eating my food and indulging in my good buddy's cakes. That alone is enough for me.

Oh, that's right! I almost forgot.

The folks from the other side have a special name for Nekoya.

They call it...

The Restaurant to Another World.

Opening Prep

I REMEMBER IT like it was just yesterday. The first time I ever visited the master's restaurant, Western Cuisine Nekoya (known as the Restaurant to Another World to the other guests), was just as the seasons were changing and winter was coming to the capital. It was a frigid night.

I recall being holed up in some ruins just outside of the city, with nothing but a dirty, tattered cloth to cover my shivering body.

What am I gonna do?

I recall nearly succumbing to tears, thinking I was gonna die there. Even though tons of people lived in the bustling capital, finding a job was impossible. I didn't have a single copper coin to my name. The only food left was the meager rations I had for the evening. At the rate I was going, I would be dead long before winter arrived.

Maybe I should've never come to the capital, I thought.

I recall shivering from the cold air, as I had no wood to start a fire. I gently massaged the hard horns I hid beneath the hat I had worn since leaving my hometown. Why couldn't I have been born a human?

I'm a demon, and like all other members of my race, I received our dark lord's blessing. This meant there was a part of me that was inhuman. This varied from demon to demon. For example, some of us had strange eyes that could see things humans could not, while others had horns or a tail. There were those who grew scales from their body and demons with poisonous blood or sweat. I had even heard of demons with slime-like appendages they could stretch out.

Even if one's mother or father were human or half-elf, a member of the demon race would be born with the dark lord's blessing. That was inescapable. In my village, there was a child whose father was a human from the empire. Despite having human blood running through them, they were born with an even stronger blessing than usual. They grew lizard scales and had fangs that secreted poison.

The only blessings I received from the dark lord were small, black goat horns. According to the wise priest in my hometown, who had four large horns, demons who were born with them had a stronger connection to the dark lord than all others, giving them the right to become priests or priestesses. Unfortunately, I was born with so little power that I couldn't do the job. My own physical and magical strength was no better than your average human girl, so it wasn't as if I could do things that humans couldn't. As far as I was concerned, my demonic blessing was nothing more than a curse that brought me misfortune.

I was born and raised in a small town in the wastelands of the Kingdom. It was a poor place, with land that wasn't fertile enough to grow wheat or any other kind of meaningful crops. Mercenaries who had left to earn money in the empire came back with cobbler's tubers, the only thing we could grow in the barren fields. When I was a child, I don't recall ever having eaten my fill.

After my parents died from a disease that went around, I decided to leave. My big brother and sister had long since left home, becoming mercenaries and getting married, so I couldn't count on them for anything. I also knew that taking care of the tuber fields by myself was impossible, so I sold them to my neighbor and used the money to leave for the capital.

I think things went rather well at first. I managed to get a waitressing job at an inn at the capital, and I worked hard every day. Day-to-day life was a little tough at first, as I wasn't used to that kind of work. But they gave me the leftover vegetables, soup, and hard bread at the end of the day. If I'm being perfectly honest, it wasn't a life of luxury, but I made enough money to at least start saving.

Unfortunately, that life didn't last for very long. One day, my hat fell off my head. As soon as my horns were visible for all to see, it was over.

...I was just a young demon girl who grew up in a small town. I don't think I ever really understood what that meant to those of the outside world. I never understood how we were viewed by the humans in the Kingdom.

The night my horns were seen, I was chased out of the inn. They tossed all my belongings out as well. I was at a total loss.

Of course, I went searching for work as soon as I could. Unfortunately, my identity as a demon was already well known, so the only work I could find were day jobs for people with physical strength. There were times when even those ran dry.

I tried to be as frugal as possible, but my savings depleted faster than I expected. That's when I found myself living in the ruins of the capital, a place that not even the poorest of the poor would choose to call home. I shivered from the cold.

"I suppose I should eat."

The sun had long since set, meaning it was dangerous to walk around. I pulled out the last cobbler's tuber I bought with my remaining money in the hopes of staving off my hunger. A few days earlier, I used some abandoned fire wood I found outside the city to boil the tuber. I figured it wouldn't go bad for a while given the time of year.

Despite how hungry I was, the tuber was anything but delicious. It went without saying that it was cold, but it was also dry as sand. At one point, I half expected it to get caught in my throat. The only real flavor it had came from the dash of salt I sprinkled atop of it. I washed this all down with some lukewarm water.

Regardless of its flavor, the tuber at least helped fill my empty stomach. That alone was enough to put me comparatively at ease.

"I should go to bed."

Once I was finished eating, I had nothing else to do. I curled my body into a ball to keep warm and closed my eyes, forcing myself to sleep.

I had no way of knowing how much my own fate would change the next time I woke...

At least, not yet.

*Restaurant to
Another World*

CHAPTER 21
Fried Rice

THE RED QUEEN raised her face from the now-empty pot of beef stew that she had spent the entire day enjoying from atop her blisteringly hot, golden bed.

Hm?

In the back of her mind, she saw the image of a demon living in a human city. It was a female with golden blonde hair and two black horns. The Red Queen had no memory of such a creature.

Unlike White, who bred and took care of hundreds of thousands of humans, or Black, who was the weakest of the six ancient dragons but smart and skilled in controlling magical energies, the Red Queen had trouble discerning the differences between the humanoid races. All she knew for sure was that the creatures with long, pointy ears were crafty little bastards.

I see.

Nonetheless, the reason the female appeared in the Red Queen's mind was because she had something to do with the thing the Red Queen treasured most.

When the Red Queen first visited that mysterious place and partook of the beef stew, she loved it so much that she cast the same spell on the Restaurant to Another World and its master as she had on her own personal treasures. It was a powerful spell indeed. This magic allowed the Red Queen to see any and all beings who encountered her treasure, regardless of whether they were from this world or the other. Should they do anything to endanger her property, they would be on the receiving end of her rage and vengeance.

Years ago, a human who possessed the power of a god (the result of White dispersing their blood throughout the world) once attempted to make the Restaurant to Another World's master their own. At that time, the Red Queen was alerted to this danger and immediately visited the otherworldly restaurant. It was then that she formed a covenant with the other great dragons: "The six ancient dragons must never take or destroy each other's lives or treasures." While fatal bloodshed was avoided that day, she made sure to punish the human in question so they would never think to try something so foolish ever again.

Thanks to the Red Queen's magic, she would be made aware of any being who stayed at the Restaurant to Another World. She could see everything.

Hm, perhaps she wandered in?

Seeing how today wasn't the Day of Satur, the girl likely wandered into the restaurant the previous day and stayed overnight.

The magic that bound the two worlds together was complicated. It was incredibly difficult moving from the Red Queen's world to the master's, but returning to one's own world was extremely simple. A person could just leave whenever they wanted to. This was something the Red Queen had learned from the human who worked to connect the two worlds together once upon a time, long before she first visited the Restaurant to Another World.

In that case, I could do with a bit of a stroll.

Now that she understood what was going on and had also finished her helping of beef stew, the Red Queen had some free time on her hands. She spread her massive wings and let out a bellowing roar. Her trusty balrog butler immediately came to her, and she briefly informed him of her plans.

I'm going out for a bit. Fear not. I'm only taking a look.

The Red Queen flew off into the sky.

It was Sunday morning, just after the master had fed the young, horned girl who wandered into the restaurant on Saturday night. The master decided to prep for the next week of work.

Normally, Sundays were the one day of the week in which the master could relax, especially because of special business days. He was unmarried, which meant he was fairly laid back most of the time. On Sundays, he'd take the opportunity to check out highly reviewed restaurants for both work and pleasure or spend time on the third floor testing out new recipes and dishes. He was rarely in the basement.

But today was different. The master decided to spend his entire Sunday in Nekoya. He was going to use this time to help train his brand-new hire.

The young woman apparently had experience working as a waitress, but things in the other world were probably different than they were here. He'd have to teach her the ins and outs of the job, just to be sure.

"So today I'm gonna have you learn everything you need to know about the job. You'll be getting paid for today, so make sure you pay attention."

It appeared as though Aletta didn't expect to be paid

for this time period. After looking positively shocked, she replied in a loud voice, "Huh? O-oh, okay! I'll do my best!"

The master broke into a smile after hearing the young woman's response. "Excellent answer. Now, let's see. First..." He looked her up and down and quickly decided on the first order of business.

"First thing's first. I'll show you how to use it, so how about taking a shower and washing yourself off? After that, I'll get you some fresh clothes and shoes."

While the master understood that Aletta was from the other world, it still didn't quite explain how dirty and tattered her clothes were. They were unbefitting of a young woman her age. If she was going to work as a waitress at Nekoya, her outfit simply would not do. That's why the first order of business was to get her cleaned up.

Things got busy from there on out. While Aletta bashfully cleaned herself off in the shower, the master had to go about readying her uniform.

I have no clue what her shoe size is... For now, I'll just roll with twenty-four centimeters, I guess. Ah, crap. She probably doesn't have underwear, does she?

The master quickly made his way out the back exit and dropped by the closest convenience store in the area. He grabbed the cheapest stuff he could find, went back to

Nekoya, and passed her the goods through the door. It ultimately took about two hours to get everything ready for Aletta.

"U-um, I'm finished changing..." she said.

Aletta emerged in her uniform, her cheeks still red from the hot shower, but her body clean and her hair nice and dry.

She wore a short-sleeved white blouse and a black vest over the white underwear the master bought for her, and a black flared skirt that rested just above her knees. Over that she wore a white apron with a black cat appliqued on it. Completing the look were a pair of white socks and black shoes.

Nekoya's uniform was traditionally black and white, which went quite nicely with Aletta's red hair tie and thick blonde hair. Even her tiny black horns, proof she was a demon, looked like strange but charming hair decorations. He had to admit, she was adorable.

"H-how do I look?" she asked.

Due to her poor lifestyle, Aletta was thinner than most. She'd never worn clothes like this before, never mind those from another world. This was the very first time in the young demon girl's life that she had ever worn completely fresh, clean clothes, and she felt both bad for it and slightly embarrassed. Her eyes quivered in fear as she sought the master's opinion. Her cheeks were red, the rest of her face turning pale from a mix of terror and nervousness.

As a man running a business, the master made sure to carefully inspect the young woman's appearance to confirm that she'd be all right to be out in front of customers. He nodded affirmatively.

Everything looked in order. Whether she'd be able to do the work properly or not was a different problem altogether, but she looked as respectable as any of his regular student part-timers. He'd have to teach her all sorts of things about waitressing, but in terms of cleanliness, she passed with flying colors.

"Perfect. You pass. How do the shoes feel? Do they fit? And did you make sure to clean yourself up real good?"

"Y-yes! The shoes also fit perfectly! I washed myself just as you instructed!" Aletta answered, her body still tense.

O-oh my gosh, what if this is the kind of place that nobles frequent?! she thought, feeling a wave of anxiety wash over her.

Even when she had worked at the inn, she never cleaned herself as thoroughly as this. Of course, she made sure to wash to prevent herself from smelling, but her old boss never had her wear a set of completely fresh clothes.

According to the master, everyone working at the restaurant had to make sure to keep themselves clean. If anyone were to bring filth or sickness into Nekoya, they could potentially pass it along to the customers, which would be a big problem. For someone like Aletta, who could barely find food to eat in the capital, never mind clean herself, perhaps it was inevitable that the master would find her too dirty. He ordered her to use the magic tool in the other room to clean herself, and even taught her how to use it.

Of course, Aletta knew how to wash with regular water. But this being another world and all, there were all sorts of bizarre magical tools she'd never seen before. The master explained how to use most of them, but it still took some time before she would do so herself.

There was something called a "shower room" with a strange device that rained down hot water. Apparently, it was a tool specifically designed for cleaning one's body. The master taught her how to use it and gave her permission to use the "shampoo" and "body soap" in the room to clean her body and hair. They were both scented oils of some kind that Aletta had never used before. She used a strange towel to spread the oil across her body, stunned by the amount of suds generated by the sticky fluid. Even the most expensive of bar soaps didn't bubble like this.

Aletta was embarrassed to find that she was much filthier than she realized. She washed herself under the hot water until there wasn't a speck of dirt left on her. She was stunned as she looked at her own beautiful skin and shiny hair. It was almost as if she were looking at a different person entirely.

Next, the young demon girl used the towel the master prepared for her to dry her body off and moved on to the strange magic tool that spit out hot air to dry her golden blonde hair. Aletta's dirty clothes were tossed into a device that could automatically clean them (they'd apparently be ready by nightfall). Meanwhile, she put on the strange, stretchy, white underwear the master bought for her, and then slipped on the somewhat suggestive waitress uniform.

It was now time for her to learn the ropes.

"All right. That's enough cleaning up for now. On to the next matter at hand," said the master, having concluded that it was about time to teach his new otherworldly worker how to do her job. "Let's see. I'm thinking of teaching you all sorts of stuff, but...can you read?"

"Huh...? Um, I... I'm sorry..." Aletta lowered her head as she replied.

In her hometown, the only ones privileged enough to be taught how to read and write were the elder's son and the priest's children. Most of the other children were too busy battling day-to-day life and didn't have the free time necessary to devote to studying. It went without saying that Aletta was in the latter group.

"Hm, well, I was gonna have you carry out food and take orders from the customers. You think you'll be okay?"

"Yes! I most definitely will! I can remember ten orders, even twenty if you need me to!" Aletta loudly responded to the master's question.

If nothing else, Aletta was confident in her ability to remember things. Not being able to read was a normal thing at the inn she used to work at, so having the ability to memorize a customer's orders was an absolute necessity.

"All right, if you say so."

The master knew this issue was going to pop up, but after seeing how determined the young woman was, decided to move forward without worrying too much about it.

"Then first, before we even talk about taking orders, let's start with the cleaning. Before the restaurant opens and right after it closes, we have to make sure there's no food on the floor. And since we're doing this now, we may as well clean the places we normally don't," said the master.

"You got it!" Aletta nodded her head in response.

"Aye. That's what I like to hear." The master couldn't help but smile in response, and the two began their first day of work together.

"Phew, that about wraps things up."

Aletta finally finished cleaning, more exhausted than usual. Part of this could be blamed on the fact that there was no way to tell what time it was in the basement. It certainly didn't help that she was still nervous about the whole job thing.

The master gave her a special rag just for cleaning the walls and floor, as well as a special liquid of some kind specifically for getting grime off surfaces. Aletta was amazed by how simple it was; she simply applied the liquid to the cloth and ran it over the dirty spots. She would then go back over it again with a separate, cleaner cloth, and just like that, no more stains. After wrapping that up, the master instructed her to clean the rooms outside of the dining hall and kitchen. These were places like the staff changing room that weren't usually cleaned all that often. Aletta did her best to make the place nice and sparkly while also learning the layout of the restaurant.

After all that hard work, Aletta's stomach was once again empty. She smiled happily, rubbing it through her uniform. "Mm... I'm definitely hungry," she said.

The master had informed her that once she wrapped things up, they'd be taking a break for breakfast.

"Um, Master? I'm finished!" Aletta reported to the older man in the kitchen.

"Good work. Once we finish eating, I'm gonna teach you all about how to interact with customers. But first, go wash those hands of yours." The master was standing in front of a magical device of some sort, holding a large black pot as he spoke to her. The device in question could create flames without firewood. How useful!

"Okay! I can wash them here, right?"

Aletta did just as she was taught, standing in front of the faucet and turning the golden handle to get the water running. After wetting her hands a bit, she applied some of the green cleaning liquid to them and rubbed them against each other, creating countless suds. She made sure to clean under her nails and the spaces between her fingers.

This other world is amazing, she thought as she rinsed her hands.

Aletta couldn't help but think to herself about how strange this Restaurant to Another World was.

After that first magnificent breakfast, the master had explained the truth of Aletta's circumstances to her. This strange place called "Western Cuisine Nekoya" was referred to by some customers as the Restaurant to Another World. The reason being that it was an eatery that existed in a world separate from the one Aletta lived in.

Once every seven days, doors connecting to the restaurant appeared across Aletta's world. Specifically, this occurred on the Day of Satur. Inhabitants of her world used these doors to visit the restaurant.

When Aletta first heard the master's explanation, she was surprised, but felt his explanation made sense. With all the strange contraptions and delicious food, it was only logical that this place wasn't from her world.

I have to do my best, she thought. *I'll never find a job this good ever again!*

Not only was she getting ten silver coins just for one day of work, she was even getting fed. If the previous meal was any indication, this would be nothing like the partially rotten vegetables, old soup, or hard bread she used to get from her old job.

I wonder if it'll be anything like that amazing breakfast from earlier...

Aletta gulped. She'd had breakfast at the Restaurant to Another World earlier in the morning, and it was incredibly delicious. In fact, it was the first time in her life she'd ever eaten something that good before. Just thinking back on it was enough to make her mouth water all over again.

"Heeey, Aletta!" the master called, with impeccable timing. "It's time to eat, so grab a seat in the dining room."

"Okay!" she energetically responded.

"Here we go. This is today's lunch." He set a plate in front of her.

"Wow..." She sighed at the sight.

The dish in front of Aletta caused her eyes to sparkle. Obviously, she'd never seen the food before, so she had no clue what it tasted like, but it looked amazing nonetheless. The aroma wafting up from it was more than enough to tickle her taste buds.

The meal in question was best described as "golden." Sitting on the large plate was a mound of small white grains dressed in egg. Its delicious smell filled the air around it, and she could see small bits of chopped meat and green vegetables mixed inside of it. Next to that dish was a small bowl filled with a brown soup of some sort and then a transparent glass filled with ice and a type of brown tea.

"It's a rice dish," the master said. "Is that okay with you?"

The master sat down at the same table as Aletta, placing down his own dish. He'd used the leftover rice and ingredients from Saturday, as well as the remaining wild boar meat he'd received from a hunter of the other world. While it wasn't something he'd feel comfortable serving customers, it was the perfect dish for him and his employees.

"No problem at all! By the way, what is this called?" Aletta's eyes sparkled.

"Ah, this is called fried rice," the master replied, a smile on his face. He explained that it was a dish he frequently made for himself on Sundays.

When he was still in high school, he worked part-time at a local Chinese restaurant as part of his training. Even after that, he continued to polish his wok techniques. He was secretly confident in his ability to make fried rice.

"C'mon. Eat up before it gets cold. Fried rice tastes best while it's still hot!" The master grabbed a spoon from off the table and put his hands together. "Let's eat."

And just like that, the older man began digging in to the fried rice in front of him.

"Oh, um... Thank you, oh god of demons, for this, my daily bread. I offer you my gratitude."

Aletta followed in the master's stead, offering a quick prayer before beginning her journey into the golden hills of deliciousness in front of her. She dug her spoon into the mountain of fried rice and brought some up to her mouth.

And then there was silence. The two coworkers quietly continued eating.

Th-this is delicious!

Those three words were the only things to pop into the young demon's head. She continued filling her mouth with the hot fried rice, letting none of its warmth escape.

Aletta had never eaten a rice-based dish before. Its flavor utterly charmed her. The grains of rice had absorbed the flavors of the aromatic grease, sweet and sour meat that still had a touch of its gamey taste, and the uniquely sweet vegetables. All these combined to make the rice taste incredible.

Each spoonful unraveled in her mouth, its savory quality exploding as though it were dancing across her tongue. Every bite she took only brought out its flavor even further. And then there was the golden egg that gently wrapped itself around that flavor, bringing together the entire dish.

Meat, vegetables, rice, and eggs. Every spoonful was an absolute delight.

Her hand wouldn't stop. She would swallow down some fried rice, occasionally stop to take a sip of her soup, and then wash it all down with cold tea. Despite how well she'd eaten that morning, she could feel her now-empty stomach filling up all over again.

Aletta spent her lunch time quietly eating her fried rice alongside the master. The young demon finished her meal, and just as she washed it all down with some cold tea, she let out the simplest of opinions on the dish.

"Wow... That really was amazing!"

They were simple words, but they came from the bottom of her heart. That much was clear.

"Really? Well I'm dang glad to hear that." As far as the master was concerned, having a young lady such as Aletta say something like that felt pretty good. He flashed her a smile.

"All right. Once you've finished resting for a little bit, we can start your afternoon training. First thing's gonna be...handling the dishes."

"Okay!" Aletta answered, her eyes filled with determination.

That night...

"Ahh... That was delicious."

How to handle the plates, the best way to carry food to customers, how to hand over menus, and even what words to use. Aletta learned all manner of things from the master, and after finally going over all there was to go over, it was dinnertime. This time, it was a dish of meat fried in breadcrumbs.

"That minced meat cutlet stuff was wonderful..." Aletta simply let herself stew in the aftertaste of the dish while she waited for the master to return from the back.

She was stunned when she found out she'd be getting paid for today's job training. The idea of getting paid to learn seemed bonkers. In fact, it almost seemed too good to be true. Part of her wondered if maybe she was being tricked.

"Yo, sorry for the wait." And then the master returned, bag in hand.

"N-no, not at all! Thank you very much!"

Aletta abruptly stood up and bowed deeply to the master, an expression of gratitude that he had taught her earlier in the day. No matter how much she thanked the man, it would never be enough.

"Now, now," he said, waving it off. "No need to get all stiff on me. Here, this is today's pay. If I remember correctly, you wanted three silver coins' worth to be in copper, yeah?"

"That's right! Thank you very much!" Aletta's tone was light compared to the heavy bag the master handed her.

Her stomach was full and her body warm. The horned demon girl couldn't have been happier.

"All right then, be careful now. I'll see you next week! Remember, the morning six days from now."

"Okay!"

The master watched the young woman as she passed through the door and back into the slums of the capital. The black door shut behind her and vanished.

Wow... she thought. *So that really was another world.*

Seeing the door vanish behind her hammered in just how mysterious the past day had been. But while the door may have disappeared, she knew it was real and not a dream. She had proof.

She was still wearing the brand-new uniform the master gave her, while in her hands she held her old battered clothes, now cleaner than they had ever been. Even her hair was still tied up neatly with the mysterious, stretchy string he gave her. In her pouch were seven silver coins and thirty copper coins. Just as promised, the master paid her a grand total of ten silver coins. If her experience had been a dream, she wouldn't have any of this.

Ah, that's right. I have to be careful.

Aletta immediately took the silver coins out of the pouch and began hiding them in her clothes and shoes. She was alone here in the capital, but she had long since learned how to live in the slums. She laid out her rough blanket and thought about the day's happenings while getting ready for bed.

Today sure was incredible...

She'd been treated to not one, not two, but *three* wonderful meals in a single day. She even got paid more money than she'd ever received in her entire life. Her life up until yesterday seemed like a strange dream.

"I'll have to work even harder starting tomorrow."

Overwhelmed with exhaustion from such a fulfilling but tiring day, Aletta wrapped herself up in her old blanket.

Starting tomorrow, I'm gonna start looking for more work... If possible, something other than waitressing.

After having such an incredible experience in the other world, she couldn't imagine herself being able to go back to waitressing in the capital again. It'd probably just be terribly disappointing by comparison.

As those thoughts raced through her mind, Aletta quietly drifted off to sleep, her soft breathing the only sound audible in the old ruins...

The young demon had no way of knowing. She had no way of knowing that the Restaurant to Another World had a special protective spell cast over it by a certain regular customer.

Aletta had no way of knowing that this specific spell would alert that regular customer whenever something happened to her treasured restaurant. No way of knowing that through the contract she made with the master, the girl was now considered a part of that treasure.

Three days later, the capital was faced with an unprecedented incident. Moving like some sort of massive, living castle, the great crimson dragon of legend crossed through the sky directly above the capital. Legend had it that on the day the great beast showed itself to the world, it would mean the destruction of the country. The great dragon would burn the nation to the ground.

The king, nobles, knights, and sorcerers fell into panic for a time. (Among them, only the legendary sage, Altorius, remained calm. "She's not going to do anything. She's just here to look is all," he said, calm as always.)

Fortunately for all, the great dragon simply cut across the sky. It launched no attacks against the Kingdom, and by nightfall, calm had settled throughout the city. Things eventually went back to normal. Not a single person had noticed what happened.

As the great dragon cut across the sky, it glanced down at a weak demon girl, who stared up at the sky in return.

*Restaurant to
Another World*

CHAPTER 22
Fried Seafood

EVENING CAME AS GARD, a dwarven glassmith, trekked up the mountain with his friend Guilhem. He turned to the other dwarf.

"Hey. Can I ask you a question?"

"What?" Guilhem replied, his beloved beard rustling in the wind while his eyes sparkled.

Gard took a deep breath and asked what had been on his mind for a while now.

"Why in God's name are we climbin' a mountain?" This was the only question that really mattered.

"Why? Didn't I tell you before we got here? Today's the Day of Satur, which means I'm gonna go grab a bite," Guilhem replied, unsure of why his friend was even asking such a foolish question.

Gard was annoyed. "Guilhem, have you forgotten?

You invited me to go partake in some delicious spirits and fish."

Guilhem was a dwarf who loved both booze and his work, like many of his race. Additionally, he also made his own spirits. In fact, among the dwarves with a passion for making spirits, few had the talents he did. It certainly helped that Guilhem had invented some new types of alcohol, making him a household name among his people. If this same dwarf spoke highly of someone else's alcohol, it had to be delicious.

"You got that right. The restaurant we're headed to has fish and spirits so damn delicious that it's out of this world, friend. Hell, the fish I had there was the first time I ever understood just how good fresh fish could be. Color me surprised!" Guilhem pumped his chest out proudly.

This caused Gard to explode.

"You still ain't answerin' my question, dammit! I'm askin' you why we're climbin' a mountain to go eat fish, you numbskull!"

Quite some time had passed since they began their trek up the mountain. At no point had Gard spotted a single fish, never mind water. Where could this fish Guilhem spoke of possibly even come from?

"That's an easy one! There's a restaurant up ahead. We'll be there soon."

Like hell there is!

Gard held in his rage. If there were an idiot out there willing to open shop on a mountain like this, he'd love to bust their head open and take a look inside. The same went for the idiot in front of him.

Just as Gard reached back for the beloved battle axe he'd wielded for over ten years...

"We're here!" Guilhem pointed his short, fat index finger at their objective.

As soon as Gard looked at where his friend was pointing, his hand gripped the handle of his battle axe.

"Hey, Guilhem. All I'm seein' over there is a busted old shack."

Indeed, it was a small shack that had been carved out of the mountainside. While a human might be impressed, to the trained eyes of a dwarf, it was nothing more than a ramshackle shed.

"Yup! I made it myself! You know I ain't so good at big construction work, so cut me some slack, eh?" Guilhem smiled and explained to Gard, unaware of the feelings building inside his friend.

"Guilhem, I always *thought* we were friends..."

Other races often said dwarves were incredibly hard-headed when it came to their work. They were also short-tempered in regard to getting into fights. This was in fact quite true, and they hated being made the fool more than perhaps anything else in the world.

If he's going to be like this, I have no choice but to show this idiot the error of his ways.

Gard slowly began pulling out his trusty battle axe. But then he noticed something odd.

"What's with that door?"

Inside the old shack that didn't even have a proper lintel, Gard saw something that caused him to pause. It was a beautiful, well-kept black door with a brass handle. Its construction was exquisite, and Gard realized it must have been made by a talented craftsman. It stood out like a sore thumb in a place like this.

"Didn't I tell you? That's the door to the restaurant with the delicious booze and food." Guilhem peered at his friend's surprised face. "The entrance to the Restaurant to Another World."

The shocked expression on Gard's face as he heard his friend's words was exactly like the one Guilhem had after accidentally stumbling upon the door.

A bell rang as the pair of dwarves stepped through. "Welcome!"

"I'm here!"

As soon as Guilhem turned the slightly too-high handle of the door and stepped through, he was greeted like always by the middle-aged master of the restaurant.

"...This is another world?" Gard asked.

Since this was Gard's first time visiting, he couldn't help but glance around. Despite it already being evening, the inside of the restaurant was well lit, and there were already multiple customers seated. Most of them were races you'd never see in a dwarf town, but there were also monster folk and demon-like beings that you'd be hard-pressed to find in human villages. None of them seemed the least bit belligerent, focusing instead on enjoying their delicious-looking food and sipping their booze.

I see... So this is what it means to be in another world.

Seeing was believing. Gard found himself completely believing his friend's words after seeing all the different races in one place. It was clear this wasn't any ordinary restaurant.

"So, what's in the fried seafood today?" Guilhem asked the usual question, all the while keeping tabs on Gard off to the side.

"Cod, squid rings, and scallops!"

"I see, I see. Then I'll have two servings of that. One for me, and one for this guy here. I'd also like two mugs of beer and a bottle of whiskey with rocks. That'll do for now!"

"Aye, you got it," the master nodded.

"And make that as quick as you can. We're dang tired from climbing up the mountain. Hey, Gard. Over here."

After making his order, Guilhem directed his friend to an empty table.

"Phew, we can finally take a break."

While it was frustrating that their feet couldn't touch the ground because they were too short, the chairs were nonetheless quite comfortable. The two dwarves leapt onto their respective seats.

"By the way, Guilhem, what was that 'beer' and 'whiskey' stuff you ordered? Are those the delicious spirits you told me about?"

"Aye, that they are."

Gard was far out of his comfort zone, which meant he had to leave everything to his friend. He was filled with questions, and Guilhem was more than happy to oblige.

"You see, there are all sorts of spirits we ain't never heard of here. And guess what? They're all damn delicious. You know I wouldn't lie about that."

"Say what? Are you serious?!" Gard raised his voice, stunned by the sudden revelation.

As far as Gard knew, Guilhem made the best spirits in

the world, bar none. His friend was the one dwarf in the world who knew what the best booze was.

A few months ago, Guilhem had begun selling a rare liquor called fire spirits he'd created after days upon days of testing. Once the aging process had finished and the liquor went on sale, dwarves in town fought each other over trying to buy up as much of it as they could. The demand far exceeded the supply, making it hard to get. Additionally, fire spirits were too strong for races other than the dwarves, so it hadn't been very popular—but this new stuff had a completely different flavor to it, which led the human merchants who were familiar with the dwarves to buy some for themselves. Of course, these same merchants were unable to buy enough to resell once they returned home. The dwarven heavy drinkers would never allow it.

So far, there was only enough of the new fire spirits for the dwarves. That was steadily changing, however. It was believed that production would soon be able to keep up with demand, and the other races would be able to indulge in this brand new liquor. It certainly helped that Guilhem did not keep his recipe to himself. He was more than willing to teach anyone and everyone how to make the new fire spirits, which meant that brewers all over town were working on it.

Guilhem was the one who had perfected the brewing of the new liquor, so if he said this booze was amazing, he was telling the truth.

"Really? I can't wait to try some." Gard shook his tiny legs underneath the table in excitement. Guilhem couldn't help but smile at his reaction, responding in kind.

It only took a few moments of waiting.

"S-sorry to keep you waiting! Here are your beers!"

A young waitress dressed in otherworldly clothes with a bizarre hair accessory brought the two dwarves their drinks. Despite being something of a regular, Guilhem had never seen her before. In her left hand were two large glass mugs. She carefully placed them down on the table before the duo.

"Ah! Many thanks! We've been waitin' for this!" said Guilhem.

"Oho! So, this is booze from another world? It's beautiful!"

The men raised their voices in excitement at the alcohol in front of them. Unlike the humans, the dwarves paid no mind to the young girl who was far too tall and thin for their liking. They instead focused on the layer of white, mist-like foam at the top of the mugs.

"The rest will be out soon! Please take your time and enjoy!" The young lady seemed nervous. Perhaps she was new? After letting the men know about the rest of their order, she quickly shuffled off to grab the empty dishes of another group of customers.

"Well then!"

"Let's drink!"

The two dwarves lightly clinked their mugs together. As the sounds of the glass clashing filled the air, the men guzzled the golden beer. Their noisy gulps as they downed the foamy liquid echoed throughout the area surrounding them. It didn't take long before the beer had settled in their stomachs and their mugs were empty.

"Whew!" the dwarves said in tandem.

"Ooooh, that was damn delicious! This beer stuff is incredible!"

"Didn't I tell you so?! It's not particularly strong, but it feels great goin' down the gullet. Plus, it's nice and cold! Every time I have a beer, I can't help but think that ice-cold is the way to go!" Guilhem responded to his wide-eyed, satisfied friend. He remembered well how surprised he had been the first time he drank beer. It was inherently different from other, stronger types of alcohol. It had a similar, wheaty bitterness, but just cooling it made it taste that much different.

It was clear that an ice-cold beer was the perfect drink to cool down a tired body that had spent the whole day trekking up a mountain. Guilhem made it a point to order one first every time he came to the Restaurant to Another World.

"What say you, Guilhem? Another beer?" Gard asked.

"You got that right! Hey, little lady! Sorry, but could we get another two beers over here?" The dwarves wasted no time asking the waitress for refills while she took care of the dishes.

"Ah, y-yes! Right away!"

"You know what?" said Gard. "These glass mugs are something else, too."

While the men waited on their drinks, Gard took a moment to inspect the empty mugs in front of him. They were not ornate in any way, but the glass handles on them had no visible air pockets to be found. The mugs were so transparent that one could see through all the way to the other side.

"It's so clear that you can really enjoy the beautiful color of the beer. Hm, I'm gonna have to try making one of these," he said.

As a glassmith, he was earnestly fascinated by the object in front of him. As hardheaded as Gard could be, he was equally patient and capable of putting together marvelously detailed works when it came to glassmithing. The glass mugs he made were typically intricate works of arts.

But looking at this simple glass mug in front of him, he realized something.

"The alcohol is a decoration in and of itself. Anything else just gets in the way," said Gard.

"Oh? I figured you'd say something like that."

His friend had clearly arrived at the same conclusion he had. Guilhem smiled at Gard. And so, the two of them waited for their refills to arrive.

"Sorry to keep you waiting!" the waitress said. "Here are your beers and orders of fried seafood!"

"Oho!" the men shouted in unison after seeing what the waitress brought to them.

"Hm, let me have a look... So, this is the delicious fish meal you recommended, eh?"

Gard took a close look at the food in front of him. Piled on top of the white dish were three different types of fried foods, golden brown and quietly sizzling atop some bright green vegetables. One was large and leaf-shaped, three were shaped like hoops, and the last three were small, round balls.

"Hm. This does look delicious, but is it really fish?" he whispered to himself after taking a closer look. His expression was one of both expectation and doubt. Gard couldn't believe that a restaurant with booze this delicious could possibly serve nasty food. And yet he also couldn't wrap his head around this supposed fish being any good. Gard's common sense was getting in the way of his own expectations.

The dwarf village that Gard lived in was surrounded by mines. Due to its proximity to mountains, it was great for folks who wanted to begin working as blacksmiths. High-quality coal and iron were readily available. The only problem was that it was far from the ocean. Quite frankly, unless you became an adventurer and traveled with humans, halflings, or those cursed elves and half-elves, you'd likely never see the ocean with your own two eyes.

This meant that while fish were imported into town, they were often caught in local rivers and ponds, and then heavily salted to preserve them as long as possible. They were functional as something to nibble on when drinking but not much else. While it was certainly possible to catch fish that were born in the rainwater that gathered at the foot of the mountains, they often tasted like dirt and had far too many bones, perhaps due to the location in which they were born.

As far as Gard was concerned, where he grew up, he had two options when it came to fish: either overly salted or dirty and bony. Either way, he'd labelled fish gross. Sure, dwarves had strong jaws and stomachs, but just because they could eat fish didn't mean they enjoyed it. Gard had not once in his life ever found them to be any good.

"Now, now. Give it a shot," urged Guilhem. "The leaf-shaped one is fish, those are scallops, and those are some strange sea creature called squid."

Guilhem had awoken to the pleasures of booze and fish over ten years ago. Back when he first set out on his own, an older dwarf he drank with made the recommendation. Guilhem reached over for the small red and blue containers on the table and brought them close to himself, eyeing the white sauce next to him as well. He was trying to decide which one of the three to use, all the while urging his friend to begin eating.

"If you say so," said Gard.

If nothing else, the spirits of this other world were delicious. Based on that fact alone, Gard decided to give the fried seafood a fair chance. He drove his fork through the fish and lifted it up. Through his large nose, he could smell the fried food's tempting aroma. Gard opened his mouth wide and bit into it with a loud *crunch*.

Whaaaaat?!

It was a flavor unlike anything Gard had ever experienced in his life. The first thing that struck him was the coating used on the fried seafood. It was clearly made with both high-quality oil and wheat. The flavors struck his stomach like a delicious arrow.

Y-you're telling me this is fish?!

What came next could not be put into words. After biting through the layer of breaded coating, Gard was struck by yet another flavor he had yet to experience. He couldn't believe this was fish. The lightly prepared seafood was fried to a crisp, the heat of the oil helping to spread the savory flavor of the fish throughout Gard's mouth. As he chewed into it, it gently fell apart across his tongue. It had a light but pronounced flavor. Gard could tell that the fish had been ever-so-slightly seasoned with salt and pepper, but unlike the fish caught in their rivers, it lacked any rawness or taste of dirt. It also seemed as though the bones had been taken out! This tremendous fish flavor, combined with the taste of the light breading...

I can't believe this!

After encountering such a culinary delight, Gard's instincts took over. His open left hand immediately grabbed the handle of his mug, and he took a huge gulp of his beer. In his mouth, the flavor of the hot fish came face to face with the ice-cold beer. They danced together in tandem, creating what could only be described as a perfect alliance of flavor. This was exactly what Gard expected and had hoped for.

I must have more!

Gard devoured the fried fish almost immediately and then turned to the remaining items on his dish. First, he took two pieces of the strange circular "squid," drove his fork through them, and guided them to his mouth.

Madness! he thought. *This is delicious, too!*

Unlike the fried fish he ate earlier, the fried squid had a familiar, cozy "toughness" to it. Thanks to the dwarf's hardened teeth, he cut right through the squid. While the flavor was altogether different, it too was as delicious as the fried fish. Gard couldn't stop shoveling squid into his mouth, his hand stopping for nothing. It didn't take long before the squid was all gone.

What about the last... Whooooaaaa?!

And so, Gard turned his attention to the last item on his dish, the fried scallops. These, too, were absolutely marvelous. The flavor that emerged from beneath the thin layer of breading was much more intense than the previous two items. The moment he bit into one, it dissolved into what felt like a series of strings, leaving behind a unique aftertaste. This mouthfeel and the comparatively small size of each piece left Gard wanting for more. It was but a moment before the scallops were gone.

"That was delicious! Both the booze and fish!" Gard's impressions came late, only after he had devoured his meal and emptied his mug. "Damn you, Guilhem. Have you been hiding this from me the whole—huh?"

Gard was prepared to shower his friend in bitter words of jealousy when he noticed something. Guilhem was eating the same fried food that he had, but he was using three different sauces.

"Ah, that's the trick," he sighed "Nothing goes with fried seafood quite like tartar sauce! The other sauces are great and all, but at the end of the day, nothing else goes with white fish meat quite like this!"

In addition to the fish's naturally light taste and the flavor of the aromatic breaded layer, Guilhem was enjoying a third taste: a gentle sourness. This made for the best possible combination as far as Guilhem was concerned, crunching away at his fried food.

"H-hey, Guilhem. What is that stuff?" Gard asked, shaking ever so slightly.

Guilhem didn't seem to notice his friend's loss of composure as he went on to explain one of the restaurant's other charms.

"Great question! This stuff is called tartar sauce. It's basically the best topping you could ever use on fish. It's made using tons of boiled eggs and has just a hint of sourness to it. When you combine it with perfectly fried fish like this, it's so delicious you could hardly believe it was from this world. The sauce in this red bottle here is called 'soy sauce.' It's a wee bit strong on the saltiness, but it makes up for that in terms of savoriness. It goes aces with fish dishes. Just puttin' a little of it on standard cooked fish'll make it taste that much better. This last blue bottle is another type of sauce, but it's got a pretty complicated flavor. I'm talkin' sour and spicy, even. This stuff goes with all sorts of fried foods. You could argue it's the best all-around sauce. So yeah, you can put any one of these on the fried seafood and try 'em out. Because the master uses different fish each day he serves the dish, I always end up struggling to pick a sauce..."

"How could you not tell me all of this sooner?! Agh, you fool!" Gard couldn't help but shout in rage. The dwarf could hardly believe the delicious meal he ate was still in its unfinished form. This meant the fried seafood could become even more delicious. He would never be able to forgive his friend for withholding that information, but there were bigger fish to fry.

"Excuse me, could I get some whiskey over here?"

"Hey, young lady! I wanna place another order. Three dishes of fried seafood, and make it quick!"

"Wh-what?!"

After the young waitress brought them two glass cups,

each with a large, round ball of ice in them, along with a bottle of brown spirits, they quickly placed their final orders.

"Excellent! Young lady, let me get another three plates as well! The food here is amazing, but the serving size isn't quite enough for us dwarves!" Guilhem did as always, requesting seconds on his meal.

"Let's drink and eat to our heart's content! Today is on me!"

"Haha! I knew you'd say that!"

The two dwarves partook in their whiskey and chatted among themselves while waiting for their next orders to come in.

"Whew! All the booze from the other world is damn delicious! Is this the land of the gods?"

"It might be! Ain't nothin' here that tastes like it's from our world!"

It didn't take long for the whiskey to disappear as the two men drank and drank and drank. They still found time to talk in between sips, somehow.

"Wait, don't tell me there's still more delicious fish and booze here."

"Of course there is! Especially that seishu stuff made from rice on the Western Continent. It's great! Oh, and the wine here tastes completely different. They also serve more than just fried fish, too. Hell, I'd come here every day if I could!"

"Here, here!" Gard agreed with his friend. He finally understood why Guilhem built the tiny shack around the door.

The next morning...

Gard woke up, quickly raising his body off the shack's hard, stone floor.

The dwarf initially panicked, thinking all the amazing things he experienced the day before were a part of a long and elaborate dream. But he had proof it was all real. He was cradling a bottle of unopened whiskey in his hands as if it were his child.

Looks like that wasn't a dream. Eh, not like that was enough booze for a dwarf like me to really get drunk.

The two men had continued to enjoy their alcohol and fish throughout the night. Gard eventually got to try all three of the different toppings, which led both dwarves to furiously debate over which one went the best with fried seafood, all while indulging in different types of other-worldly booze. The plates just kept stacking up on their table. This lasted until a large demon woman carrying a massive pot that even the dwarves couldn't have easily lifted appeared in the restaurant. The man who appeared to be the master of the restaurant informed them that it was closing time, and they promptly left.

...I owe him big time.

Gard peeked over at his friend, who laid next to him. Delicious food and drink. His wallet was empty, but in exchange, he had gotten his hands on an amazing bottle of alcohol.

Having received this much, he had a whole lot he needed to give back.

First, I should fix this place up a bit.

Gard began putting together his plan.

And so, the beautiful stone cabin that popped up in the middle of the mountains like a sore thumb would eventually become a beloved resting spot for visitors to the dwarf town. Its dwarf caretakers made straw beds and left heavy, warm blankets inside so anyone could come in and catch a bit of shut-eye.

There was just one strange thing about the cabin. In the back of it was a metal door so thick that even a strike from a dwarven axe was not enough to break through.

The only ones with the key to the door were the dwarves who built the cabin in the first place. According to them, there was nothing beyond the metal entrance; just a small, empty room.

Why, then, would they build a vault-like door to protect nothing? The only ones who knew the answer to that question were the dwarves who made it...

Restaurant to Another World

CHAPTER 23
Cheesecake

HILDA, THE "NIGHT STRIDER," kept guard in the woods. She was a mercenary who operated out of the imperial capital.

"...Geez, they were a real pain in the ass."

She watched the last fleeing goblin of a group of thirty-four jerk its head back and fall to the floor through her crystal goggles, and finally let herself relax.

In her hands was her trusty crossbow, powerful enough to pierce even steel armor. Hilda bought this weapon for herself when she became a first-rate mercenary back in the day. The nice thing about it was that, despite its power, it was still light enough for a woman like Hilda to hold with little issue. On her head she wore a hat with a hood made from tough beast hide attached to it. Her eyes, which made the difference between life or death as far as she was concerned, were protected by translucent crystal goggles. She wore sturdy leather pants, a leather, sleeveless jacket so she could feel the wind on her skin, and mythril gauntlets that ran from her elbows to her fingertips.

Hilda was a mercenary who primarily operated on her own. She was born with eyes that could see well in the dark, as well as ears that could hear even the tiniest of noises. It was honestly less that she worked alone and more that there were few mercenaries who were able to keep up with her in the pitch-black night of the woods.

"I'll come back and loot them later. For now, I should probably head back." Having taken care of the goblins in question, Hilda began talking to herself. It was a bad habit she had picked up due to operating alone for so long.

Hilda's experience as a mercenary told her that goblins and treasure went hand in hand. Defeating such a large band of them would mean a hefty payday. Of course, goblins didn't really understand the worth of any of the things they collected, so about half of their belongings ended up being trash. But, on occasion, they would collect copper, silver, sometimes even precious jewels and stones they took off their poor victims. You never knew what you might stumble upon. Hilda would be paid for slaying the goblins, but that was an altogether different payoff from looting their dead bodies. Being able to cash in on those goods was necessary for mercenaries like Hilda, who operated alone.

Over twenty years ago, the cobbler's tuber was discovered by the great emperor. This strange food could be grown even in cold regions where wheat couldn't be harvested. Even better, tubers grew beneath the ground, meaning that birds couldn't damage them like they did other crops. This nutritious staple could be eaten boiled or roasted, leading it to eventually be referred to as the "crop of the gods." All across the country, frontier villages were built to grow cobbler's tubers and sell them to other towns.

It was from one of those villages that Hilda had received a job offer. They wanted her to eliminate a group of goblins that had moved into a nearby forest. It took three days for her to eliminate the thirty-four creatures calling the woods their home.

"Goblins are easy pickings nowadays," Hilda whispered to herself as she shouldered her crossbow and quickly made her way back to her camp. It was a simple enough location; she had already gathered some firewood together so she could get a campfire going. She'd be heading back to the village come morning, but for now, she wanted to enjoy some dried fruits and rest as a reward for a job well done.

Or at least, that's what she planned on doing before she discovered *it*.

"...Hm?"

Hilda stopped in her tracks.

"Is there something there...?"

Her eyes began darting across her surroundings. Despite how dark it was outside, she was able to see as clearly as if it were the middle of the day. Her eyes unconsciously narrowed.

"Is that a door?"

Directly in front of her eyes was a large, black door with a golden handle. Its construction was magnificent, with an illustration of a cat on its front. It made zero sense that this would be in the middle of some random forest.

"This wasn't here yesterday. I'm sure of it."

Hilda had passed this way the previous day, so she knew full well that this object was out of place.

"I don't know what's going on," she muttered. "But I smell treasure."

Her instincts were yelling at her to press forward. She placed her hand on its cold, black surface.

Rarely were the mercenary's instincts wrong. While she barely had any of her equipment on, and all she currently carried was her old crossbow, she believed in them.

She had long since left her small hometown in the middle of nowhere, refusing to spend her life as a fisherman, and found her way to the imperial capital. It was there that she began calling herself a mercenary, and it was her instincts that got her through all kinds of life-threatening situations, as well as earned her her nickname and her relative fame around the nation. She trusted her eyes, ears, and instincts more than anything else in the world; they were her partners.

She squeezed the door handle in her hand and turned it.

"Ah! W-welcome!"

Hilda found herself loudly greeted by a young girl in a strange uniform. While the sounds of a bell ringing filled her ears, she was surprised by the presence of the girl in front of her. Through her crystal goggles, Hilda saw a young lady wearing a short skirt and a top with short sleeves. Not altogether uncomfortable-looking at all. That was all well and good.

The problem was what was on top of the girl's head.

"You're...a demon?" Hilda asked the girl in a low voice.

Indeed, the young lady in front of her had two black horns growing out from her head of blonde hair. If she were a human, they may have just been an accessory of some kind, but Hilda couldn't be fooled.

"Huh? Oh, um..."

"Ah, no, I'm sorry. I didn't mean to—"

The young demon girl in front of her immediately shrank in response to Hilda's words, as if she were used to that kind of treatment. Hilda panicked and quickly took off her goggles and hat, revealing her identity.

With no goggles blocking them, Hilda's green eyes were visible for all to see. In reaction to the bright light of the interior she was in, her pupils narrowed...vertically. No longer hidden by her hat, Hilda's dark brown hair covered her similarly colored, pointed ears. They twitched slightly.

"...I'm also a demon. My name is Hilda."

She, too, was a demon who had received the blessings of the dark lord. Except in her case, they took the form of cat eyes and ears.

"...Oh, my. Thank goodness. I thought you might hate me or something!" The young demon girl smiled at Hilda as she let out a sigh of relief. "I'm a waitress here at Western Cuisine Nekoya! My name's Aletta. It's a pleasure to meet you!"

"I see. Aletta... By the way, what exactly is Western Cuisine Nekoya? It would appear to be some sort of bar or eatery, as far as I can tell."

Taking a quick glance around the interior of the shop,

Hilda figured it must've been one or the other. Open tables and chairs lined the inside of a room with no windows. Despite the latter, it was bright as day. There were also a host of customers already present, munching on a wide variety of dishes.

"That's right! The master told me this is a restaurant that doesn't exist in our world. To be honest, I'm not really sure what that means!"

With a hint of nostalgia, Aletta explained to Hilda the circumstances in which she found herself working at Nekoya about a month before. While Hilda didn't quite grasp the concept of there being "another world," she at least understood that this was a special place.

"I see," she said. "Well, a restaurant serves food, right? So long as we agree on that much, I don't see the problem."

"Yup! And all the food here is super-duper delicious!" Aletta explained to Hilda with a huge smile on her face.

It was very clear to Hilda that the young girl wasn't being forced to say this by her master. No, Aletta truly felt that way.

"Well, in that case, I'm looking forward to trying some," she said.

Hilda sat herself down at one of the open tables and took a sip from the glass of slightly fruity ice water that Aletta brought her from the back, completely free of charge. She unlaced her mythril gauntlets and wiped her hands clean with the warm, moist cloth on the table.

This is quite the nice spot, she thought to herself.

The water went down smoothly, and the cloth was nice and soft. Hilda's instincts told her this was a good restaurant.

Plus, everyone's meals look great.

There was all manner of seated customers around her, eating their food. The one thing Hilda noticed was that every one of them had a smile on their faces. Just as Aletta said earlier, it seemed as though the customers were quite fond of the food here.

As Hilda's narrowed eyes drifted around the restaurant, they suddenly widened and rapidly blinked in shock.

Is that the great samurai master Tatsugorou sitting there? And wait...could that be the great sage Altorius next to him?!

The former was a legendary mercenary from the Western Continent. The latter was the greatest sage not only in the Kingdom, but among all of humanity. As a fellow mercenary, Hilda had heard all manner of tales about both individuals, and here she was, looking at them in the flesh. If this meeting had happened in her world, it would be massive news.

"Will you be ordering something?"

"Yes. Um, what do you have?" Hilda asked Aletta.

"Um, let's see... Hilda, can you read Eastern Continent characters?"

"I can. I learned how after becoming a mercenary."

Aletta's expression brightened upon hearing Hilda's answer.

"Ah, then hold on just a second, and I'll bring you a menu!" She vanished into the back before reappearing just as quickly.

"We can serve you everything written here. Once you've made your decision, just call for me!" Aletta handed Hilda a thin but large book of some sort and shuffled off to deal with another customer.

"...Wow, there's so much here." Hilda, now alone, calmly opened the menu. Inside, she found careful explanations of what each dish was. Most of them were things she'd never heard of before.

"They serve croquettes and french fries here? Wha...?!"

The demon mercenary was considering ordering one of the few items on the menu she recognized: the thinly cut cobbler's tubers often served at bars and eateries alongside alcohol. When she turned to the next page, however, Hilda felt like she'd been hit in the head with the softest of pillows.

"They serve sweets, too?!"

Under the section labeled "desserts" was a host of different sweets. Parfaits, pudding, pound cake, pancakes... None of them were remotely familiar, but she did recognize one thing.

"...They're all cheap."

The sweets on the menu of this otherworldly restaurant were all fairly inexpensive. The lowest-costing sweets were only a handful of copper coins, while the most expensive on the menu were still only ten copper coins. Normally, even the smallest of confectionaries would cost multiple silver coins at the very least. That was just the way it worked in Hilda's world. Sugar and honey were both expensive and hard to come by, so sweets in general were considered food only nobles could afford.

When she was just a child, Hilda had risked being stung by bees with her friends to get honey from their beehives and pour it over sour fruits. As an adult, she'd use copper coins to buy the season's fruits. But she'd only ever actually eaten a handful of real sweets in her life.

"Hmm... At this price, I gotta go with sweets."

All the other food on the menu was around the same price. Considering how expensive sweets were where she came from, the choice was clear. Hilda had spent so much time being poor that she was strict about spending.

"But which one should I order...? Ooh, soufflé cheesecake?"

Hilda had felt that learning how to read Eastern characters would be key to her success as a mercenary, so she'd asked a comrade to teach her. Outside of that, however, she had very little education to speak of. Nonetheless, she trusted in the instincts that had kept her alive this far.

Which is how she decided on her order. She skimmed the list and went with the one that "felt" right. There were three different types of cheesecakes on the menu: rare, soufflé, and baked. She chose the one that was described as soft, with a cheesy flavor not unlike a fried confectionary. Cheese was Hilda's absolute favorite food.

"Hey, Aletta! I wanna place my order!"

"Of course! Right away!"

"Get me one of these soufflé cheesecake things, would you? I'll also have some of this black tea stuff, too."

In the corner of the dessert page was a little section that read, "When you order any dessert item, including pudding, all drinks are half off." Hence, Hilda decided to get a drink with her cake.

"Coming right up! Thank you very much!" Aletta took Hilda's order and disappeared into the kitchen.

"I wonder what it's gonna be like..."

Hilda waited impatiently, excited to see just what sort

of confectionary she'd be treated to. Fortunately, all the sweets at the restaurant were apparently premade, so Aletta returned with the order on a clean white plate and a handled cup with tea in no time at all.

"Sorry to keep you waiting!" Aletta said. "This is your soufflé cheesecake and black tea set. The blue container over there has sugar in it, so feel free to add as much as you'd like to your tea."

"Oh? I'm allowed to use the sugar...? Thanks."

Hilda was already shocked that the sugar was free to use, but nonetheless took it. In front of her was a beautiful, ceramic white cup filled with reddish tea and a cheese-colored, triangular confectionary topped with violet sauce. Both were things she'd never seen before.

Let's see, first... Wow, it's so white. I'd heard sugar was typically brown.

The first thing Hilda did was open the lid on the blue container. Inside was pure white sugar and a small spoon with which to scoop it up. She had heard that sugar was brown, so when confronted with the salt-like, white grains, she grew suspicious. Hilda never thought to buy any for herself, so she wasn't exactly knowledgeable on the subject. She scooped some of the sugar out of the container and placed it in her palm, then licked it.

...This is definitely sugar.

All it took was a single lick for the sweetness to spread across the top of her tongue, confirming it as sugar. Hilda dropped three scoops of the stuff into her tea before taking a sip.

"Mm, this is good."

The tea itself was sweet with just a hint of sourness to it. Hilda wasn't used to drinking this sort of thing, but she could nonetheless feel it making its way through her tired body. It was quite delicious.

"Let's see. Next is..."

It was time to dive into the soufflé cheesecake. She took hold of her small fork and cut off a corner of the triangle that had no sauce on it.

"A cheese-flavored confectionery, eh? Wha...?!"

The moment Hilda took a bite of it, she raised her voice.

While the cheesecake undoubtedly had the aroma and sour flavor of cheese, it was also sweet. What really stunned her, however, was its texture.

No way. I know the menu said it was soft, but this is insane!

Indeed, the confectionary Hilda was currently indulging in was far too soft. It was both moist and light, quickly falling apart in her mouth. The only thing that remained was the sweet, cheesy aftertaste. She was sure she'd eaten a piece of the cheesecake, yet nothing remained of it in her mouth.

"This is incredible!"

Unable to forget that amazing texture, she quickly took another bite, this time a much bigger one. Just like before, it was soft and fluffy before fading away and leaving behind the flavor of sweet cheese. But that wasn't all.

Hm?! This violet sauce is awesome, too?!

The next piece she cut from the cake had some of the violet sauce on it, and it, too, tasted brilliant.

Wait, is this sauce made from sugared, boiled berries?

The sweet and sour berry sauce paired perfectly with cheesecake. It had a thick sweetness to it that fresh fruits simply didn't have. Both the cheese and the berries were sour in completely different ways, but the sauce brought them together in harmony.

The moist cheesecake even partnered well with Hilda's tea.

"Excuse me, Aletta! Could I get another order of... No, *two* more orders of cheesecake? And a refill on my tea, too!"

It was inevitable that Hilda would order seconds.

"Of course! Hold on just a moment!" Aletta responded cheerfully.

"Phew... I can't believe they even let me order takeout."

Hilda walked through the forest at night, her breath still smelling of cheese. In her hand was a round cake (six slices worth) she had purchased from the Restaurant to Another World. She even received a little glass jar of sauce (apparently called jam) to use on it. The fact that this all cost a single silver coin was incredible.

Quite happy with her purchasing decisions, Hilda hurried back to camp.

"I can't wait for tomorrow morning."

The man who proclaimed to be the master of the restaurant warned her that if she didn't eat the cake by the next morning, it might go bad. Hilda wasn't in the least bit concerned. She'd be able to devour six slices of it in one sitting, no problem at all.

C'mon, Hilda. Patience. Wait till tomorrow!

Hilda shook her head at the thought of sneaking just one more slice for the evening. She knew she would regret digging into her new cake when she was still enjoying the aftertaste of the previous slice. She trusted her instincts.

And so, Hilda turned away from the cake and closed her eyes.

I guess, well... One of these days, I can tell them about that place. One of these days.

Hilda pictured the other female demon mercenaries who called the imperial capital their home. They were her rivals, but they were also easy to spend time around. While she wasn't going to say anything yet, she figured it might be worth telling them about the Restaurant to Another World eventually and getting them to owe her one.

As she mulled over these thoughts, she slowly drifted off to sleep.

*Restaurant to
Another World*

CHAPTER 24
Natto Spaghetti

"Wow..."

Fardania, an elf born in the Shiena woods, looked up at the massive tree towering over her and found herself completely overwhelmed.

Long ago, two of the great dragons known as the "Seven Overlords" had used their fierce breath to carve great scars into the giant tree. Those dragons were Gold, renowned for its immense greed, and Red, whose ravenous nature was legendary.

Half a year had passed since Fardania left her home and began her journey. This time, she found herself in the center of the great sea of trees, a place that had prevented all non-elves from entering for many years. There were all types of monsters roaming the forest, not to mention the many magical barriers the elves had set up. If one didn't know how to make use of the forest's blessings, there would be no way to survive the journey to its center. It was so vast that it took half a month for Fardania to make her way there.

The giant tree that made this place its home was the reason Fardania traveled here. It was the entrance she was searching for.

The forest capital.

It was the one remaining elven city from the time when the elves ruled the world, when they did battle against the Seven Overlords and the races that worshipped them. During that era, some thousand years ago, the elves had a magical civilization far more complex than the present. But then a great pestilence wiped out most of their population, civilization collapsed on itself, and humans took over as the dominant species. It was then that the elves began to dwell in small villages in the lush forests around the world, choosing to live their lives closed off from the other races. The forest capital was the closest thing they had left to a "nation" of their own.

"So, this is where Dad's friend is..." Fardania said.

Inside her bag was a letter her father had sent after her with his familiar. Fardania gently placed her hand on it. He was clearly worried about his young, impulsive daughter and her journey alone, so he'd sent her a letter of introduction to his old friend in the capital.

When I was but a child of a hundred years old, I traveled across the human world with this man as my guide. I recall him being quite the foodie. In fact, he's still researching food to this very day, I imagine. If you have nowhere else to go, I recommend paying him a visit.

So her father had written in the letter.

If she was going to surpass the master's otherworldly cooking, she had to know her own world first. In order to do that, she had to pay a visit to the capital of the elves, the place where her people's wisdom dwelled.

"Great," she said. "I should at least be able to get through this myself."

The massive tree in front of her was the entrance to the capital. Fardania approached and sighed in relief after inspecting the magic cast on it. It was a type of barrier magic designed to keep monsters away and prevent outsiders from entering, and it took someone with immense magical talent to even temporarily break. One could say it was the pinnacle of all elven knowledge.

The barrier essentially warned that those who were not practitioners of the magical arts were not worthy of entering the capital. Fardania, who had trained in the magical arts under her father, was at least capable of opening a hole big enough to enter.

"Dad wanted me to contact his friend via telepathy

once I got here so he could open the door for me," she thought. "But...it's faster if I just do this myself."

Fardania began to work on breaking the magical lock. She figured that once she broke through the barrier, a second kind of magic, perhaps a warning of some kind, would activate. This would inform the people on the inside that she had come, which worked out quite nicely.

Fardania was a pure-blooded elf of the Shiena woods. There shouldn't be any issue with her visiting the capital. And so, she weakened the barrier for a brief period, stepping foot into the elves' last true domain.

Meanwhile...

"Oh? The barrier's being tampered with."

Christian noticed the disturbance while working on research inside his mansion, which was built into the massive tree.

"Hrm, they appear to be quite skilled."

The elven man was currently in charge of monitoring the barrier protecting the forest capital. As an elf now in his fifth century, Christian was among the youngest in the city, but his magic and sword skills were second to none. His time in the human world had been quite fruitful. The barrier protecting the city was also equipped with another high-level spell that would automatically trigger a warning.

"They're not even trying to hide their presence. My guess is that we have an elven guest," Christian said aloud, pondering his own theory.

It was clear that whoever tampered with the barrier only did so temporarily to allow themselves time to enter. Christian couldn't imagine that the visitor hadn't noticed the warning magic, given their skill, theorizing that this was a sign that they didn't mean to hide their presence. A sign of their intent, so to speak.

"Something about their technique feels familiar..." he muttered. "Ah, could it be that she's finally arrived?"

Christian noticed that the caster's technique resembled an old friend of his that he traveled with some fifty years prior. He had received a letter from this man via his familiar half a year ago.

My daughter has left on a journey, seeking to invent a new type of food. I imagine she'll probably head to the forest capital first. When she gets there, please look after her.

There was more to the letter, but that was undoubtedly the most important part. The rest of it was filled with Christian's friend talking about how adorable his daughter was and how she'd come to resemble his wife.

It even included a warning about how he wouldn't show his friend any mercy should he try to lay his hands on the young lady.

"Well then, I'm sure if I wait here, she'll find me eventually. Now that I think about it, the door should be appearing today..."

If she's trying to invent a completely new cuisine, that place might be a good place to start.

After all, it certainly had done so for Christian. It was that very restaurant that propelled him to begin his search for something new in the first place.

After breaching the massive tree's barrier, Fardania stepped foot into the forest capital for the first time.

"This is the place, right?"

The capital was filled with countless houses made from the wood of the living tree. One of them belonged to her father's friend, Christian. It didn't take long to locate his home after asking a fellow elf walking by.

"Christian's house has had this weird smell coming from it for the past ten years," she was informed. "You'll recognize it immediately."

Fardania wasn't entirely sure what the elf meant by

this at first, but after walking around for a bit, it became clear. She could smell his house from a distance. It was like something was rotting.

"Excuse me..." she called. "Long time no see, sir."

Fortunately for the young elven woman, the master of the house made his presence known immediately. He had golden hair and green eyes, and wore a thin mythril sword at his waist, no doubt infused with some type of magic. To the average human, who had trouble discerning elven ages, the man only looked to be a year or two older than Fardania. However, to the eyes of an elf capable of seeing the flow of magic, it was obvious he was even older than her father. His strong magical power spoke to that.

According to Fardania's father, Christian was some hundred years older than him. He also lived alone. Elves also typically didn't hire help, instead choosing to make helper golems for themselves. Considering the man standing before her looked just like the person in her memories from when she was thirteen years old, she was certain this was Christian.

"Yes, Fardania, was it?" the elf said. "I heard everything from Edmond. Your lifting of the entrance barrier was quite clever. There aren't many elves who can undo it at just past a hundred years old, even here in the forest capital. You truly are Edmond and Matilda's daughter. I'm quite impressed."

"Thank you very much, sir." Fardania accepted Christian's honest praise, albeit a bit shyly.

"Please, relax. There's no need to be so formal with me. You are my best friend's daughter, and you're already an adult, correct? Treat me as you would a friend," Christian responded, voicing what had been on his mind since she'd arrived.

"Underst—okay. Glad to be friends, Christian."

"Likewise, Fardania."

The two elves shook hands, symbolizing their new friendship.

"So, uh, what's with the smell? Is there something rotting in here?"

It didn't take long for Fardania's eyes to sparkle with curiosity. She immediately asked Christian what was on her mind, and the older elf couldn't help but grin on the inside.

Christian laughed. *I see. She's rather outspoken.*

"I suppose you could say that I'm doing research on rotten elf beans."

Fardania raised her eyebrow in response. "...What?"

She knew what elf beans were. Long, long ago, when the elven armies were off on an expedition, they had discovered a crop with strange powers. The crop had the ability to revitalize dry ground when planted and grown in it. The beans were used to regrow barren forests as well. As such, it was a popular crop to grow among elves, and frequently eaten too. Fresh elf beans were a beautiful green color, while the dried beans were closer to a light yellow. Boiling would give them a gentle sweetness, and they were quite delicious. Even Fardania's hometown had a stockpile growing in the forest, though not in great quantities.

"But why would you rot them?" she asked.

Despite her knowledge of the beans, Fardania didn't see the point in rotting them. Drying them would prevent rotting from ever happening in the first place, and most elves could use magic to prevent foods from rotting at all.

Preserving foods for hundreds of years required the use of magical tools, but if one wanted to save something for a few days, it wasn't very difficult. At least not to a race full of talented magic users. Fardania herself had done this multiple times, often using magic to preserve the rice balls she purchased from the restaurant so she could enjoy them over multiple days. If she could use that kind of magic, there was no way Christian, an elf more long-lived and powerful, couldn't.

"Well, I'm not really rotting them." Christian took a moment to think before rewording his answer. "Do you know what cheese is?"

He'd decided to start with the basics, a food that most elves had little contact with.

"Cheese?" she asked. "That's a food that humans make, right? I believe it involves taking beast milk and letting it sit in the dark for a long period of time without any kind of preservation magic, cultivating mold in it. Normally, it should just go bad. But apparently it doesn't, and humans even find it delicious."

Fardania had traveled the human world for quite some time before finding her way to the forest capital. While she wasn't terribly familiar with the food, she had at least heard of it. Needless to say, she'd never felt the need to eat it herself, so she didn't have the slightest idea what it tasted like.

Christian nodded. "Precisely. Humans call the process 'fermentation.' Human alcohol is apparently made in a similar way. It's one of the preservation methods they came up with due to not being able to use magic as easily as we can. I'm currently trying to use that technique on elf beans."

Christian spoke to Fardania about the details of his current objective. Because elves could use magic to preserve a food's freshness, the concept of "fermentation" would never cross their minds. Christian was the only one doing research into it.

"So, does it work?"

"Indeed it does… I've eaten the real thing before," Christian nodded his head and responded. He had seen what the "finished" product looked like. All that was left was to replicate it.

"Wait, where? They have them here in the capital?"

Fardania's curiosity was on the receiving end of a shock after discovering the existence of something she'd never heard of before. "Fermented" elf beans… Perhaps they could be of some use in her own food quest.

"Not in the capital… Er, well I suppose it's sort of in the capital?"

Fardania was confused by Christian's vague answer. Unable to parse his meaning, she asked for an explanation. "What do you mean?"

Christian cleared his throat. "About ten years ago, a door to another world appeared in the forest capital. This door is connected to a restaurant on the other side, and it serves a dish using fermented beans."

As the man in charge of monitoring the city's barrier, it was Christian's responsibility to inspect the door. This was what led to his new research.

There was also one other thing that Christian wanted to confirm. A question had appeared in his mind when he first read Edmond's letter.

What exactly could cause a proud, young, passionate elf woman, talented in the culinary arts, to suddenly leave her peaceful home in search of making a "new food"? Christian thought it highly possible that, like him, she had eaten something delicious made by someone other than an elf.

"Wait, you can't mean..." Fardania immediately knew what Christian was referring to. It was the very same thing that had become the trigger for her own journey.

"Judging by your reaction, you must be familiar with it as well. The Restaurant to Another World."

And just like that, Christian's theory was proven true.

Christian and Fardania entered the Restaurant to Another World, greeted by the sounds of the magical bells ringing.

"Welcome! Oh, this is a rare pairing," the master remarked upon seeing the two elves.

On one side was the young elven man, a regular at the restaurant. On the other was the elven girl who had been popping up every now and then over the past year. He'd never seen the two of them come together.

"Yes, she's the daughter of a good friend of mine," Christian explained. "I'm treating her today. Can I get the usual? Two orders of natto spaghetti, no eggs. Much obliged."

Christian once made the mistake of eating the spaghetti with eggs, so he now made it a point to bring them up every time he ordered.

"You got it!" The master nodded his head and went into the back.

"Natto spaghetti... That's something us elves can eat?" Fardania asked Christian after watching him take care of things.

Elves couldn't eat meat, fish, eggs, or milk. Fardania had incorrectly assumed the only dishes at Nekoya that didn't utilize these ingredients were the tofu steak and the fried rice balls.

Just how many dishes does this place serve?!

The depths of Nekoya's menu made Fardania anxious.

"Natto spaghetti has a unique smell to it, you see. It's not very popular with the other customers. I'm the only one who orders it, actually."

Christian explained the dish to the young lady in front of him. It took a great deal of courage to order something

97

described in the menu as "a noodle dish topped with rotten beans." When he first visited Nekoya, the current master had just taken over. If he hadn't recommended the dish to him as something without meat, fish, eggs, or milk, he likely would have never thought to order it for himself. That said, Christian had been the dish's number one fan ever since that fateful day.

And so, their food finally arrived.

"Sorry to keep you waiting! Here are your orders of natto spaghetti!"

A young demon waitress who looked about the same age as the two elves set their meal down atop the table. Both plates were full of slim, yellow noodles. Sitting on top of them were thinly sliced, black, paper-like objects, dark green herbs with a strong scent, and some sort of sauce with beans that looked surprisingly similar to elf beans but darker in color.

"Let's eat. Fear not, it's quite delicious." Christian held his silver fork and lightly mixed the natto at the top with the spaghetti below it. He then wrapped a helping of spaghetti around his spoon and took a bite. It was as delicious as always.

Natto spaghetti was always a treat. Christian only recently managed to replicate natto's unique stickiness and scent in his own research. The rich flavor was a combination with something salty, likely mixed in with it beforehand. Then there was the uncooked herb with its unique flavor and the black, paper-like substance. It had the same savory taste as the grass of the sea. These flavors fused with the light, wheat taste of the noodles to form a singular new flavor profile.

It looks like she's taken a liking to it as well.

Christian glanced up at Fardania while he ate his spaghetti. She also ate in dead silence. Her own eating speed matched Christian's, the spaghetti disappearing off her plate in front of his very eyes. She was clearly enjoying her meal.

Hm. She seems to be contemplating something.

Christian almost immediately realized what Fardania was pondering while she ate her serving of spaghetti.

She's analyzing the flavor?

That made sense. If she were truly researching food as she said she was, of course she'd focus on the flavor. Christian turned his focus back to his own meal.

Christian had no way of knowing. He had no way of knowing what she was really thinking, or what she would soon do.

❦

The incident happened after the pair had finished their plates of natto spaghetti. Fardania turned her attention to the waitress collecting their plates.

"The natto stuff in this dish, um... I'd like to try it with rice. Is that possible?"

She asked as though it were the most natural question in the world.

Wh-what?!

Meanwhile, Christian was stunned into silence by Fardania's words. Natto was a type of sauce used on noodle dishes. For ten years, the researcher had simply assumed this to be the case. And yet, here was this young lady, completely flipping that idea on its head after a single sit-down.

I-Impossible! There's no "natto rice" anywhere on the menu!

However, the demon waitress simply tilted her head in response to the question.

"Um... Hold on just a moment. I'll go ask the master," she said, retreating to the back.

It wasn't long before the master reappeared, carrying a small bowl filled with white rice, a plate with sliced, thick green herbs on top, and a dish with some sort of yellow sauce. There was even a glass bottle similar to the ones already on the table. Last but not least, he carried a bowl filled with natto. "Geez. We're supposed to serve western cuisine..." he muttered as he approached their table.

The master lined the various dishes up in front of Fardania.

"Make sure to stir the natto thoroughly," he instructed "Once you've done that, mix in some of this dashi soy sauce and pour it all on top of the rice. Feel free to use as much onion and mustard as you'd like. Just be careful. Too much of the latter and you'll feel it in your nose. Take it nice and easy."

"Got it," Fardania said. "Oh, and could I also get two fried rice ball sets? Make one of them miso flavored. Nice and strong."

"You got it. Sit tight." The master turned to leave for the kitchen.

"E-excuse me! Could I have the same...? I'd like an order of natto rice, please!" Christian simply couldn't help himself.

"Roger that. It'll be right out."

And just like that, Christian found himself face to face with the same dish that Fardania ordered.

"Mm, I knew it! Natto pairs super well with rice!" Fardania looked like a small child happily enjoying her food.

Christian couldn't help but feel slightly panicked watching her eat, so he began digging in, too. First, he stirred the natto, making its texture that much stickier. He didn't care and continued stirring. Next, he mixed in some of the dashi soy sauce. Christian had a hunch that this was the same ingredient used in natto spaghetti. The elf continued stiring it all together. Finally, he added a dash of the green herbs and yellow stuff, taking care not to use too much. He took a quick bite of his mix so he could make the right adjustments.

This is definitely natto. And this...

The saltiness of the dashi soy sauce fused nicely with the sticky texture and taste of the natto. Meanwhile, the addition of just a wee bit of onion and mustard—used as a secret flavor in the noodles—gave it all a bit of a punch. This was Christian's first time ever eating natto by itself in this world, but it was quite delicious. After making sure it was just to his liking, he added it to the bowl of white rice.

All it took was a single bite. Christian trembled from shock.

It was good. The natto had the flavor of the earth. When paired with the warm, white rice, it became that much tastier. If he were to put it into words, it reminded him of his friendship with Edmond... The feeling of traveling with a close friend for years on end. That's how well they went together. The vaguely sweet but simple flavor of the rice fused with the strong flavor and aroma of the natto to become its own new, delicious experience. Natto existed to be eaten with rice. The flavor Christian experienced was so strong it led him to this very conviction.

At the same time, this was also the taste of defeat. The young woman sitting in front of him, his best friend Edmond's daughter, had yet to even live a third as long as he and was still so far ahead of him in terms of her pursuit of flavor. She had a powerful appetite, refusing to be tied down by common sense and, perhaps most importantly, had the reckless bravery to boldly take on new challenges...

Ah, to be young again.

Christian made peace with himself. The young woman in front of him was already a full-blown connoisseur of flavor.

After leaving the Restaurant to Another World, Christian informed Fardania of something important.

"What?! Rice exists in our world?!" Fardania was dumbstruck by her new friend's words.

She simply didn't expect rice to exist on their side of the door. She'd been traveling for a year now, stopping by various elf villages and human towns, but not once had she come across the fluffy, white grain.

"Indeed it does. Across the ocean on the Western Continent, dishes with rice are quite common," Christian explained, nodding his head in response to Fardania's outburst.

The older elf had spent many more years of his life, a century or more, traveling across the world. While rice was extremely rare on the Eastern Continent, it was more common than wheat over on the Western Continent. People there ate it daily. While it didn't taste much like the rice served in the Restaurant to Another World, it was most certainly a similar crop.

"Wow... I had no idea." Fardania's eyes sparkled.

Rice.

This was the crop she sought. If she was going to make a dish better than anything at the Restaurant to Another World, she was going to need rice. This was the very moment Fardania's next objective was decided.

Haha, she really is quite young.

Seeing Fardania burn with passion, Christian decided to give her something.

"Fardania, here. Take this." He handed her a small pot filled with his prized treasure.

"What's this? Wait, it's a little different from the stuff on the rice balls, but this is miso, isn't it? You can make miso by rotting—er, fermenting elf beans?!"

It took only a single peek into the pot for Fardania to figure out what it contained. Its red and brown earthy color made it obvious. The research into fermenting elf beans Christian was conducting had already born fruit. Fardania never imagined for a moment that one of that restaurant's staple foods could be made in her world.

"That is correct. After many long years of research, I accidentally stumbled upon the recipe for elf bean miso." Christian nodded. His current goal was to find a way to purposely make it. But at the moment, this was all the elf bean miso in the entire world.

"Take it with you," he said. "Your favorite food is miso, is it not?"

"Thank you so much for everything," she said.

Fardania politely accepted the pot, clearly moved by his actions, and stuffed it into her magic bag. This was something truly precious. She had to take good care of it.

"Well then, I'll be going."

"Yes, take care. Even with the life span of an elf, it's a wide world out there."

Fardania began her journey anew as Christian watched from afar. Her destination was just beyond the ocean. The young elf's pursuit of flavor continued.

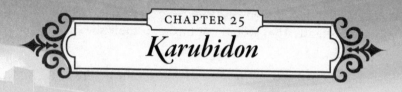

CHAPTER 25
Karubidon

JUST BEFORE THE SUN ROSE in the southern hemisphere, Fairey was in her private quarters deep within the Ocean Nation's palace, preparing to go out. Her servants were normally in charge of dressing her, but she had made sure to pick a time when they'd be gone. Fairey began dressing herself.

She was changing into a standard court lady uniform, the cheapest of all the clothes she had access to. It didn't have a single spell cast on it by any diviners, lacking the protection normally provided for those of royal blood. As it was forbidden for anyone not of Fairey's family to use certain strong perfumes, she picked something several measures weaker. She forsook her favorite earrings, as black as her own hair, and the sapphire hair piece, the same color as her mother's eyes. Fairey's mother was originally a princess of the Kingdom in the Eastern Continent before moving to the Ocean Nation to be wed. Such jewelry would cause her to stick out too much. None of it was needed where she was going, and more importantly, they would not fit the costume she was trying for.

All right. This should be good enough, she thought.

After getting dressed, she looked in her long mirror built from a single piece of silver by the palace's craftsman. Reflected back at Fairey was a young, fourteen-year-old girl with the mixed blood of a foreign-born mother. The palace jesters and bards had less than kind words for how they described Fairey's unique beauty, but there was little she could do about that. Still, everything else about her outfit was impeccable.

Perfect. Now nobody should be able to tell who I am. I look just like a commoner girl.

Fairey was pleased by her flawless disguise. As far as she was concerned, this was exactly what a commoner girl looked like. Of course, she'd also never seen a commoner girl in her entire life, but that was a small detail.

I should be on my way.

With her preparations finished, Fairey made sure to not get caught by her annoying attendants as she made her way outside. Her destination was the flower garden in the center of the palace yard. It was there that flowers bloomed across all four seasons and also where she would find the "path" to her objective.

The flower garden was filled with all kinds of mingling scents. Fairey made her way into a grove off to the side. As she stepped into the grove, she noticed the spell that was always cast there, designed to make one grow lost and confused, was gone. Her steps grew lighter.

...So, she was telling the truth. That fox of a man is at a party today.

The rumor the young girl had heard from one of the gossip-loving attendants she was close to in the palace was true.

While the palace diviner was undoubtedly extremely capable in the magical arts and quite smart, something about him was suspicious. He reminded Fairey of a devious fox. On this day, he was away from the palace, attending a party hosted by the prime minister who handled foreign affairs. Whenever the diviner had to leave the palace for a party or some sort of public affairs business, the shrewd man released the spell he normally cast to prevent people from getting near the place.

Days like that overlapped with the Day of Satur rarely, once every few months at best. Fortunately for Fairey, today was her lucky day.

And so, the young girl came face to face with her objective.

...It's been three long months.

Fairey stared at the large black door with the cat illustration on its front. This was what she disguised herself as a commoner for. This was why she had to avoid the diviner's ever watchful eyes. Just thinking about the food waiting for her made her mouth water. She wrapped her hand around the door's handle and turned it.

The sound of bells ringing greeted Fairey as she stood in place just beyond the entrance.

"Oh? Welcome! It's been a while."

"Yes, it has. You have done well to greet... Er, may I have the usual?" Fairey smiled at the master.

One fateful day two years ago, Fairey had shown mercy to a mouse-like halfling who had snuck into the palace garden, letting her go without alerting the guards. In exchange, the small person had led her to this place, where she would eat *it* for the first time. Since then, she only ever ordered the same dish.

"Aye, you got it. Hang on just a moment." The master accepted her order as usual and left for the back.

This was the Restaurant to Another World, the one and only place in the world where Fairey could eat *that* dish.

I see this place is as bustling as ever, she thought with a smile.

The young lady sat down at an open seat and surveyed the hustle and bustle of the restaurant while she waited for her food to arrive. People from completely different backgrounds shared the space, eating their respective meals. Among them were even high-class customers like Fairey.

For example, there was the Witch Princess. Fairey had seen her once when she was a child. The great sage's student had bluish silver hair and light, sky-blue colored eyes. Her pointy ears were proof she was a half-elf, and she was as beautiful as a doll. She was indulging in some sort of soft, yellow treat.

Then there were the siblings from the Desert Nation, just like her father's concubine, who indulged in some sort of black coffee with white ice cream atop of it. They also had beautiful, green-colored drinks with soft cream sitting on top. The pair wore flashy clothes over their stunning bronze skin. They had black eyes and smooth black hair as well.

The pair seemed to be paying attention to another high-class visitor, a beautiful girl with white skin and light blonde hair, who carefully ate some sort of large and colorful confectionery in a glass cup.

Fairey laughed to herself. *You've all got it quite wrong.*

They were all eating things that were far from being Nekoya's most delicious menu item, at least as far as Fairey was concerned. The young girl cradled that slight feeling of superiority in her chest as she waited for her food.

And then...

"Sorry to keep you waiting! I have your meal right here. Um... This *is* correct, right?"

"Yes, it is," Fairey replied and nodded her head to the newly hired demon servant who seemed altogether puzzled.

The dish the servant held was undoubtedly her most beloved of foods. The aroma had already made its way to her nostrils, causing her mouth to water.

"Excellent!" Satisfied with her answer, the demon servant placed the dish of food down in front of Fairey, along with a bowl of miso-flavored soup and a glass of tea.

The meal consisted of a single large bowl. Across it were a series of white and blue stripes. The bowl itself was filled with white rice and a host of colorful vegetables. On top of that was carefully seasoned and cooked beef.

"Oh, how I have longed for this day! How I have

longed to partake in a 'karubidon' from the other world!"
Fairey couldn't help but voice her delight aloud.

Three months had passed since she last had the opportunity to enjoy a karubidon. Even longer had passed (two
years) since her chance encounter with the halfling who
brought her to the door. To Fairey, karubidon was the
greatest of all feasts.

"Please take your time and enjoy! I'll bring out your
dessert as soon as you're finished." With that, the demon
servant hurriedly returned to waiting on the other customers. Fairey watched her leave and then turned her
attention to the karubidon.

I must enjoy its delightful aroma before anything else.
The day Fairey first came to the restaurant, she had
lacked any real worldly experience (not that she had any
now). She barely trusted the mouse-like halfling who described to her the most delicious way of eating karubidon
at the Restaurant to Another World. Regardless, even
now Fairey followed the halfling's instructions.

Fairey lifted the bowl. She could sense the heat of
the bowl on her hands, and it was just heavy enough for
Fairey's slender arms to feel its weight. It was undoubtedly

a meal meant for royalty. Her face near the karubidon, she was entranced.

There was so much food in the bowl that Fairey could barely make out the rice beneath it all. She could see the sweet, bright orange karoots and dark green boiled pieces of spinach. She spotted white elf bean sprouts and, of course, brown beef seasoned with some sort of juice and a dash of white powder.

Fairey kept the dish close to her face and breathed in deep. The aroma of the sweet rice and freshly cooked meat found their way into her finely shaped nose along with the stimulating scent of the juices. These three elements came together to make Fairey's stomach grumble and rage for food.

Ooooh, I can wait no longer!

Anyone who grew up learning classic manners in the Ocean Nation would look at the Restaurant to Another World's eating practices as rather barbaric, but Fairey cared little. She began digging into her food. She scooped up a piece of meat drenched in juices and took a small, almost bird-like bite of it.

Oh, this miraculous taste! How I have seen and felt it in my dreams!

The flavor of the meat and its juices danced across her tongue along with the taste of the fat and its light mouthfeel. The meat and fish served at the Ocean Nation's palace were typically boiled for a long period of time to excise any "extraneous" elements from the meat. This beef was different, however, as its delicious juices spilled out into her mouth as one. Supporting that flavor was the juice used to season the meat in the first place. It helped elevate the meal to the realm of art.

The juice had a fruity sweetness to it, accompanied by the faint spice and salt of some unknown ingredient that reminded Fairey of fish sauce. Mixed into all of that was a sort of aromatic, greasy something or the other. While this complicated sauce was too strong to enjoy on its own, it went perfectly with the meat.

It tasted nothing like what was served in the palace, which was why it so easily captured Fairey's heart and stomach.

But now it's time for the main attraction!

Fairey couldn't afford to let her guard down just yet. It wasn't just the meat that made this dish so exquisite. No, the karubidon was not a complete dish with that alone. Now that Fairey had begun her journey through the wonderland of taste, there would be no stopping for detours. In her quest for further deliciousness, she stuck her chopsticks into the bowl.

By taking a piece of beef earlier, Fairey had uncovered a trove of white rice hidden beneath. She grabbed a small but comfortable amount of rice with her chopsticks and proceeded to eat it.

!!!

There were no words left. No more ways to express what Fairey felt in that moment. The warm, fluffy rice spread throughout her mouth, its sweet taste and flavor in a completely different league than the rice served in the Ocean Nation. The meat that trampled through-out Fairey's mouth then turned its attention to the rice, courting its favor and mixing together. The flavor that came out of that divine encounter was the true treasure that Fairey sought and desired most.

This was the flavor that captivated Fairey, turning her from a high-born princess of the Ocean Nation into a commoner girl.

Fairey !et herself slowly enjoy the array of tastes in front of her. She indulged in the contrast of the colorful vegetables against the white rice and meat. She could feel the heat on her hands through the bowl.

First, she ate some meat, then some rice, carefully so as to not dirty her clothes. She then took bites of the thick, green spinooch, the faintly sweet karoots, and the crunchy elf bean sprouts. All of the vegetables were lightly seasoned with salt but otherwise barely had an actual flavor to speak of. This meant they worked perfectly as a palette cleanser between bites of rice and meat.

Next, it was time to eat the vegetables together with the meat and rice.

By adding vegetables to the complete flavor that was meat and rice, the karubidon once again revealed a brand-new character it kept hidden up its sleeves. The texture the vegetables provided to the taste and seasoning of the meat juices was irresistible. After taking several bites from the karubidon, Fairey then turned to the miso soup, a piece of seaweed floating across it, and sipped directly from the bowl. This new flavor let the tongue relax, energizing it so it could go back to the front lines of the karubidon at maximum capacity, ready to win.

There was no more room for words.

Fairey's tongue was being used for tasting and nothing else.

But eventually, that performance came to an end.

"Phew."

Fairey took longer than most customers to finish her dish, taking the time to enjoy her glass of cold tea and letting out sighs infused with the aroma of meat. All that remained was a tremendous feeling of satisfaction. No ordinary meal provided the same feeling of fulfillment and happiness that this one did. Fairey was quite possibly the happiest young lady on the planet in this moment.

Karubidon really is the other world's most delicious food of all.

While Fairey lost herself in thought, the demon servant from before returned to her table.

"Um, I'm here with your soft cream! I'll take your plates for you."

"Much obliged."

Fairey's empty plates were replaced with a small container filled with white, soft cream.

"Ah... It's so sweet."

The cold, rich sweetness of the soft cream made for the perfect way to close out her climactic battle with the karubidon. Like with her main course, Fairey slowly partook in the desert, taking each spoonful slowly and meaningfully.

All good things must come to an end, and Fairey finished off her soft cream.

"Phew, I am rather satisfied. Well then, I'll be taking my leave," said the young girl to the servant, quietly leaving behind the payment on the table.

Truth be told, this was the only time and place in which Fairey had use for silver coins. She asked one of her female attendants for access to multiple coins, but the whole meal only cost a single coin. Indeed, the karubidon, tea, and soft cream all totaled up to naught but a single silver coin.

Is that really enough?

She couldn't help but wonder this to herself every time she visited. Fairey knew for a fact the master refused to take more money than that, so she complied with a single silver coin. It was the one way she could express her gratitude to the restaurant. It didn't feel like an equivalent exchange though.

Fairey watched the demon servant take the coin off the table and begin cleaning up, before leaving through the door she came in.

Karubidon should be eaten in one sitting and capped off with soft cream. Once the soft cream is finished, one must leave immediately.

These were the instructions the halfling had given Fairey two years ago when the halfling first led the young girl to the Restaurant to Another World. Fairey continued to follow those words as she returned to the grove in the palace garden.

I have no need for lunch today.

Fairey gently rubbed her stomach and returned to her quarters to change.

It was just about lunchtime, but she hardly felt the need to put anything else into her mouth at this point. She would simply explain that she felt ill.

Considering how full she felt, eating anything else would be rather boorish indeed.

As the sun shone bright in the sky above, Fairey gathered her determination for the day as a single crow looked down upon her.

This crow was, in fact, a familiar created by its master to specifically watch over the princess as she went on her little "adventures."

"It's important for the princess to be able to spread her wings every once in a while, lest she start to feel cramped," Doushun whispered. He smiled to himself as he watched the princess from the eyes of his crow familiar, slowly rocking to and fro in the carriage on his way to the party.

CHAPTER 26
Assorted Cookies

I T WASN'T YET the Day of Satur, so Aletta was visiting a certain building just outside of the royal capital.

"Um, this *is* the place, right?"

The young demon girl had made her way to an old district of the capital, directed by the employment agency. This part of the city used to be quite lived-in, and ultimately was much nicer and well kept than the ruins Aletta currently called home. But because the citizens began moving to the newer districts of the capital, the area was now mostly empty.

Through the employment agency, Aletta had been introduced to a potential job as a housekeeper. The residence was home to an adventurer named Sarah who frequently left on journeys. She wanted someone to take care of the house and chores while she was away.

The person at the office said she was a good person, if more than a little odd...

The older woman working at the agency was rather kind to Aletta, and even presented her with this job opportunity, claiming it to be a good chance for her.

Apparently, personality had been more important than skill set for this particular job.

"To be completely honest, I don't really trust you demons too much, ya hear?" said the agent. "But recently you've really cleaned yerself up. Plus, ya always make sure to do the work. More importantly, ya ain't no liar. I figure it might not be a bad idea to introduce someone like ya to the young...er, to Sarah."

And so, Aletta received a letter of introduction and directions to Sarah's house. Apparently, she'd be the one to decide whether or not she wanted to hire the demon girl for the job.

Aletta stood before the door of the house, hopeful but still a bundle of anxiety. She checked herself to make sure everything was in order. While she was still wearing the same old clothes as before, the master gave her expensive smelling soap along with her pay.

"Keep yourself clean, got it?" he'd said.

And so, the young woman made sure to wash her body, hair, and clothes much more thoroughly than usual.

In fact, Aletta was significantly cleaner than the average commoner at this point.

"Excuse me! Gelga from the employment agency sent me here!" Aletta strengthened her resolve and announced her arrival to the master of the household in a loud voice.

Even if things don't turn out so hot, I'll make it thanks to my job at the restaurant.

Aletta was nervous but not panicked. With a click, the door in front of her opened, and the master of the house appeared before her.

"Huh?"

"Wha?"

Both the demon girl and the women at the door immediately recognized one another and voiced their surprise in tandem.

Three days quickly passed following Aletta's hiring at Sarah's home. It was the Day of Satur, and the demon girl was working her hardest at the Restaurant to Another World. Like always, she arrived early in the morning at Nekoya, washed herself thoroughly, changed into her uniform, and began waiting on customers until just after midday.

"Okay. It's your thirty-minute break," said the master. "You're free to relax until the long hand on that clock over there points straight up."

"Yes, sir!"

The master usually looked for an opening when there weren't too many customers present to give his waitress her break time. Aletta gripped the hot cocoa she received from him with both hands and took a seat in the small break room.

"Whew. Delicious."

Aletta was careful to take small sips of the hot cocoa, so as to not burn her tongue. The liquid warmed her tired body. This sweet but slightly bitter drink had become a personal favorite of Aletta's ever since she first tried it. Apparently, it was a product of the other world. Aletta had never seen the drink in the royal capital before, and that was said to be the most advanced and prosperous city in the entire nation. That's why whenever she had the chance to get a free drink from the restaurant, she always made sure to order cocoa.

"I feel so happy!"

Aletta let out a satisfied sigh. In the last month, she'd had so much good fortune that it felt like some sort of dream. That wasn't all though. Aletta herself had also changed.

Since getting hired by the Restaurant to Another World, the demon girl stopped wearing her hat even when in the capital. The primary reason for this was that every time she worked at the restaurant, she was able to wash herself with scented, otherworldly oils twice, once in the morning and once at night. As a result, her formerly unkempt hair looked quite beautiful, and she felt it'd be a waste to hide it. Through taking her hat off, Aletta also realized that it was better to work without one on.

Aletta was a demon, which was why she had two small black horns on her head. Choosing not to wear a hat meant the humans around her would be aware of her lineage. On the other hand, leaving them out in the open also seemed to signal that she was an honest young lady who wasn't hiding anything. Much to Aletta's surprise, this helped with finding work on her side of the door. Of course, this didn't suddenly mean that there *weren't* people who gave her dirty looks or refused to hire her. It was, however, easier for Aletta to outright avoid work with those kinds of people, instead finding places that were okay with hiring demons. In truth, the amount of trouble she ran into had gone down significantly.

A large part of this was due to how clean and well kept Aletta had become through simply washing herself and her clothes more regularly. The kinds of problems she encountered were completely different nowadays: the beautiful demon girl now found herself on the receiving end of human and demon men trying their best to pick her up.

Three days ago, Aletta began working as a housekeeper at her employer's house. Her employer, a self-proclaimed treasure hunter, had her doing a variety of things around the small abode, such as cleaning, laundry, and other household chores. When Sarah went out, she entrusted Aletta with holding down the fort.

The house had a room full of the treasure hunter's precious magical tools and the like. While this space was locked, allowing anyone to watch over a house with a room like that meant trusting the person. It only took a single glance at Aletta for the treasure hunter to place her trust in the girl, offering a total of eight copper coins a day as well as a room to live in. There was a single reason for the way Sarah treated Aletta.

She already knew Aletta quite well. Sarah, lover of minced meat cutlets, was a regular at the Restaurant to Another World.

And so, Aletta had said goodbye to her poor life in the ruins of the old city, moving into the spare room of Sarah's house. Every seven days, she'd work at the

Restaurant to Another World and then spend the rest of her time fulfilled and happy.

She even had a little time to relax.

"Is it really okay for me to eat this?" she wondered.

After taking a breath, Aletta reached over with her hand. Her target: a large metal box with an illustration of a puppy with white bird wings against a background of clouds and a rainbow. She slowly opened the container.

Inside were baked sweets from the other world called "cookies." According to the master, they weren't particularly common at restaurants like his. One would normally find them in shops designed for drinking tea. They were special sweets, so to speak.

"Which one should I pick?"

Faced with the assortment of brown baked goods, Aletta found herself lost.

The master told her that the cookies in the back were leftover samples his friend had given him, so she was free to eat as many as she wanted. Each baked cookie was crunchy and delicious, and the demon girl was fully confident she could just keep eating them forever. Nonetheless, Aletta didn't have the courage to just go through all of them, free or not.

She decided to take as many cookies as she had fingers on one hand and limit it to that.

Aletta was practicing self-control.

"There! That should do it!"

After puzzling over her options for a little while, Aletta finally picked out five cookies from the box.

Her first pick was a cookie with white cream in it made from butter and sugar. In between the pieces of dough were dried grapes with just a pinch of alcohol in them.

Aletta also grabbed a large cookie whose dough was mixed with a spice called cinnamon and a bunch of ground bean-like things called almonds. Additionally, she picked out a cookie that shared the same color as her cocoa. According to the master, it was made using a black powder referred to as chocolate and a dried fruit called "banana," which came from a mysterious nation where it was summer all year round.

The fourth cookie Aletta picked out was baked using sugar brewed from bright red berries. The final one the demon girl selected was made of cookie dough fused with leaves of black tea. It was extremely crunchy and came apart quickly in her mouth.

Of the fifteen different kinds of cookies in the box, Aletta managed to narrow down her picks to the five, painful as it was. She carefully ate one after the other, taking her time to enjoy their individual flavors.

Fruit ain't got nothing on these! Aletta couldn't help but think, after enjoying the flavor of the sweet cookie rolling around in her mouth. She thought back to the words of her new demon friend, a mercenary named Hilda.

"Sweets get more expensive by the season, often becoming more expensive than fruits at the market," said Hilda. Aletta finally understood what she meant.

As she bit into the cookie with cream in the middle, the flavor of butter and sweet, white cream filled her mouth. The two different tastes left behind a rich flavor when combined with the airy texture of the cookie itself. Additionally, mixed with the sweetness of the cream was a spiciness, courtesy of the dried grapes, that brought the whole package together.

The large cookie with the "almonds" in it smelled sweet. This went well with the unique flavor of the dough. Just one of these cookies was enough to be satisfying. While it was slightly harder than the other sweets that Aletta picked out, it could also be dipped into the cocoa she was drinking to make it easier to chew on. It was delicious regardless of how she chose to eat it.

Meanwhile, the dark brown cookie was ever-so-slightly bitter. However, the bittersweet chocolate and the banana flavor came together perfectly. Additionally, both the banana and the chocolate shared a sweetness that was still different in nature. The two flavors worked together to further strengthen the cookie's deliciousness.

The cookie with the bright red sweet and sour berry sugar was less sweet than the others, and even a bit hard to the touch. It was beautiful to look at, not unlike a small piece of art. The transparent berry sugar looked like small gemstones. It was pretty enough that Aletta almost felt bad about eating it.

As for the cookie infused with black tea leaves, it quickly came apart after a single bite, spreading its delightful aroma and the thick, buttery sweetness throughout Aletta's mouth. The dough was much more fragile than that of the other cookies, absorbing the liquids in her mouth and quickly dissolving. It didn't take long for the aroma of tea to occupy the inside of her mouth. This was a definite plus.

With each cookie Aletta ate, she was reminded of just how delicious "sweets" truly were. This was especially the case given that she'd never had the chance to eat them in her short time in the world. They simply couldn't be compared to your average fruits. That was why Aletta simply sat in silence, enjoying their flavor.

At the Restaurant to Another World, Aletta was treated to three amazing meals, and this singular moment in time felt just like those. She couldn't have been happier.

Of course, all good things must come to an end.

Despite taking her time with each cookie, it didn't take long for all five of them to eventually take up space in Aletta's stomach.

"Aw, all done already?"

With her cookies now gone, Aletta sipped on her cocoa and glanced over at the cookie container in the corner. At least half of the cookies remained in the box. In fact, there were still some of her favorites left over.

"...Nope! I can't!"

But there are still so many left. I'm sure I could have a few more...

Aletta quickly shook her head and said goodbye to her temptations. If she were to go back in for more, she knew for a fact she'd end up finishing off the box. She'd completely fill herself up on cookies.

Regardless of what the master said, Aletta felt it was a bad idea. Now was the time to practice self-restraint.

She sighed. "Back to work I guess."

After confirming that the long hand on the clock was nearly pointing directly up, Aletta stood up and tried to forget about her internal strife. While she still had some time left, when she thought of the master out in the dining area handling both the cooking and customers simultaneously, she felt bad just sitting around.

"Excuse me! I've finished my break."

"Gotcha. You know, you could've taken a little more time. Ah well. Could you take this to the young lady over there? You know the one."

"Of course!" Aletta happily replied as she grabbed the fruit parfait from the master.

Seven hours later, Aletta's time at the Restaurant to Another World came to an end.

"Um, I've finished changing."

Like always, Aletta made sure to take a shower after work and change into her freshly washed normal clothes. When she checked in with the master, she was still slightly pink from the hot water.

"Great. You did good today. Here, your pay...and a congratulatory gift, too."

After checking to make sure Aletta was nice and clean, he handed her a brown paper envelope with her pay alongside a light blue bag.

"What's a congratulatory gift?"

Aletta instinctively took the bag in question, but she was confused. The bag had characters from the other world written on it, as well as an illustration of a puppy with wings. The light blue paper bag had a handle on it and was quite heavy. Aletta was curious as to what was inside.

"Oh, I'm guessing you folks don't do this over there, eh?" The master came to this conclusion after seeing her reaction to his words. While the world over there had the concept of "years" based on how long it took to revolve around the sun (he wasn't actually sure if the other world was round or not), and the notion of "months" existed (thirty days equaled a month, and there were twelve months in a year), the concept of "weeks" did not exist. This meant there were probably other customs and standards that didn't exist there as well. The master turned to his employee.

"Aletta, this morning you told me you found a steady job over on your side, right?"

"Huh? Oh, yeah. That's right, but..."

She vaguely remembered mentioning this to the master earlier that morning.

The master nodded and explained, "On this side, we give a gift when something good like that happens. Not every single time, but you get the idea. Sorry I couldn't get you something better."

"N-no, this is wonderful. Thank you. Wait, this is...?!"

Aletta listened to the master's explanation of his world's strange customs as she peeked inside the bag in her hands. She raised her voice in surprise.

Inside the bag was perhaps the one thing in the world that Aletta currently desired.

"I could tell you were holding back in the break room, so I figured you might like this. You enjoyed the cookies, right?" The master cracked a smile after seeing Aletta's response to her gift.

A month had passed since hiring Aletta at Nekoya, and he'd figured out a handful of things about her. For example, he noticed she would pick at the cookies little by little every time she took a break. It took about three days for a large bin full of cookies to empty out. The master wished his regular staff had that kind of self-control.

"U-um, yes, but...isn't this really expensive?"

Aletta had grown used to seeing the symbol on the box in her bag: a puppy monster of some kind with wings. The container itself was smaller than the one in the break room, but judging by its weight, it was packed with cookies.

The master nodded in response to Aletta's well-meaning question. "Ah, well, yeah. It is pretty expensive. It's supposed to be a gift after all."

According to his childhood friend, the same man who made these cookies in the first place, this assorted selection of cookies was one of the Flying Puppy's long-term sellers since it first opened shop during the time of the previous owner. Sometimes he would change the types of cookies inside the box, but it was always beloved by the people who went out of their way to buy one. In fact, they were so popular that his friend often got requests from department stores and even weddings. The master knew the cookies tasted good, as he'd been eating them since he was a wee lad, but generally speaking, he tended to buy them not for himself, but as a gift to others. They were quite a bit more expensive than the cookies you'd find at a convenience store or a market.

According to the man behind the cookies, "We can't produce at the same levels as those big makers can, so all we can do is offer a taste worth the price of admission."

"Is it really all right for me to accept something so valuable?" Aletta asked.

The master gave Aletta ten silver coins for her work like it was no big deal. If this same man was saying the cookies were expensive, they must be terrifyingly pricey. Just going by the taste alone, she could certainly see how that'd be the case. Aletta trembled just a bit as she looked to the master.

"Of course it is. My pal said he'd love for you to grab a box for yourself one of these days if you enjoy his work, but that there is a gift from me. You've got no reason to feel bad. You're my only staff member on Saturdays, so

I don't see any problems with spoiling you from time to time," the master explained, confidently nodding his head.

Over the last month, Aletta had worked steadily and seriously. While there were certainly elements of the master's world that she wasn't quite used to, she was excellent with the customers and had proven herself to be a reliable worker. From what the master had heard, the young woman was living in some poverty on the other side of the door. It couldn't hurt to do at least this much for her, right?

"Um, um, thank you so much. I'll take good care...er, I'll make sure to enjoy it!" Aletta accepted his generosity.

"Haha, try not to take too long on that, all right? If you keep the container sealed, the cookies should last about three months or so. But once you open it up, you got about two weeks to finish them off. Oh, and the silica gel... There's some translucent pellets at the bottom. Those aren't edible, so be careful," the master cheerfully explained, chuckling.

This was how Aletta got her hands on "otherworldly cookies."

...Little did she know that they would lead her to yet another fateful encounter that would change her life.

A small but sturdy and beautiful horse carriage stopped on the corner of the old city district in front of a certain house.

"We've arrived at Lady Sarah's abode, Mistress," the coachman and butler informed Shia, who had been sitting in the back of the carriage.

"Is that so? Thank you. I'll be on my way, then. Come pick me up in a little while," the young lady delivered her orders to her butler.

"Understood. Take care, Mistress Shia."

Whenever Shia visited this particular house, or her family in general, she preferred to be left alone, even by her butler, who had long served the Gold family. He was well aware of this fact as he helped her off the carriage and left her to her business.

"I hope you're doing all right, Sister," said Shia.

Shia quickly adjusted her dress and looked at the house in front of her. It was one of the many homes her family owned throughout the royal capitol and had renovated to make into livable spaces. After succumbing to her "fever," Shia's older sister proclaimed to her family that she would make a living on her own. This was the house they had pretty much forced upon her.

Yes, this was the house that Shia's "fever-stricken" older sister, Sarah Gold, lived in.

⚜

Sarah was Shia's elder by five years, and the unfortunate victim of their family's dreaded sickness, "William's Curse"—also known as adventure lust. While Shia was the fourth generation of the Gold family, the tale of the curse had been passed down through the ages like a lullaby. Hearing those anecdotes, or perhaps because the blood of a true adventurer ran in their veins, many Gold children who grew up hearing the story of how the first generation would go on to abandon their connections to the family business (one tied to nobility no less) in favor of becoming a treasure hunter or adventurer.

Rather than live a rich and luxurious day-to-day life in the capital, those afflicted with the curse opted instead to spend their time crawling through old ruins and caverns filled with all sorts of dangerous monsters. They worked alongside the sketchiest of folk but also operated by themselves. In most cases, those afflicted by the "ailment" eventually lost their lives. That's how terrifying William's Curse truly was.

The legendary William had started the family business

from pretty much nothing. Even his son and second generation of the Gold family, Richard, didn't have it particularly easy. At the time, they weren't close to the business giant they would eventually become. It was necessary for them to do that sort of dangerous work, especially considering they mostly dealt in selling precious elf relics and magical items that they found on their own.

But the times had changed.

The Gold Firm had long since established itself as a business that treasure hunters and adventurers could trust not to screw them out of a fair payment, unlike others that preyed on their lack of business acumen. When a treasure hunter or adventurer got their hands on a valuable relic and ended up in the capitol, they would almost always head straight for the Gold Firm. The Golds would then purchase those items off of them and use the appraising skills they'd honed over years of experience to figure out what sort of object they were dealing with. Once the object was identified, the Gold Firm sold it to a collector or perhaps a knight or mercenary seeking magical equipment. They would occasionally even sell to high-level adventurers. If an adventurer or noble requested it, the Gold Firm would contact one of their mages and have them make comparatively simpler magical items to sell.

These practices were what allowed the Gold Firm to

accumulate the massive wealth they did. There was no longer any need for a family of nobles to go digging through dangerous ruins in search of treasure.

Being a treasure hunter meant encountering danger at every turn. The only members of the family to become treasure hunters, retire in peace, and pass away due to natural causes were William and his son Richard. It was terribly ironic that the two men who became treasure hunters out of necessity managed to survive the job, while the many others who came after them met their ends at the hands of monsters or all manner of ruins. Some left for adventure and were simply never seen again.

To Shia, William's Curse wasn't just some nebulous, distant threat. If things had gone according to plan, Shia's uncle, her mother's brother, would have become the next head of the household. Unfortunately, before the young girl was born, he had been eaten by a monster. Meanwhile, Shia's beloved cousin, in many ways like an older brother to the girl, went to explore some ruins and never returned. Even now, his body remained undiscovered. But perhaps closest to home was Shia's older sister, Sarah.

And so, Shia made it a point to check in on Sarah whenever she heard Sarah had returned home in the capital. She had to see for herself that her older sister was okay, that Sarah wasn't pushing herself too hard.

"Um, I'm terribly sorry. Lady Sarah is currently out right now."

...Though on occasion, Shia was met with days like this. Shia had never seen the girl in front of her.

"Um, you're Lady Shia, are you not? It's a pleasure to meet you. My name is Aletta. I'm Lady Sarah's housekeeper."

The housemaid likely saw Shia's resemblance to her older sister and came to the logical conclusion. The girl named Aletta did her best to politely introduce herself. She wasn't clad in the traditional uniform of a Gold family servant but was instead in her own clothing. It was damaged here and there but was clearly well washed and clean. Over her clothes, she wore a simple apron.

Judging by the black horns peeking out from Aletta's strangely well-kept blonde hair, she appeared to be a demon. They weren't terribly common in the capitol, especially not as normal shopkeepers or artisans. Most of their kind were found doing sketchier jobs, things like treasure hunting or mercenary work. Aletta seemed disconcerted by the sudden visit from her master's family.

"Might I enter and wait inside?" asked Shia.

"Oh, of course! Please, come right in!" Aletta nodded her head not once but twice to the young girl's proposal.

Shia entered the guest room and immediately sat down upon one of the cushioned seats.

"I'll be right out with some tea!" Aletta, still not quite used to the job, hurried into the back.

Shia watched the housekeeper retreat, tilting her head internally. "Sarah, when in the world did you go and hire a demon girl?" she muttered.

One normally didn't hire a demon as a housekeeper, particularly because the job required a certain level of trust.

As the youngest daughter in a family that dealt in buying and selling magical items to a large number of adventurers, it made sense that Sarah didn't particularly fear demons. Still, their kind often lived in rough conditions, which meant they were frequently ill-mannered and crude. Those of the species who went on to become relatively well-known mercenaries or adventurers with money to spare might have been different, but demons like Aletta who lived in poverty and had no power to call their own tended to be that way.

"Poverty is the start of all evil," she said. This was a well-known saying in the world of business that Shia inhabited. "But if Sarah hired her, she's probably all right."

Shia sorted through her thoughts as she whispered to herself. Three years had passed since Sarah became afflicted by William's Curse and left home to become a treasure hunter. While she was several generations removed from the blood that flowed within his veins,

Sarah undoubtedly had talent. It only took three years for the clueless young noblewoman to become a talented treasure hunter.

In that time, Sarah had developed an eye for people, perhaps even more so than Shia, who worked for the family business. If her older sister thought this demon girl was a good person worth trusting, than perhaps she was. Still, Shia couldn't help but wonder how Sarah came to that conclusion.

"Sorry to keep you waiting!"

Aletta returned to the guest room holding up a tray carrying a cup of tea and...

"Are those baked sweets?"

Shia tilted her head as she saw the five baked sweets sitting atop a rough-looking plate made of wood. After Sarah became an adventurer, she devoted herself to her work and saving money on her own as a treasure hunter. She wasn't exactly one to indulge in sweets. They typically didn't last very long, and this was the first time Shia had been served something other than tea upon visiting.

"That's right! They're called cookies. I guess you could say they're a special sort of treat."

Since Shia was a "special" guest, Aletta decided to offer her the last five cookies from her box, as much as it pained her to do so. She wore her best "business" smile.

"Please, help yourself," she said. "The tea is hack tea."

Hack tea was known for its bitter yet refreshing flavor. It was also relatively cheap to obtain compared to others of its kind. Aletta placed the plate of cookies and tea down in front of Shia with a surprising smoothness and grace. She had honed these skills at her other job, thanks to the master.

"Really? Well, thank you."

Truth be told, Shia wasn't terribly fond of hack tea without any sugar or honey. It was too bitter for her tastes. That said, she knew it would be rude not to touch what had been offered. She was the daughter of a merchant, and she'd been taught not to make the people she shared company with uncomfortable. Shia grabbed the tea cup and took a sip. Just as expected, the bitter flavor of the tea filled her mouth and nostrils.

I don't completely hate it, but...

She preferred it with some manner of sweetness. This prompted her to look down at the baked "cookies."

...They must be sweet, right?

The young woman once again glanced at the plate of treats. They appeared to have been baked with wheat or some sort of flour. The light and dark brown cookies were relatively few in number, all things considered.

They appear to all be different types. As far as I can tell, they seem well crafted if nothing else.

Shia, having never heard of "cookies" before, took her time analyzing the food in front of her.

One of the cookies was leaf-shaped, with white sugar scattered across its surface.

One had some sort of dark brown paste sandwiched between two thin pieces of light-yellow biscuit.

Another cookie had a dollop of bright orange in its center.

Yet another was shaped like a puppy with wings and had what appeared to be dried grapes in it.

The final cookie had a black and white pattern checkered across its surface.

It went without saying that each of the five treats on the plate in front of Shia was far more carefully crafted than the average confectionary. They were beautiful, and if they tasted anywhere near as good as they looked, they'd be more than fit to serve to nobles.

So, what do they taste like?

After analyzing the beautiful, mysterious treats in front of her, Shia couldn't help but feel a bit excited. She grabbed the leaf-shaped cookie with the translucent sugar scattered across its surface. With the aftertaste of the hack tea still lingering in her taste buds, she brought the cookie to her mouth.

What?!

Shia's eyes widened in shock. The cookie was far less sweet than its appearance suggested. Instead, it tasted of baked wheat and butter. In terms of what was expected from sweets for nobles, its sweetness was subdued. But Shia knew.

This... Why, it's magnificent.

Shia took another bite of the cookie. What surprised her most was its texture. By stacking multiple thin layers atop one another and baking them, the cookie was easy to bite into, while also soft enough that it came apart without much resistance. The subtle sweetness also fused together with the strong butter and wheat flavor.

Shia couldn't help but take a sip of her hack tea. Its refreshing bitterness helped to clear her mind and tongue as she thought to herself.

...Are all these just like this one?

Upon realizing that this might very well be the case, Shia adjusted her posture and stared at the remaining four cookies. Could these all truly be just as delicious?

With that question running through her mind, Shia reached out to grab another cookie.

Is this really baked? It's so much more lightly colored than the others. And what is this dark brown stuff?

The next cookie Shia decided on was the light yellow one with the dark brown paste sandwiched in the middle.

She couldn't even begin to theorize what the stuffing in the middle tasted like. Filled with a sense of expectation and anxiousness, she bit into the cookie and once again nearly lost her balance in surprise.

What is this?! The stuff in the middle pairs wonderfully with the cookie!

Indeed, the crispy outside layers were intensely sweet, tasting of butter and milk. Meanwhile, the dark brown stuff in the center was distinctly sweet yet bitter. By themselves, either one of these would be an excellent confectionary in and of itself. Together, however, they brought out the best in one another, creating something truly special.

Th-these "cookies" really are incredible!

Filled with a sense of pure excitement, Shia looked at the remaining cookies...and ate them.

I knew it!

Her gut instinct was right on the money.

The treat with the orange dollop in the center—just as Shia had suspected, the orange bit was brewed mikun sugar. She surmised it was likely made through boiling a mikun together with sugar, resulting in a tremendously refreshing flavor. Before this cookie was even made, the pâtissier most certainly mixed mikun skin into the cookie dough itself: it was a concentrated mikun assault on her senses.

The puppy-shaped cookie had dried grapes mixed into it, but they weren't just any dried grapes. They had been soaked in fairly strong alcohol of some sort, which gave the sweet fruit an additional bitter bite. This proved to be a good match for the cookie itself, which was far sweeter than the rest. Needless to say, it was delicious.

And then there was the final cookie, the one with the checkered pattern. This, too, was impressive. Unlike the other treats, it was rather simple; it seemed to be made from heavy dough. It was tougher to bite into than the others, and the black parts of it had a unique sweet and bitter flavor to them.

Shia eventually finished all the cookies on her plate and closed out her cup of tea. As it turned out, the hack tea, with its refreshing, unsweetened taste, was the perfect way to cleanse her palette.

"That was delightful…" She let out a satisfied sigh.

No matter how one looked at it, these weren't any ordinary confectionaries. They were nothing like the "high-class sweets" that prized volumes of sugar over all else. These were perfectly balanced.

"Where did you get these?! Did Sarah buy them herself?"

Shia immediately began questioning Aletta, who was standing nearby. These weren't the sort of delicacies a commoner, never mind a demon, could easily get their hands on. Whoever made these treats was at least as skilled as any one of the cooks at the famed Alfade Company, said to be an equal match for even the king's own chefs.

No, whoever made these may very well be even more talented than them.

"Huh?! Um, well..." Aletta stumbled over her words.

Shia didn't know about the Restaurant to Another World, and Sarah had asked her to keep it a secret from her little sister. The young woman wasn't sure what to say.

"...If you don't want to answer, I understand."

Shia could tell with one glance that it wasn't that the demon girl didn't know, it was that, for one reason or another, the girl couldn't answer her question. If news got out about these confectionaries, it would cause something of a stir. All the gourmets across the capital would rush the store in question.

While this may be great for business, there were those who hated being mobbed by insistent customers. If these cookies were made by the hands of one such craftsman, Aletta's reaction made plenty of sense.

Hopeful, Shia asked Aletta, "Then let me change the question: Do you think you could get more of these?"

"U-um, probably. But I think they might be super

expensive. They filled a lovely metal box about this big. There were all kinds of other cookies, too."

Aletta used her hands to describe how large the box was. Since the master had said, "buy a set from him if you enjoy the cookies," she assumed they were for sale.

But at the same time, he also described them as being "quite pricey." If from the master's perspective they were "quite pricey," they must've been "impossibly pricey" for someone like Aletta.

"Really? Might I see the box?" asked Shia, her interest peaked by Aletta's description.

"Yes, of course! I'll be right back" Aletta nodded and scurried to the back, returning with a light blue metal container.

"Here. You just had the last of the cookies that were inside." Aletta's cheeks were bright red as she placed the box in front of Shia.

"I see. You're right, this does seem quite expensive."

Shia opened the box with the drawing of a winged puppy monster on it and felt a tinge of disappointment upon seeing its empty insides. She imagined what it would look like filled with cookies like these, then did the calculations in her head. She sighed at the results.

Sweets were, by their very nature, expensive. Just the five cookies served earlier would run about one or two silver coins. While they weren't nearly as heavily sweetened with sugar as what Shia was used to, they were clearly made using all manner of wonderful techniques. The ingredients had to have been first-class material. Shia wouldn't be terribly surprised if they cost two or three times more than the average confectionary.

This was especially the case when one considered that the treats were being sold in a beautiful metal box that would be worth purchasing by itself. It might be worth even more than Shia imagined.

"...All right."

After listening to Aletta's explanation, Shia came to a decision. She calmly pulled her wallet from her person and took out a single coin.

"You don't have to rush. Whenever you have the chance is fine. Could you buy me one of these?" Shia gently handed Aletta the coin.

"Huh?! But this is a gold coin!" Aletta let out a sound not altogether dissimilar from that of a scream as she looked down at the gold coin in her hand.

Gold. The demon girl had only just recently seen it in person for the first time. The one demon regular who dropped by the Restaurant to Another World every time it was open, giant pot in hand, always paid for her meals with gold. A single bowl of the woman's favorite soup ran one silver coin. To fill the giant pot she brought with her ran two gold coins. Just one alone was clearly an incredible amount of money.

"Yes, it is. It's my whole allowance for one month, so please don't lose it. I doubt a box will cost an entire gold coin, but...I imagine it'll probably run you somewhere between forty to fifty silver coins for a single box. That one gold coin should be more than enough to cover that, since it's worth about hundred silver coins, give or take. You can give me the change back afterward, but don't worry. I'll have some more to thank you for completing the job."

Once Shia made a decision, she acted on it immediately. This was the one thing she had in common with her older sister. While Aletta may have been a demon, Aletta was also Sarah's trusted housekeeper. She highly doubted Aletta would just run away with the money.

"I-I understand," Aletta replied and nodded, seemingly overwhelmed by Shia's determination. She took the gold coin from the girl.

Shia looked Aletta straight in the eyes. "I'm really counting on you."

"Oh? Well, if it isn't Shia! What're you doing holding my housekeeper's hands?"

Shia's original objective, seeing her older sister, had completely and utterly slipped from her mind.

Days later, Shia would once again find herself shocked by not only the amount of cookies in the metal box but also the types and the overall cost.

It was understandable. Aletta came back to her with a box of ten different types of cookies for a mere single silver coin. She found out that a box twice as big, with fifteen different types of cookies, only ran two silver coins. These prices were affordable even by Aletta's standards.

And so, the Restaurant to Another World's counterpart of sorts, the Flying Puppy, gained a brand-new fan.

Not that the man who ran the place had any clue...

Restaurant to Another World

CHAPTER 27
Ham Cutlet

IN THE CORNER of the continent was a small village, and in that village was a tiny old log house. In the corner of said house was a married couple's bedroom.

It had been a month since Ellen last pulled her best clothes out from her chest. She changed into them and prepared to go out for the day. Since she didn't have a mirror, Ellen brushed her dark brown, ruffled hair and checked to make sure her clothes were in order. That was about all she could do to make sure she looked presentable.

All right. This should be good. Not much more I can do!

Ellen wasn't wearing her usual worn-out clothes, but rather the set she put on when going to a festival or wedding ceremony. She even had on a pair of silver earrings she received from her mother. They were equipped with small gems the size of her pinkie fingernail. When Ellen first got them as a gift, her mother told her that if she was ever pressed for money to sell them immediately. Folks like Ellen didn't have access to expensive shops dealing in pricey makeup, so she used the red she decocted from flowers in the spring to add a little color to her lips and lightly dabbed her cheeks with white powder she created from flowers she picked in the mountains.

Despite everything Ellen had done to prepare herself before heading out, she still wasn't terribly confident about her looks, considering where she was headed. Her destination was a place where numerous high-class women, both younger and more beautiful than the now thirty-year-old country woman was, often visited. But the reality was that Ellen was the wife of a poor woodcutter. She didn't have any other items to pretty herself up with. She made peace with that fact and left her bedroom.

"Sorry for the wait!" she said. "Well? How do I look?"

Ellen's family was waiting for her outside the room. Her husband and kids had also neatened their dark brown hair and wore their best clothes. Ellen posed flirtatiously.

"Ya look fine!" her husband said. "Now let's get movin'! The kids are workin' up quite the appetite, sounds like."

"Yeah, c'mon, Mom! Hurry up!"

"I'm hungrrrry! Let's gooo!"

Unfortunately, reality was unkind to the housewife. Despite her best efforts to pretty up, Herman barely looked at her before giving her the most basic of compliments. Ellen's husband was just over thirty years old himself and had begun showing signs of his age. Meanwhile, her two children, Kai and Bona, were in a rush to reach their destination. Kai looked much like Herman and had turned eleven years old this year. Bona, on the other hand, looked more like her mother, and was only eight.

"Yes, yes, I know! Now listen up, everyone! Y'all better behave yourselves over there, got it?"

Ellen would be lying if she said she wasn't at least a little annoyed with her family after she went through all the trouble of dressing up. Couldn't they afford to give her at least a compliment or two? In the meantime, she lectured the children about their manners.

"Yeees, Moooom," they answered in harmony.

As always, there was no way of really telling whether the kids understood her, but at least they had the energy to respond properly. Ellen always had to warn the children whenever it came time to head over there.

"Shall we be off then?"

"Yup!"

And so, the four of them exited their log cabin and went next door to the small barn.

"All right, I'm opening it up."

Inside was a single donkey Herman used to carry trees that he'd cut down. It stood quietly in the barn, sipping water. Herman's family watched him as he approached the door in the back of the building. He placed his hand on the handle of the black door with the cat illustration on it and turned it.

And, like always, the door opened to the sound of bells ringing.

"Welcome, Herman, Ellen!"

The couple had been coming to Nekoya on and off for fifteen years, since before they were married, back when the previous master was still alive. They'd known the current master for quite some time.

"Gonna have the usual today?" he asked.

The master immediately went to take their order. Due to his long relationship with the pair, he already knew neither of them could read, so there was no need to hand them a menu. Plus, Herman's family only ever ordered one thing.

"Yup. Same as usual. Four daily specials. Oh, by the by, what's on the menu for today's special?" Herman asked as usual.

As made apparent by its name, the daily special changed every time Herman came to the restaurant. It was about two copper coins cheaper than anything else on the menu, which was part of the reason why they ordered it every visit. Not to mention that, despite being cheaper, it was in no way less delicious than any of the other items on the menu. Plus, since it changed with every visit, this meant they tried all sorts of different foods.

"Today is ham cutlet. I think bread pairs quite well with it, by the way."

The master had no problems recommending rice with ham cutlet, but as far as he was concerned, it went best with bread.

Satisfied with the master's explanation, Herman made his usual request. "I see. Then we'll have that with the bread. Could ya bring out the bread and soup first? Like always?"

"Absolutely. I'll be back out in a bit."

The master finished taking their orders before they even sat down and returned to the kitchen to prepare their food.

"Let's grab a seat."

Herman took a breath and looked for an empty table. There were all sorts of customers at the restaurant, ranging from nobles to monsters to demi-humans.

"Oh, that one looks open. C'mon, let's go."

"Aye."

"Okaaay, Dad!"

Herman led his family to a table, and they all took a seat.

"Hey, Mom! I want ice cream! Can I order some?"

"Oh, oh! I wanna drink cola! The black fizzy stuff!"

The moment they sat down, the children began excitedly making requests. Ellen didn't blame them; this was the one time every month the family got to indulge. Kai wanted the ice-cold confectionary that was only available at this particular restaurant. Bona, meanwhile, was a little bit of a special case. On one of their previous visits, a group of kids who apparently came to the restaurant on their own had let her try some of this cola drink, and it quickly became her favorite.

Ellen shook her head. "Nope! Not today. We ain't got the money. Right, Dad?"

Unfortunately for the children, Ellen had a firm grip on the family wallet. While she couldn't read or do math, she had a precise understanding of just how many coins the family had to their name. She looked to Herman for backup.

He shrugged. "Hey, Mom. I'd kinda like a beer. Mind if I order one?"

"...This is the part where I wanted you to nod your head."

As usual, reality was unkind. Ellen wasn't sure if Herman had any knowledge of their finances, but either way, he couldn't help wanting the cold and delicious, otherworldly alcohol that resembled ale. Ellen knew full well that the "beer" drink went amazingly with any of the menu items that had "cutlet" or "fried" in its name.

"No fair, Dad! Then I want ice cream!"

"Then I want cola! The black fizzy stuff!"

"C'mon, are ya sure we can't cut loose just a li'l? I'll cut more firewood startin' tomorrow, promise?"

Now that the children had gained a strong ally in the form of their father, the united front continued putting the pressure on Ellen.

She sighed.

"Either you order cola or ice cream, but not both. The two of you are gettin' the same thing, got it? If you end up orderin' separate stuff, you're just gonna end up wanting the other one, too. I know how this goes. And Dad, if you're gonna order beer, make it a bottle. I want some, too."

"You got it!"

"Yay!"

And so, the children proceeded to debate over what to order, eventually settling on the cola.

"Sorry to keep you waiting! Here's your soup and bread."

A young new waitress wearing a somewhat strange black hair piece placed down the food in front of the family.

"Much obliged. Oh, and I'm sorry to ask so suddenly, but could we get a bottle of beer and two servings of cola?"

"Of course! Thank you for your order! I'll bring those out with your ham cutlets!" The young waitress happily responded to their order and disappeared into the back.

"Let's dig in..." Ellen said to the kids, then elbowed her husband. "C'mon, Herman. Really? Right in front of me?"

"Wh-what?"

Herman was staring at the waitress's backside. Ellen shook her head and finally started eating.

Ah, it smells delicious.

At the Restaurant to Another World, just ordering a regular meal gave you the right to eat as much soup and bread as you wanted. Those two items alone were far more delicious than anything Ellen ate in her world.

It was even better than the white bread that was only available during special occasions like festivals.

Long ago, before they were married, Herman had accidentally stumbled across the door to the restaurant. He began inviting Ellen to come with him around that time. Back then, she found herself ordering all manner of sweet desserts that made her feel like her body would melt away. Nowadays, she came here specifically with the intent of eating bread and soup, almost always ordering the daily special. They were worth the price of admission alone.

Ellen picked one of the freshly warm pieces of bread up off the white plate and bit into it. Underneath the shiny brown crust was soft, white bread that resembled fresh snow. Ellen took a small bit of the butter from the side of the plate and spread it on the bread. She took yet another bite.

It's so sweet.

The first bite of bread with plentiful butter spread on it was something else. The thin and crunchy outer layer and the light sweetness of the soft, white crumbs spread across the insides of her mouth. Meanwhile, the scent of wheat and butter mixed together and filled her nose. The combined flavors filled Ellen with joy, and it wasn't long before the small piece of bread disappeared down her gullet.

The housewife then turned her attention to the soup. Mixed in with the pale liquid were vegetables and thinly cut meats. Ellen used her spoon to scoop up the soup and took a taste.

Ah, this really is the best. This place is the best.

The overwhelming deliciousness of salt, meat, and vegetables filled her mouth, but that wasn't all. Even Ellen could tell there was far more to the soup than just those ingredients alone. She wasn't sure if it was the way the master made it, or perhaps what went into it was just that different, but the soup had a complicated, thick, and wonderful flavor that Ellen could not replicate. While the soups changed every visit, every single one of them was delicious in their own way, and she once again had no complaints for the chef.

Ellen continued sipping at her soup on the side while enjoying her bread. A bite of bread, a sip of soup, repeated time and time again.

She looked up for a moment and saw that Herman and the children were doing the exact same thing.

We really are eating some delicious food, aren't we?

The rest of their food arrived just after the four of them, feeling truly happy, finished their bread and soup.

"Sorry to keep you waiting! Here are your ham cutlets and drinks!"

The young waitress reappeared with orders in hand, including refills of bread and soup. Either the master told the waitress from earlier or she was just being downright thoughtful.

"Ah, thank you kindly," said Ellen.

Ever grateful, Ellen and the others came face to face with the true main attraction of the day. On top of a single plate were four round, fried objects, crispy brown. Next to them was a little mountain of pale green vegetables. In the corner of the plate were three small, red fruits of some sort and some faint yellow mayonnaise. Today's daily special, "ham cutlet," looked delicious.

"All right! Let's feast!"

Herman poured beer from the brown bottle into two translucent glasses and handed one of them to Ellen. He then reached for the blue bottle and spread the sauce inside all over his ham cutlets.

"Here you go, Mom," he said, passing it to her.

"Thanks."

Ellen grabbed the beer and sauce from her husband and began eating. At first, she only put a dash of sauce onto her cutlets. Herman had poured so much sauce onto them that they turned black, but Ellen was a bit more conservative. She liked a bit of crunch to her cutlets.

With her knife, she cut a slender piece from the round

ham cutlet. Pink meat and milky white cheese peeked out from the cut.

Looks like there are two types. Those with cheese and those without, Ellen thought to herself. She took her fork and stabbed it into the portion without cheese, where the meat was much thinner. She brought it to her mouth and felt the aroma of the oil and sauce fill her mouth and nose. Ellen bit into the ham cutlet.

"Mm!"

She inadvertently raised her voice. After a deeply satisfying crunch, the flavor of the salt, herbs, and lightly seasoned meat filled her mouth. The way it blended together with the sauce from earlier was magnificent.

"It's so tasty!"

"Delish!"

The kids were eating their ham cutlets without any sauce, but they, too, raised their voices in satisfaction.

"Whoo-ee! Ain't nothin' like a beer with some fried food!"

Herman had already finished off his first beer while devouring his sauce-drenched ham cutlets. All four of them couldn't have been more satisfied with their meals. They had today's special, the ham cutlet, to thank for that.

Ah, the cheese ones are great, too!

Ellen took a bite of the cheese ham cutlet and was

immediately struck by how fresh the pairing of the meat and melty cheese was. Combined with the frosty cold beer, it was like nothing else.

Indeed, when it came to any fried foods here at the restaurant, there was one important thing to pay mind to when eating. First, Ellen cut a vertical opening down through the bread that the waitress brought to their table earlier. She then carefully stuffed the opening with vegetables and the thinly sliced pieces of meat. Ellen finished off her prep work by topping it all with mayo.

The housewife took a bite of her newly complete "ham cutlet sandwich."

I wasn't wrong! This is why I can't stop coming here!

Ellen couldn't help but let out an internal shout of glee as she happily munched on her food. The sweet, soft surface of the bread and the crunchy fried meat were having a party with the fresh vegetables in her mouth. Moreover, the bread was all-you-can-eat!

A while back, the master taught her all about how to best enjoy fried food. Ever since trying it for herself, Ellen made it a point to do it any time the daily special ended up being something fried. Not once had the master's advice steered her wrong.

Ellen's husband and two children had also shifted to eating their food as a sandwich.

Herman covered his cutlet in sauce, while Kai sandwiched his ham cutlet with plenty of mayo. Meanwhile, Bona made her sandwich with just vegetables and cutlets with cheese. All four members of the family had their own unique way of eating ham cutlet sandwiches, in accord with their individual opinions of the most delicious way to enjoy ham cutlets.

"Whew! This sauce is dang great!" said Herman.

"It's all about the meat! The cheesy ones are great, but nothing beats a big piece of meat!"

"Kai, Kai! I'll give you my regular ones if you give me your cheesy ones!"

Yet they were all undoubtedly satisfied with their meals.

And so, the family continued eating away at their ham cutlets, ordering refills of bread and soup all the way until the sun had set.

"Whew!" the family sighed in unison, their bellies filled with good food and an overwhelming feeling of joy.

It was about time to head home. Ellen pulled out her wallet and called for someone from the restaurant. "'Scuse me! Check, please."

"Aye, you got it. Hold on just a moment." Instead of the young waitress from before, the master came out from the back himself. Apparently, she wasn't terribly good with counting money.

"Then I'm countin' on you."

Ellen handed the master her wallet. If the man in front of her had been like the usual merchants who looked down on Ellen and Herman for being poor, she would never hand him her wallet for fear of being ripped off. But having known the master for years, she knew beyond the shadow of a doubt he would never do something like that. He had her absolute trust.

"No problemo!"

The master reached into the wallet and pulled out two silver coins and thirteen copper, the exact amount for the meal, before giving Ellen back her wallet.

"Thanks as always!" he said. "We're looking forward to your next visit."

"We'll definitely be back. C'mon, everyone. Let's get goin'."

Ellen put her wallet, significantly lighter than before, back into her bag and led the other three out of the restaurant. The moment they stepped out of the door, they were back inside their barn.

"Today's special was delicious, Dad."

"You got that right." Herman sighed. "I'm guessin' the next time we'll be able to go is next month... If only we had more money."

"When I grow up, I'm gonna marry somebody so rich that I can go there every day!" said Bona.

"You big dummy! The restaurant only appears once every seven days!"

The family chatted among themselves over how delicious the food was as they returned to their home.

"All right, y'all. Get undressed before you get your clothes dirty."

"'Kaaay!" her family answered.

The three quickly changed out of their fancier wear and back into their usual beat-up clothes.

"Right. I'm gonna go get some firewood. C'mon, you're with me, Kai. The sooner we can dig up the money, the sooner we can go back to the restaurant."

"Okay!"

"Bona, come help your mother with her mending."

"'Kay, 'kay!"

After everyone finished changing, it was time to get back to work, all the while chattering about the delicious food they had just finished eating.

And so came the end of the Herman family's special, once-a-month feast, marking their return to everyday life. This also came with renewed anticipation for the next time they'd get to go back to Nekoya.

*Restaurant to
Another World*

CHAPTER 28
Pork Soup

"**M**EAT DAY" always came near the end of the month.

Meat Day. It was a special service day at Western Cuisine Nekoya that came without fail at the end of the month (excluding February). Back when the previous master was around the age of the current master, and before the place became the Restaurant to Another World, he began doing special service Meat Days. He hadn't discounted the meats or anything like that though.

"Special service at restaurants should come in the form of food, not money!"

The previous master had lived off his cooking abilities alone after the war. This was one of the principles he lived by, and his grandson agreed. That's why the current master made his way downstairs a little earlier than usual, finished with the usual beef stew order, and got to prepping for Meat Day.

"...That should just about do it."

The master nodded to himself as he looked at the color of the cooked pork meat and moved on to the next step.

He dumped the vegetables he'd cut earlier into the pot: thickly sliced carrots, wide cuts of onion, boiled taro free of sliminess, and daikon radish cut slightly thicker than the carrots. While the master normally also included burdock, the Saturday customers found its taste too earthy. They weren't fans.

The master sautéed all these ingredients until the pork was browned just right. He then took blended stock made of tuna and kelp, mixed it into the pot, and began heating it all together. The master carefully removed the scum, and once the whole mess was boiling, stopped the flames and mixed in the miso, then placed the pot on a warmer to keep the temperature steady.

"That's done!"

The master carefully stirred the pot's contents and placed the lid over it, sighing to himself. Suddenly, the entrance bell rang, almost as if it had been waiting for him to finish.

"Good morning!" Aletta, the Restaurant to Another World's sole otherworldly waitress, entered Nekoya and greeted the master with a big smile as he exited the kitchen.

"Yo. Before you take a shower, make sure you grab breakfast first. The rice just finished up."

"Wow, thank you!" Aletta grinned with excitement upon hearing the word "breakfast." She always made sure not to eat on mornings she'd be heading into work, so her stomach was completely empty.

"Hang on just a sec. I'll go get things ready." The master grinned at Aletta and began readying breakfast, complete with the day's special menu item. He prepared fresh white rice for them both, as well as leftover grilled salmon from the previous day's daily special. The master also placed down two empty bowls and began preparing the final touch: just a dash of butter and a bit of freshly cut scallions. A long time ago, the previous master heard from a Hokkaido native that including these two items in the recipe would make the flavor that much more "western."

"Sorry to keep you waiting. Feel free to use whatever spices you'd like."

As the butter melted into the miso soup and fused with its ingredients, its gentle fragrance filled the area around it.

"What a wonderful smell... Um, this is miso soup, right?"

The scent alone was enough to rattle Aletta's empty stomach as she glanced down at the soup in front of her. It was a food with a unique taste to it that utilized something called "miso." Whenever she had rice with a meal here, it typically came with miso soup. But there was something different about the bowl of liquid sitting in front of her, even if she couldn't quite pin down what that was.

"Is it just me, or is there more stuff in there than usual? I can even see meat."

Indeed, while the ingredients in miso soup seemed to differ every single time she came, there only tended to be two main additions to the dish. Meat was never involved either. However, it was clear to Aletta from a single glance that not only was there meat, but all kinds of different vegetables in the soup.

"You're right on the mark. It is 'Meat Day' after all." The master nodded while replying to Aletta.

"Meat day?"

It was one of Nekoya's traditions.

"For as long as I can remember, 'Meat Day' is the one day where we swap out miso soup for pork soup."

It was a special menu item that only appeared on this specific day. This was the special service that Nekoya offered to its customers near the end of every month.

That day, Aletta's other boss, Sarah—aka Minced Meat Cutlet—visited the Restaurant to Another World for the first time in twenty days.

"Wow, so today's soup is really that good?" she asked.

"It's awesome!" said Aletta. "It's full of meat and veggies."

Sarah listened intently while Aletta told her all about the day's menu. Supposedly, the pork soup being served was in a tier all its own. It was apparently so good that many felt it deserved a spot on the proper menu.

"Well then, I guess I'm decided. I'll have an order of rice, pork soup, a minced meat cutlet, and a minced meat cutlet sandwich, please."

After hearing Aletta's excited thoughts, Sarah couldn't help but order some soup for herself. She was normally more of a bread kind of girl, but she felt rice went better with miso soup.

"You got it! Thank you for your order!"

As soon as Sarah finished making her order, a voice erupted from the table over. "Say what?! If there's pork soup, that must mean today is 'Meat Day,' is it not?!"

"Hm? Know something, Fried Shrimp?" asked Sarah.

The origin of said voice was the knightly man known as "Fried Shrimp," whom Sarah had become ever-so-slightly close to during the great "Sandwich Incident."

"Indeed. I heard about it from Lord Tatsu...er, Lord Teriyaki. Supposedly, pork soup is an ephemeral dish served only on 'Meat Day.'"

Heinrich, known to the regulars of Nekoya as "Fried Shrimp" and a knight of the Duchy, explained to Minced Meat Cutlet the story he had heard from the swordsman he looked up to.

Pork soup only appeared once or twice a year on "Meat Day." It was as mysterious as it was delightful. Outside of utilizing the same miso used in miso soup, it was on an entirely different level of flavor. It had quite a few fans among the many regulars who had been frequenting the Restaurant to Another World for decades. The problem was that none of them had any way of figuring out when exactly "Meat Day" was, so being present when pork soup was available proved to be a puzzle in and of itself.

After chatting with Minced Meat Cutlet for a moment, Heinrich placed his usual order.

"Young lady! I would also like an order of rice and pork soup! Of course, I will be having that with fried shrimp! Oh, and a fried shrimp sandwich to go, thank you!"

"Yes, right away, sir!" Aletta scurried to the kitchen with the pairs' orders. She returned a little while later with their food in hand.

"Sorry to keep you waiting. Here are your orders of minced meat cutlet and fried shrimp. And these are your pork soups. The red spice here is quite hot, so be careful."

A faint sizzling sound could be heard from both plates of fried food alike. And then there was the pork soup.

It looks as delicious as usual, thought Sarah.

Indeed, this looks as scrumptious as always. Heinrich echoed her thoughts.

Though neither Sarah nor Heinrich took their eyes off the hot, fried foods in front of them, they first started with the pork soup.

...This is splendid.

As soon as Sarah took a sip of the soup, she immediately understood Aletta's gushing appraisal. The savory flavor of the boiled pork meat had melted into the soup itself, and the vegetables were hot and soft. The unique flavor of the miso paired well with the gentle flavor of butter that wrapped itself around all of the soup's ingredients.

This reminds me a little bit of knight stew.

The soup's flavor reminded Sarah of her hometown, the royal capital. Knight stew was developed just before she was born, quickly becoming the city's most famous food. Much of its popularity came from how it utilized knight sauce, which was also quite different from the lightly salted soups Sarah was used to. Its rich, buttery flavor was one of its main characteristics.

Sarah had indulged in knight stew often when she was a child, being from an affluent family and all. But ever since she broke out on her own as a treasure hunter, her pockets were far less deep than they used to be. She hadn't eaten the stew in a long time.

Oh, this is pepel, is it not? It really brings the flavors together.

Meanwhile, Heinrich was thinking back to his hometown by the sea as he looked at the bottle of pepel. Pepel was a crimson-colored, fiery spice from the Western Continent that was easy to come by in the port town that he grew up in. It was a town filled with all sorts of goods from the Western Continent, but because pepel wasn't native to the Duchy and had to be imported from the Ocean Nation across the sea, it was rather expensive. Fortunately, cost was never much of a problem for Heinrich's family, considering they were nobility.

As a boy, he hadn't been particularly fond of the pepel in his soup or noodles. It was so hot that it burned his tongue. As an adult, however, it became one of his favorite additions to almost any dish.

But wait, there's just a hint of the sea in this. Some sort of hidden flavor?

Deep within the thick flavor of the miso was just a hint of the sea. Heinrich could spy no fish within the depths of the meat and vegetables, but there was most certainly a hint of fish-like flavor.

It's been three years since I last went home... Heinrich thought.

The faint taste of fish, a flavor unavailable to him at his fortress, reminded Heinrich that he hadn't been home in a while. In fact, the last time he visited was to report to his parents that he had been entrusted with a squad of knights all his own. Since then, he had received a long vacation but was unable to return home due to the long journey.

Maybe I should head home for once, thought Heinrich.

I could just drop by and see how everyone's doing, mused Sarah.

Sarah and Heinrich couldn't be from more different worlds, with personalities that were nothing alike, and yet the pair came to the same conclusion at precisely the same time.

"What?! What's with this crazy soup?!" The young hunter was stunned.

That same day, "Ginger Pork" Yuuto and his master visited the Restaurant to Another World. As always, before he swung by, he made sure to wash his trusty hunting dog, Taro, cleaning all the muck off him. Yuuto went on to order his usual, a plate of ginger pork with some rice. Everything up to that point was the same as it always was.

But something was different about today...

"There's never meat in the miso soup! What is this, Master?"

Chunks of meat and vegetables floated in the miso soup. The meat was nice and fatty, while the vegetables had been carefully simmered. The soup itself had been seasoned differently than the usual miso, too. Each time Yuuto chewed the meat and veggies, the delicious flavor of the soup filled his mouth. The onions were the only ingredient that hadn't been simmered, and still maintained a satisfying crunch.

Long story short, today's soup was on a whole different level than usual.

"Looks like today's Meat Day, I'm guessing!"

Mashira, Yuuto's master, smiled down at the soup and

took a big bite of ginger pork and rice. He patted his own hunting dog, a beast several times larger than Taro, and explained to his student what the deal was.

On Meat Day, the master of the restaurant served a special pork soup. It was filled with all manner of meat and vegetables, and, as always, came with free refills. According to Mashira, he had only stumbled upon Meat Day a handful of times.

"Wait, if this comes with free refills, then..." said Yuuto.

"Exactly," Mashira answered. "You can have your fill of pork soup for today and today only."

Mashira gave his student a firm nod of his head and began digging into his food once again. Yuuto also focused his attention back on his ginger pork.

The pair would go on to eat two servings more than usual.

"Oho, today's Meat Day?"

Taking in the reactions to the soup by the other customers, many who typically adored rice, the former Duchy commander "Curry Rice" Alphonse pieced together the situation. He knew of pork soup; hell, he'd spent twenty years of his life coming here every week, through rain or snow. Alphonse had tasted pork soup more than a handful of times.

"I'll have a large order of curry rice. Same as usual. But before you serve the main dish, could you get me a plate of rice and a bowl of pork soup, too? Lots of butter, please."

Like a true veteran, Alphonse ordered pork soup. Before eating the curry rice, he would match some white rice with the pepel-filled pork soup. He would then proceed to eat some of his curry with pork soup. This was what he always did on Meat Days.

"You got it!"

"Yo, young lady! Let me get in on that, too!"

As soon as Aletta took Alphonse's order, she found herself on the receiving end of yet another booming voice. It came from the man who furiously sat down next to him.

He was a strange-looking man. From the neck up he resembled a fierce lion, his body covered in beast hair. His light clothes revealed scarred, bulging muscles. On his back was a massive steel sword covered with the marks of battle damage. While at a first glance, one might think he was a beastman, nobody had ever heard of one that understood human customs, nor were there any stories of a lion man who lived on the continent. In truth, he was a demon who had received an incredibly strong blessing upon his birth.

"I'll be havin' the usual! Two large orders of katsudon! But before that, could ya bring out some rice and pork soup? Cheers!"

"O-of course!" Aletta responded to the unfamiliar demon in front of her and retreated into the kitchen.

"Hey, long time no see," said the lion-faced man to Alphonse. "I thought you might've gone and finally kicked the bucket on me."

Lionel, also known as "Pork Cutlet Rice Bowl," flashed what could only be described as a menacing smile at Alphonse. The imposing man thought little of death. After all, he came face to face with it every single day of his life. Lionel was the strongest and most renowned swordsman in the demon capital, and he had the track record to prove it.

"Oh, shut your trap. You really think I'm gonna up and die that easily?"

The average warrior might shrivel in the face of such a threat, but Alphonse was as calm as could be. A long time ago, he, Teriyaki, and Omelet Rice had even gotten into a big verbal argument over which rice dish was the best. While the only common link they shared was this restaurant, the lion man was one of the people he had no trouble calling a friend.

"I just went home is all. Took me a while to find a door after that," he explained to his old friend.

"Oho! Ya managed to get home? That's fantastic!" Lionel was genuinely happy to hear the news. In the colosseum, Lionel was a creature of destruction and death, but outside of it, he was normally quite friendly. "So, I guess ya got that city life thing goin' now, eh?"

"Indeed. To be quite honest, compared to life on the island, it's almost too uneventful. I'm quite bored."

The two men chatted about their individual circumstances to one another. Lionel spoke about his recent battles, while Alphonse told stories of his boredom after returning to the Duchy.

"Um, sorry to keep you waiting! I brought you your rice and soup first," said Aletta.

And so, their first set of orders arrived.

"Ah, much thanks!"

"You have my gratitude."

The pair gave their thanks to Aletta and grabbed their food.

"Shall we..."

"...Dig in?"

The feast began.

Mm, the pairing of butter and pepel is splendid.

Alphonse wasted no time topping his pork soup with pepel and was not disappointed by the immense wave of flavor that washed over him. The savoriness of the meat and soup warmed the insides of his body, with the pepel stretching out the experience. While the aftertaste remained in his mouth, he took a bite of rice. The previous master taught him this particular eating style. The light flavor of the rice fused with the heavy flavoring of the soup and its aftertaste to create a sublime experience.

...Hmph, I'm ready.

Even after eating all that food, Alphonse's stomach was still empty. He patiently awaited the main attraction.

"..."

Compared to Lionel, Alphonse had taken his time enjoying his food. The lion man downed the rice and pork soup in what seemed like one gulp. All that was left was the wait until the rest of the food arrived.

Psh, it's all this smell's fault.

Lionel had intended on taking his time with the pork soup, especially because it had been a while since he last had the opportunity to eat some. Sadly, he was done in by the rich fragrance of the melted butter and the simmered pieces of fatty meat and vegetables. Before he could come to his senses, Lionel had annihilated the rice and soup, leaving himself hungrier than ever.

"Dammit, now I'm just hungrier!" he growled.

The pork ended up reminding Lionel of what he felt was the most delicious dish in the entire restaurant. He impatiently waited for his order.

"Sorry for the wait! Here's your curry rice and katsudon. Oh, and I brought pork soup refills, too."

"Ho, ho! Now this is what I've been waiting for!" said Alphonse. "Time to feast. Ah, and can I get another order of curry rice, please?"

"Argh, so slow! Goddamn, it smells so good! Tell the master to bring me another katsudon, wouldja?!"

With their primary objectives in sight, the two men simultaneously began digging in. It only took five minutes for them to demolish their first round of orders.

"Today's 'Meat Day,' eh? I'll have an order of teriyaki chicken and seishu with a bowl of pork soup. Hold the butter."

"Teriyaki" Tatsugorou's long years of patronage at Nekoya had honed his senses somewhat. As soon as he entered the restaurant, he had his suspicions confirmed and placed his order. While he certainly agreed that the butter made the soup that much richer and more delicious, he also felt that when paired with rice, it tasted better sans butter.

A sip of the butter-free soup, a bite of white rice, a sip of seishu.

"Mm, mm."

Tatsugorou instinctively nodded to himself. It'd been about half a year since he'd had the chance to enjoy his food and drink with a side of pork soup. The finely simmered meat and vegetables had soaked in the savory juices of the soup perfectly.

"I knew I was right. There isn't anything like booze and pork soup without the butter."

The butter was undoubtedly good on its own or when paired with other western cuisines, but when it came to booze with a kick, the pork soup went better without it. Tatsugorou came to this conclusion after years of testing on his own terms.

"Pardon me, young lady. Might I get a soup refill?"

This time, Tatsugorou spent his time at the restaurant until closing hours, enjoying his alcohol, teriyaki chicken, and fried rice.

After all the customers had returned home and the

cleanup was over, the master handed Aletta an envelope and a box of cookies. "Yo, good work today. Here's your pay and the cookies you asked for."

"Wow, thank you so much! Is it just me, or were things pretty busy today?"

"They were. It was Meat Day after all."

On Meat Days, the master typically used more rice than normal. Despite the work it took to make pork soup, it disappeared many times faster than the miso soup. The master ended up making three whole pots of the stuff before the day was done. While it wasn't quite as busy as a weekday Meat Day, Aletta was right: today had been pretty busy. In fact, they were only just getting around to having dinner.

"I suppose we should get to eating, eh? Let's see, how about grilled butter soy sauce rice balls, pork soup, and... Oh, I know. Japanese omelets!" The master held up a pot with one hand.

"Oh my gosh, thank you!" Aletta nodded not once, but twice.

"Great, then buckle up. I'll get to cookin' up some food for us."

And so, the master returned to the kitchen once more to prepare the final meal of the day.

CHAPTER 29

Pizza

THERE WASN'T A SINGLE SOUL in the royal capital who didn't know the name Sirius Alfade, the next in line to inherit the Alfade Company. His father, of course, was the current head of the Alfade Company, while his mother came from an affluent family of nobles. So while Sirius was the next in line to inherit the business, he was also a genuine nobleman with the blood of his parents running through his veins.

When he was born, the Alfade Company had already earned the position of purveyor to the king and the castle. Before Sirius grew out of infancy, his uncles were sent to the empire and the duchy to start up branches of the business there, eventually leading the company to further success.

It was about half a year ago that Thomas, his grandfather and the "Restorer of the Alfade Company," revealed to him a very surprising secret.

For many years, over twenty in fact, Thomas had kept this secret close to his chest, hiding the existence of a certain restaurant that one could describe as the savior of his family's business. Thomas entrusted the door to that place to his grandson, Sirius.

At first, the young nobleman was positively stunned. As the heir to his family's business, Sirius had dealt in all kinds of food products. But even he was shocked by just how many unknown foods the restaurant had to offer. Perhaps even more stunning was that they were all delicious. He unabashedly smacked his lips at the meals on offer, never failing to enjoy himself.

And that's when it hit him. If the Alfade Company further "stole" the flavors on offer at the restaurant, it could advance their world's culinary techniques even further. However, Sirius was also aware that he wasn't the only one thinking along these lines.

There was the info gathered from the various Alfade Company locations around the world, and then there was the info that Sirius gathered himself with his own eyes and ears at the Restaurant to Another World. By combining those two networks, it was much easier to see the bigger picture.

He had heard word that an extremely talented, young high priestess in the church of the Lord of Light, the largest of all religions on the Eastern Continent, had established a convent. According to the rumors, in said convent was a priest-in-training with almost zero talent for the job outside of being able to bake delicious bread. Meanwhile, in the restaurant, Sirius frequently crossed paths with a high priestess of the Lord of Light who always brought her female disciples with her to enjoy some pound cake.

Sirius had also heard tales about the Sand Nation from the Western Continent, who had just made inroads with the empire after sending an envoy over. This guest presented them with something called cafa, a drink that was magically cooled and greatly resembled the coffee of the other world. In the restaurant, Sirius often spotted a pair of noble Sand Nation siblings who couldn't get enough of coffee floats.

Sirius had also heard rumors of the new, deliciously strong whiskey the dwarves had developed. The Alfade Company was still trying to figure out how to reproduce this drink. Meanwhile, in the restaurant, Sirius noted the presence of two rowdy dwarf men who always seemed to be talking about booze.

Indeed, there were a handful of people in Thomas's world who had the same idea as he. Sirius knew better than anyone that if they put real effort into making those ideas a reality, they would undoubtedly bear fruit. That's why he couldn't afford to sit on his butt and watch.

And so, Sirius began to act. He began by doing the one thing Thomas was unable to do before the Alfade Company grew in size, mostly for fear of his secret getting out.

With the Alfade Company now one of the most reputable in all the Kingdom, Sirius had a single, close friend who was exactly what he needed for this mission. It was because of their current situation that this was a trump card he could use.

"Young Master, could you please tell me what's going on?"

Jonathan, one of the Alfade Company's young chefs, asked Sirius for answers.

"I have something important to talk to you about. Could you do me a huge favor and just quietly follow me, Jonathan?" That was all Sirius told him before leading him to the Alfade Company's old storage space. There were plenty of large storage spaces in the area these days, so the old one was barely used. *Why was Sirius dragging Jonathan here?* the chef wondered.

"...All right. It's about time," Sirius muttered.

He entered the storage space, and after making sure they were alone, called out to Jonathan. "Today, you and I are going to grab a bite to eat together."

"...I'm not sure I'm following you." Jonathan tilted his head in confusion.

Jonathan's father was a valued member of the Alfade Company, responsible for helping invent all manner of new products. Growing up, since he and the heir to the company, Sirius, were close in age, they'd gotten along well. Up until he became a chef like his father, he recalled running all around the royal capital as kids.

But he couldn't recall a single time Sirius had ever invited him to a meal. Sure, they'd eaten together at various stands and restaurants while on business trips, but he'd never formally been invited anywhere. And now, when Jonathan finally did get an invitation, it was to an old storage area? What was Sirius playing at?

"Look, if nothing else, I have no intention of going to eat there with anyone other than you," Sirius explained.

"What do you mean by 'there'?"

Sirius decided to tell Jonathan the whole truth. The secret that only Sirius and his grandfather knew up until this point.

"As far as I know, it's a place not of our world. But they serve the most delicious foods..."

Within the storage space appeared a black door with a cat illustration on it. What lay beyond it was the very restaurant that helped the Alfade Company become such a massive business over the years.

"The Restaurant to Another World."

That day, Jonathan Weinsberg became the third man in the company to become aware of the door's existence.

Jonathan felt like he had been slapped in the face as he stepped through the door, heard the bells ringing, and exited the dark storage space only to reemerge in a brightly lit room.

"Young Master, is this really another world? Wait, wha...?!"

As Jonathan surveyed the restaurant, his eyes met a lizardman's as the creature dug into a giant plate of some sort of egg dish. He screamed.

"Don't worry. Some of the customers here are monster folk, but they'll do you no harm." Sirius thought back on when he first started frequenting the restaurant and quietly laughed to himself. He led his friend to an empty table.

"Welcome," he said.

It didn't take long for the master to appear and quietly

place down a menu on the table in front of them. These days, Sirius frequented the restaurant rather often. He typically asked for a dish of spaghetti Neapolitan, along with a dish he'd yet to try. The master seemed well aware of this, so he wasted no time bringing a menu, some lemon water, and a moist towel.

"Thank you very much." Sirius took the menu as usual but gently placed it off to the side. "But actually, I already know what I'm ordering today."

He spoke his order aloud.

"I'd like two orders of onion and bacon pizza. One for me and one for my friend here, please."

"You got it." The master nodded and retreated to the back.

"What's this onion and bacon pizza thing you just ordered?" asked Jonathan.

Once the master left, Jonathan asked Sirius for an explanation, as the heir to the Alfade Company cleaned his hands with one of the warm towels. Quite frankly, the chef had no idea what to expect.

"You'll understand as soon as you take a bite. I know you will." Sirius responded with the smile of a child who was plotting something.

I suppose asking him to describe food from another world was silly in the first place, Jonathan thought.

Jonathan followed Sirius's example and began cleaning his hands, thinking back on everything that had happened so far. This place was probably in another world, just as the young master described.

First of all, the restaurant was filled with the sort of customers you would never see even in the biggest city on the continent. The internal decor was comprised of objects that completely defied Jonathan's understanding. On top of all that, there were customers that were clearly not from the capital. If anything, calling this another world was the only way to explain it all.

Wow, this water has some sort of citrus mixed into it, doesn't it?

Jonathan absentmindedly took a sip from the glass of ice water while he was lost in thought. He found his mouth filled with refreshingly easy-to-drink ice water and immediately understood something. If this were the sort of classy service this restaurant's master provided without being asked, he was clearly more talented than your average chef.

Of course he is. If the young master Sirius comes here regularly, he must be good.

Jonathan's childhood friend was the heir to a massive company that dealt in all manner of food products within the royal capital. He tasted a variety of different foods made by the Alfade Company's most talented chefs on a daily basis. There was little doubt that Sirius's palate was more discerning than even royalty's. That left little room for doubt. The chef here had to be immensely talented and the food incredibly delicious.

With that in mind, Jonathan waited with Sirius for the pizza thing to arrive.

"Sorry for the wait!" It didn't take long for a young demon girl to come out with a large plate in hand. "Here are your onion bacon pizzas!"

Is this bread with some sort of cheese topping?

The freshly baked food in front of him sizzled quietly as he took a good, long look at it. Covering the entirety of the plate was a round flatbread, stretched wide and cut into six pieces. A red sauce was spread across the top, likely made through crushing some type of red vegetable, along with thinly cut pieces of oranie. But the toppings didn't end there. The surface of the bread was covered with a layer of cheese, meats, and minced greens.

"Let's eat, shall we? Pizza is best when it's still hot."

And with that, Sirius began digging in. Instead of using a knife and fork, he grabbed a piece of the pizza with his bare hands. This was apparently the correct way to eat this particular dish.

I wonder what it tastes like...

Meanwhile, Jonathan found himself a bit lost when faced with the unknown dish in front of him. Sirius told him he'd understand everything once he took a bite, which meant there was only one clear path for the young chef to take. He reached down and grabbed one of the six slices of pizza.

Hm, it's quite hot.

It was indeed as freshly baked as it looked. Jonathan watched as the melted cheese stretched and pulled away as he picked up the slice. It was so hot he feared he might burn his fingers. He narrowed his eyebrows at the thing in front of him.

I see. It doesn't smell bad at all. Wait, this is...?!

A lovely aroma was emanating from the so-called pizza. It was the scent of the cheese and bacon juices melting together. But amidst this medley of scents, Jonathan caught a whiff of something that made him tilt his head ever so slightly.

Never mind. I'm sure it'll all be made clear once I give it a try.

While he found himself puzzled over the faint fragrance of something that seemed out of place, Jonathan nonetheless brought the slice of pizza to his mouth and took a bite.

Hm?! I knew it!

It was an orchestra of flavors. There was the sharp taste

of the melted cheese, the carefully cooked, high-quality meat, the very mild spiciness of the oranie... Then there were the minced greens sprinkled on top with their unique bitterness.

But that wasn't all. The base of the dish, a thin bread of some kind, was baked in such a way that the surface was nice and crusty, but the inside was fluffy and welcoming. Made with high quality wheat, salt, and water, the bread had a simple and light flavor to it that supported the main actors of the dish.

What surprised Jonathan the most, however, was something else entirely.

"Young Master! This... It's marmett sauce, is it not?!"

Indeed. In the layer between the topmost ingredients and the bottom crust was what appeared to be marmett sauce, with its slightly bitter yet incredibly delicious flavor. The sauce made from the very vegetable that the Alfade Company had discovered in a small country and worked so hard to be able to harvest within the Kingdom.

This pizza dish used marmett for its sauce, a vegetable still widely unknown outside of those who worked at the Alfade Company.

"Indeed. Apparently, it's called 'tomato' in this world, but yes. This dish utilizes marmett as its primary ingredient."

Sirius nodded to his friend as though he had been waiting for this very moment. As a chef of the Alfade Company, he'd fully believed Jonathan's clever tongue would be able to recognize the key ingredient of the dish. He had been correct in bringing the chef here.

"I'll explain my intentions later, but first, let's enjoy our meal," the young man said to his friend, who clearly looked ready and excited to begin his research right away.

"Y-yeah, sure." Jonathan could do nothing but nod his head and reach for the next slice.

He must've peeled the marmett after steeping it in boiled water, then crushed it... No, the process had to have been more complicated than that.

Jonathan, a world-class chef in his own right, could barely conceal his surprise as he tried analyzing the pizza with every bite he took. The base was very similar to the meat sauce he had helped develop in their world. They had created it by preparing boiled and peeled marmetts in a variety of different ways, producing an intensely flavorful sauce. Even for someone as talented as Jonathan, reproducing or surpassing this flavor would require an immense amount of time and research.

And who would have thought one could use bread like this!

The concept of using bread in place of a plate had existed for a long time. But the idea of placing the ingredients atop the bread and cooking them all together at the same time was completely new. Now that Jonathan had seen it in action, he understood why it was effective. By cooking everything together, the bread and ingredients fused in perfect harmony. The thin, crunchy, middle layer would be infused by the flavors of the sauce and ingredients, while the outer, thicker layer would taste strongly of wheat. Both were delicious in their own different ways. The bread wasn't just a bonus, but rather a core component of the dish.

If I can do some research on this back at the company... Oh, I see.

As Jonathan continued eating, he realized Sirius's intentions; the true goal.

"Young Master, I'm sorry. Before I could really get a feel for its flavor, I ended up finishing my serving. Do you think I could order another?"

"But of course. That's why I brought you here. Um, Aletta? Could you get my friend here another onion bacon pizza? I'll have my usual Neapolitan, thank you." Sirius chuckled at his friend, who had finally figured it out, and placed their second order with the waitress passing by. A fresh pizza for Jonathan, and his personal favorite dish that had the meat sauce that surpassed even his grandfather's famous work.

"Absolutely! Thank you very much!" The waitress responded with a bright smile as the two young men continued their meal...no, their research.

"That pizza stuff really is quite astounding."

Jonathan accompanied his thoughts with a sigh after the two men returned to the Alfade Company's old storage space.

By the end of the meal, Jonathan had eaten not one, but *three* full onion bacon pizzas. His stomach bulged painfully, but he made it a point to memorize the flavor remaining on his tongue. In fact, he was ready to begin his research that very moment.

"Right? The fact that you can mix and match the ingredients means it can be adjusted for all manner of situations. But I also love that it can't exist without the marmett sauce in the first place," Sirius replied to his friend.

While there were all sorts of delicious sauces made from marmetts, the vegetable itself was still relatively unknown, even within the Kingdom. The Alfade Company was the only organization that had easy access to the food, so, in other words, if the citizens of the Kingdom came to know and love marmett the same way Sirius and his grandfather had, the sky was the limit for the Alfade Company.

That's why the first dish Sirius chose for his friend Jonathan was the pizza. A brand-new recipe courtesy of a new world with all sorts of potential applications. If they could perfect this recipe, they'd have a dish on their hands that could become a showstopper for the next generation of the Alfade Company, replacing the knight sauce entirely. Sirius truly saw that level of potential in pizza.

"By the way, Young Master. About that restaurant..." Jonathan looked at his friend with expectant eyes. He already knew that if he wanted to use that door, he at least needed the permission of the man in front of him.

Sirius grinned at his friend. "Yes, I'll definitely take you back sometime soon. Though it should be said that we can only go there once every seven days."

Jonathan was one of the Alfade Company's best chefs: young but highly trained and capable. Perhaps more importantly, he would never betray Sirius. Due to the rapid growth of the Alfade Company, it had many enemies. That made loyalty like Jonathan's all the harder to come by.

Sirius knew that revealing the company's secret to him wouldn't be a mistake.

"Thank you very much." Jonathan bowed his head, unable to hide the smile on his face.

I bet there's all sorts of delicious foods over there! Sorry, but I'm gonna soak in every bit of knowledge I can!

Jonathan hardened his resolve, all the while thinking back to the delicious-looking pasta dish filled with marmett sauce that his friend had eaten before his very eyes.

CHAPTER 30

Roast Chicken

WHILE WESTERN CUISINE NEKOYA occupied the first-floor basement of a building appropriately called the "Nekoya Building," on its second floor was a bar.

That bar's name was "Leonhart."

Leonhart's master originally worked for a trading company, traveling across Japan and even abroad. But some twenty years earlier, his body finally broke down on him, and he used the occasion as an opportunity to finally retire from the busy life and move from Tokyo back to his hometown. Against the wishes of his family, he started up a little business for himself, a place where adults could enjoy their evenings. The space was large enough to build a sizable restaurant, but the master instead dedicated about half of the floor space to storing its supply of booze.

This meant that the actual bar itself was small enough so he could get around on his own. Leonhart had a single, beautiful counter. It was a small bar.

There were no young woman there to tend to the guests' needs, nor was there karaoke for the more musically-inclined visitors. But what Leonhart did have was a wide array of alcohol from all over the world, from the cheap stuff to more expensive booze. The master had spent much of his youth traveling the world, which meant he'd accumulated vast knowledge of different kinds of liquors. Since he could be trusted with his prices and drinks, he had a fair number of regulars. So long as he didn't make any stupid business decisions or live outside of his means, he was able to live a fairly satisfying life, once the house's loan was paid off and the kids were all grown up and independent. That's the type of bar Leonhart was.

There was one thing that separated Leonhart from other bars of its kind: it did deliveries, of a sort.

You see, if customers placed their order between opening time from 6 to 9 PM, they'd be able to get finger foods from the restaurant below to go with their booze. The best part was that these finger foods were more delicious than anything your average bar sold.

As far as Leonhart's master was concerned, if you were after a killer meal, he recommended going to Nekoya.

If you wanted delicious alcohol, there wasn't a bar better than Leonhart. And so, the finger foods that were available for delivery were exactly that: dishes that didn't require chopsticks or utensils to eat. Nonetheless, they were all incredibly delicious, went well with alcohol, and were made by a pro, of sorts. The combination of a wide variety of great spirits with delicious finger foods meant that Leonhart was highly regarded among bar-goers. Salarymen got to relieve their post-work stress by dropping by for a pint while enjoying their favorite snacks.

And so the master of Leonhart took a delivery order on a certain Saturday.

The freight elevator in the back of the alcohol storage area came to a stop with a metal clink. Upon hearing the noise, the master stepped away from his guests for a moment before heading to the back to collect the delivery order.

"Hiya. Oh? You're delivering the goods today?"

Leonhart's master was somewhat surprised to find Nekoya's master stepping out from the elevator holding a tray.

The man knew about the secret of the restaurant on the first-floor basement. He knew about the Restaurant to Another World.

Over twenty years ago, just after the master ruined his liver and found out he couldn't drink another drop of alcohol, he decided the least he could do was serve the good stuff to other folks. Thus he came upon the idea of opening up his own bar. He searched high and low around his hometown for attractive property options, but ultimately found himself attracted to the delivery service contract of the Nekoya Building and ended up renting out its second floor. It was then that the previous master of Nekoya informed him of the restaurant's secret, leaving him rather surprised. It was just like one of the fantasy stories his son loved reading. He had wondered whether the master was just talking about some anime movie; how could he not? He had just been told that the ordinary restaurant right below him was a place where residents from another world, human and inhuman, visited on a weekly basis.

Yet at the end of the day, that was Nekoya's business, not his. On occasion, he would sell the master alcohol to serve to his "otherworldly customers," but otherwise, there was no real effect on Leonhart. After a while, the master grew used to the whole "other world" thing.

"I just figured it'd be the usual young lady is all. I'm guessing you wanna talk?"

Over the past few months, on Saturdays, a young blonde waitress wearing a bizarre hairpiece had been delivering the orders to Leonhart. She was clearly a new hire. As far as the master was concerned, she looked much like what he expected his first granddaughter would look like in five years or so. She was a real cutie. After her hiring, she became the one to collect the alcohol in her master's stead.

Which meant that if the master was coming himself, he likely wanted to have a chat about the goods. Having known Nekoya's current master since he was a teen, it didn't take much for him to correctly guess his intentions.

"Exactly. There's something I wanted to talk to you about."

The restaurant's master handed him the tray full of food.

Bright green, freshly boiled edamame beans.

Thinly-cut fried potato chips flavored with salt and seaweed.

Homemade rum-raisin butter sandwiched between two salted biscuits.

Three different types of sandwiches: thick slices of ham and cheese, homemade tartar sauce made with a plenty of eggs, and tuna mixed with minced onions.

Recently, one of the regulars at Nekoya began requesting fried rice balls (extremely *not* western cuisine), so the master decided to offer them on the regular menu.

The set included butter soy sauce, onion miso, and seaweed rice.

The various finger foods on the tray were all requests from the post-work regulars who arrived immediately after the bar opened. In fact, they were the most popular items among the finger foods Leonhart offered.

"Many thanks. Once I hand these out, we can get to talkin'." Leonhart's master went and placed the dishes in front of the customers who ordered them.

"I'm sorry for the wait. Here's the delivery you ordered. Would you like seconds on anything?"

Upon setting down the food, the customers ordered drinks that paired well with the finger foods. Leonhart's master quickly prepared their drinks and handed them out.

Leonhart wasn't the type of bar that large groups of people frequented. Instead, regulars typically included visitors who came alone or in pairs, looking for a quiet place to enjoy a drink. It was a cozy bar.

"Please, take your time. I have some business to attend to, but I'll be back momentarily." The master informed the customers of his absence before returning to the alcohol storage area.

"So? What're you looking for this time?" he asked Nekoya's master, who was quietly waiting in front of the elevator.

"Let's see... I'm looking for two one-liter bottles of sweet shochu, nothing too expensive. Today's customers are really feeling it." Nekoya's master laid out his order.

"Shochu, eh? Lemme see what I got..." Leonhart's master took a moment to think about his options before presenting the man with the drink that best seemed to suit his needs. "I have some cheap potato and wheat shochu that I got from Kyushu. Does that work for you? The alcohol content is a little high, but the aftertaste is quite refreshing."

"Yeah, that sounds perfect. You're a real lifesaver!"

Nekoya's master wasn't particularly knowledgeable about alcohol, since he didn't drink himself, but he knew enough to understand that the man in front of him was a real pro. He could trust whatever drink Leonhart's master chose for him.

"Then this is it." Leonhart's master quickly reached for the two bottles he had described and handed them to the other man.

"I'll put it on your tab as usual. Just subtract it from my rent this month."

"Of course. Thank you so much!" Nekoya's master expressed his gratitude, two one-liter bottles in hand.

"By the way, if you don't mind my asking, who are you serving that to?"

The large bottle of whiskey he had sold to Nekoya's master was apparently ordered by two short, older gentlemen who wore large axes across their backs. He was rather curious as to who ordered these.

"Oh, well...they're an ogre couple." The master hesitated for a moment before explaining. They were a married couple with large bodies and horns who brought along with them a tiny, older man who at this point may as well have been a regular.

"O-ogres?" Leonhart's master couldn't help but stutter out the word as the other man chuckled and answered.

"Aye. Big ones with huge horns."

On the Western Continent, close to a Mountain Nation road, was a small cabin built for travelers.

"I'm telling you, we should cook him the normal way!"

"No! We gotta boil him!"

Inside said cabin were two ogres, a married couple in fact, who had decided to make the building their home for the time being. Tatsuji and Otora argued over the ingredients in front of them, debating how to best prepare them.

"C'mon, now. This is the sort of thing that tastes best when you just eat it plain! Plus, I'm guessing it's just a kid. We should skin it, salt it, and roast it over the fire. That's it."

The male ogre was several times larger than an average human. He had bright red skin and black hair, with two yellow horns poking out from beneath. Tatsuji wore clothes made from a tiger he had beaten to death himself. He was hoping to get to eating sooner rather than later.

"No way! Come on, look at the back of this thing's legs. Furry, right? It probably has all sorts of scum. Sure, we could just roast it and it'd probably be fine, but it won't taste any good unless we boil it first."

Otora was at least three heads taller than the average woman, sporting disheveled black hair and a white face with two yellow horns stretching out from it. She was thinking of using the meat to make a soup or stew of some sort. That way they could still feel like they had much to eat, even though there wasn't actually that much meat.

Neither ogre would budge on the issue. Each felt that their recommended way of preparing the meat would result in the more delicious of meals. It looked like the argument would continue for a time without a proper conclusion.

That is, until...

"My good ogre friends, do you have a moment?"

The "food" hanging from the thick ceiling beam spoke to the couple.

"What is it?" the two ogres answered their captive, temporarily distracted from their important debate.

"And just to be clear, the whole 'I'm not tasty so you shouldn't eat me!' thing ain't gonna work on us. I can cook you up into something delicious, no problem," Otora boasted.

"Of course, of course. I absolutely understand."

The unfortunate "food" that happened to be caught by the two ogres was in fact a halfling bard who went by the name Rat. He gulped loudly. Rat was currently in a bit of pickle, considering he was tied up with incredibly tough vines from the mountainside. Nonetheless, he took a moment to observe his surroundings, spotting firewood, some pots and kettles, clothes of all kind, swords, armor, and a small mountain of bones. After seeing what there was to see, he began carefully putting his words in order.

"I know I'm butting in, but it would appear to me that the two of you have quite the discerning palate. So I can't help but ask: Have either of you ever experienced cooking from another world?"

If he could somehow get the ogres to go to the restaurant, he'd be saved. He flashed his brightest smile to hide the plan he was putting together.

"Another world?"

"What're you talkin' about?"

The two ogres seemed intrigued by their meal's sudden suggestion and responded with curiosity.

"I'm talking about meals from another world entirely!" Rat said. "Let me explain. Once every seven days, today in fact, a restaurant that serves otherworldly meals appears in this very area. How's the food, you ask? Simply unbelievable! They offer tastes and flavors truly not of this world."

They were interested. Rat licked his lips and continued his explanation. There was a reason his silver tongue had kept him alive all these years. No matter how scary an ogre may be, all he had to do was get them to listen.

"Liar!"

"I ain't heard of anything like that."

"No, no, this is the pure truth! It's just up the mountain. And like I mentioned earlier, it only appears once every seven days. Oh, the alcohol over there is exquisite as well. How unfortunate! I could show you the way, but it would appear I'm not long for this world…"

It was obvious the ogres didn't yet believe him. Rat let out a deep sigh, still tied up in vines. He did everything within his power to not appear desperate, instead recalling his own memories of the food at the restaurant and using them to speak as truthfully as possible.

"Well, if you're that confident about this place, I wouldn't mind keeping you alive until you show us the way."

"You better not be lying though. If you are, we're gonna eat you alive, starting from those feet of yours."

The ogres had sensed some truth to Rat's words.

"Wonderful! How very wonderful! I'd be happy to show you the way then. Just..."

...untie me, is what Rat was about to say, right up until he was lifted up and placed on the shoulders of one of the ogres.

"You got it. Just tell us which way to go, and I'll carry you."

"We wouldn't want you escaping on us is all. If you don't wanna get eaten alive, you better show us the right way!"

"...Okay."

Nothing in this world was ever that easy. Rat let out a sigh that was half-disappointed and half-hopeful.

And so, the ogres departed from the cabin, bare feet and all. They were nearly as fast as a beast, despite one of them carrying Rat on their shoulders. Sure, he only weighed about as much as a human child, but he was still extra weight. But they didn't seem to care.

"Ah! Over there! Then take a right at that tree! Um, could you at least try not to shake me so much?! I almost bit my tongue!"

The harsh shaking up and down made for a ride that was all sorts of uncomfortable. Rat felt nauseated, but he did his best to lead them correctly. He was scared the ogres might not hear his directions properly, which could very well result in his immediate death.

After about an hour of running up the mountain, the unlikely trio finally arrived at their destination.

"This is it?"

"I didn't think it really existed."

The two ogres placed Rat down and stared at the structure in front of them in awe. He had led them to a black door with an illustration of a cat on it. This was the entrance to the Restaurant to Another World.

"Indeed it does. Sir, would you mind untying me? I'll teach you all about this place, I promise."

"I suppose that's fair enough."

Common sense dictated that there was no way there'd be a door like this out in the middle of nowhere. This alone was enough to prove that Rat wasn't lying. The ogres nodded in response to the halfling's request and untied the vines that bound him. Rat was once again a free man.

"Ooh, ow, ow." Rat stroked the painful marks the vines had left behind and then looked up at the ogre couple.

"All right. Go ahead and open that door."

"Why not you?"

Tatsuji seemed confused by Rat's instructions. The halfling's expression saddened a bit as he closed his eyes and explained his unfortunate situation to the bigger man.

"Well, you see, the door isn't particularly fond of me, if you get what I'm saying."

Rat reached for the door handle, but his hand simply passed right through it.

"It pains me to admit to it, but a long time ago, I tried to dine and dash. The second I left, the restaurant 'rejected' me. I can't open the door on my own anymore."

Rat spoke the truth. He had been regretting his actions ever since he made that critical mistake.

On that fateful day, he had entered the restaurant knowing full well he didn't have the money to pay for anything. Yet Rat made an order anyway, eating his fill and leaving without saying a word. The price he paid for that sin was large. He later apologized to the master for his actions and was forgiven by the man, but unfortunately the mysterious door wasn't very flexible when it came to its strange magic. Even now, Rat was incapable of opening the door on his own. That was why if he ever wanted to visit Nekoya, he had to use other customers in order to go. He had accompanied the swordsman from the Mountain Nation, the diviner from the Ocean

Nation, the naive princess, and even these terrifying, man-eating ogres.

"So that's why I need you to open the door, sir."

"I guess I got no choice then."

Convinced, Tatsuji placed his hand on the handle with no problem. The trio were met with the sounds of a bell ringing as the door opened up.

"Shall we, Otora? You're comin' too, pal."

"Yup."

"You got it."

Tatsuji stepped through after calling out to the others, marking the moment when they became guests of the Restaurant to Another World.

Despite the time of day, the inside of the restaurant was bright. Tatsuji and Otora surveyed their surroundings and quickly caught wind of something.

"Wait a second!"

"You…"

"No, no," Rat explained. "I swear it's not on purpose!"

The ogres had immediately understood the situation and proceeded to glare at Rat, who calmly returned their gaze. As always, the restaurant was filled with regulars who were eating and drinking their fill.

There was a large, older swordsman who gave off the aura of a warrior stronger than any Tatsuji had ever encountered.

There was also a young elf man, thin sword at his waist, directing a fierce killing intent in the direction of Tatsuji.

Also present was a clearly dangerous demon warrior, a lion-headed man with all sorts of scars across his body. He had a massive sword by his side.

Tatsuji also spotted another talented swordsman. Judging by his equipment, he must've been from a well-off family. Next to him was a fox-faced diviner. Tatsuji sensed immense magical energies coming from the man.

And then there was a young woman with a golden seal, signifying her high rank as a priestess in the church of the Lord of Light. She was accompanied by another young priestess.

The sights didn't stop there. At another table was a naga, her bottom half that of a giant red snake, eating a plate of some type of egg dish wrapped in meat. Elsewhere was a pair of vampires drinking wine as red as blood.

In the corner was an old, foreign diviner whose magical powers were so absurd that Tatsuji couldn't even get a full grasp of them.

The restaurant was filled with not one, not two, but many warriors and mages of all kinds, beings Tatsuji might have been able to take on in a one-on-one situation, but certainly not as a group. They all seemed to be enjoying their respective meals while carefully watching the new ogres.

Tatsuji and Otora were feared as powerful ogres in their territory. They had easily defended themselves against all manner of hunting squads. The pair were fearsome creatures in their own right, and they could sense the strength of their enemies. If the people in this restaurant were to turn on them, not only was victory impossible, but escaping with their lives intact was as well. They would have to play nice while in the restaurant. Any trouble would mean the end for them.

Rat smiled. "You see, the food and booze here are both so good that you can't find them anywhere else in the world! So the people who come here on the regular tend to be pretty amazing folks."

For the time being, Rat had escaped with his life. He explained the general details of the restaurant to the ogres before calling over the golden-haired demon waitress, who was probably from the Eastern Continent.

"I know this is a wee bit forward of me, but allow me to make the order. Young lady, excuse me. Could I get your biggest bottle of shochu? Oh, and three glasses of water, please. As for food, let's see... Six orders of roast chicken should do it. With gravy sauce, too. Oh, and can you bring out the alcohol first? For the roast chicken, we only need the meat, okay?"

"Y-yes, of course!"

Rat figured it'd be a bad idea to make the ogre couple any angrier than they already were, so he went ahead and ordered for them as if he were a regular himself. Meanwhile, the waitress looked up at the pair and responded loudly before heading to the kitchen to inform the master.

After watching the waitress retreat, Rat flashed a smile at the ogres. As a bard, he had thick skin that even their glares couldn't pierce. "All right. C'mon, you two. Feel free to sit wherever you'd like."

"Tch, you better watch your back later. Let's go, Otora."

"Aye."

Tatsuji let out a sigh as he glared at the small man, who stood only as tall as his knees. He and Otora found a table to their liking and sat down. It was just the right height for them to rest their elbows on. Next to them was Rat, whose feet were nowhere close to touching the floor.

"So that stuff you ordered. Those be otherworldly foods and booze?"

"Indeed they are!" Rat responded to Otora's question with a smile and a nod of his head. As far as his experience could tell him, they were the best items on the menu for his two new "friends." He went on to explain.

"So the shochu stuff I ordered is alcohol from the other world. It's strong like dwarf whiskey, but it also has a great flavor to it. Pour some of that into a glass with ice in it, and you got something truly delicious. Ah, perfect timing!" he said as Aletta reappeared.

"Um, here's your order of shochu."

The golden-haired waitress returned, carrying in her hands a large, transparent bottle of shochu. Rat could barely hide the excitement on his face. He quickly grabbed the bottle and glasses from the waitress. He then inserted the large pieces of ice she also brought into the glasses and began pouring the alcohol.

"Many thanks, young lady! Now then, grab a glass. It's quite strong, so be careful."

Rat figured he may as well warn them, just in case. He poured himself a bit of shochu as well.

"Psh. As if this much alcohol could do... Kerflah?!"

Tatsuji quickly downed his glass, only to raise his voice in shock moments later. He was used to drinking unrefined booze that you could get off traveling merchants; strong booze that would pass across the tongue smoothly but burn your throat and stomach.

"What a surprise! It's thick, but it smells wonderful and tastes great."

On the other hand, Otora took a single sip from her glass, letting the fluid roll around over her tongue.

It was in fact delicious. Despite being as strong as dwarf whiskey, it didn't have the same strong flavor to it.

If anything, it smelled and tasted slightly sweet as it slowly spread throughout her mouth.

"Damn, otherworldly booze is pretty great."

Tatsuji nodded his head, pouring himself and Otora a fresh refill of the shochu. His wife was talented in the kitchen, more than capable of cooking up the lean beasts of the winter, or even the hard-muscled samurai who wandered the hillside. She was extremely good at preparing alcohol as well. But even Tatsuji had to admit that this was far beyond anything she had made.

There was a dwarf in the restaurant that was gulping down his own drink. After having had some himself, Tatsuji totally understood.

"Aye, sir. The food here is something else, but the booze is in a class all its own," Rat remarked almost proudly.

Rat had known of this place for quite some time. As astute at reading people as he was, he could guarantee that of all the "guests" he brought here, not even one ever left dissatisfied.

"So what's the deal with the grub? You ordered 'roast chicken' or something, right?"

Around the time the first bottle of shochu had been emptied out, Otora pointed her question toward Rat. Because the booze was so good, it'd be especially disappointing if the food didn't compare.

"Aye, miss. It is basically roasted, fatty chicken breast and... Ah, it's here!"

"Sorry to keep you waiting. Here are your orders of roast chicken."

Just as Rat started to explain the dish to his companions, the master appeared with a large plate and a fresh bottle of shochu in hand. On top of the giant plate, primarily used for events, were six pieces of golden-brown, roasted chicken breast. Atop each piece was gravy made of meat juices for extra flavoring, as well as a dash of black pepper.

"Take your time and enjoy," the master said, gently placing the plate down in the center of the table. He returned to the kitchen to continue cooking.

"So this is roast chicken, eh?" said Tatsuji.

Otora added, "It just looks like cooked chicken meat to me, but it does smell awfully good."

Both husband and wife found themselves drawn in by the tantalizing aroma of the chicken breasts in front of them, their mouths beginning to water.

"C'mon, now. This stuff is best when eaten hot." Rat made sure to procure his one piece of chicken breast as he urged his companions to begin eating as well.

The two ogres each grabbed a piece for themselves and bit into their pieces simultaneously.

"Whooooaaaa!" their voices rang out in tandem.

They couldn't help but shout as their taste buds were attacked by an indescribable flavor. There was no way this chicken meat had simply been cooked over fire. It was too amazing for that. This had to be some sort of magic trick. There was just the right balance of fat, and the skin satisfyingly crumbled away with each bite, revealing its amazing smell. Because it'd been roasted seemingly perfectly, the hot meat juices were preserved as well. It was tender and tremendously delicious. Literally on top of all that was the extra gravy for flavoring that utilized the meat juices themselves. The black pepper added a bit of a kick to the whole equation.

"Well? Sublime, right?" asked Rat.

The pair of ogres couldn't help but nod their heads in response. Neither had ever eaten meat as delicious as this, certainly not prepared in this way.

"Next up is this!"

Rat took a bite of chicken and immediately poured himself some of the new shochu the master had brought over, taking a swig from the glass.

"Aaaah, this is the best!"

He wiped his mouth, a massive smile on his face. The savory flavors of the chicken were washed away by the sip of strong alcohol. As far as Rat was concerned, this was

...of the absolute best combinations of flavors available to those who frequented the Restaurant to Another World.

"What the... What is this?!"

"It's gosh dang delicious is what it is!" Rat answered. "Hey, we need more meat and booze over here! Bring us some more!"

The ogre couple decided to try out Rat's particular way of eating, leading them to immediately begin howling in ecstasy. They loved meat and booze to begin with, so it was inevitable that they'd be floored when faced with such wonderful versions of both of their favorite things.

"Come now! Eat up as much as you want. Everything's on me today, mates! Ah, for the next orders of roast chicken, could we get some teriyaki and curry flavored ones, too? You know, the super sweet and sour ones? You always gotta go with the gravy flavored chicken first, you know? Oh, and for sides..."

As Rat watched his two companions dig in, he quickly ordered the next round of dishes. And so the two ogres continued to eat and eat, never growing tired of the brand new tastes they were experiencing one after the other, drowning themselves in strong alcohol.

By the time they came to, it was already the middle of the day.

"Uuugh."

Tatsuji slowly blinked awake. As far as he was aware, he was right where the door from yesterday was.

"My head be killing me."

A direct result of drinking way too much the night before. That shochu stuff was strong. Maybe too strong. Compared to Otora's booze, the only alcohol Tatsuji was familiar with, it was tremendously easy to drink. It certainly didn't help that the halfling kept pushing them to drink more. There hadn't been much of a stopping point. The two ogres had gone through several bottles before collapsing, completely drunk.

"Heeey, wake up." Tatsuji shook the cobwebs out of his head while trying to wake his partner.

"Uuugh, I feel sick." Otora had clearly been just as done in as he had. She was moving quite slowly.

"Looks like that little guy ran off."

Rat was nowhere to be found. No matter how much they looked for the small man at this point, it'd probably be impossible to find him again. They weren't even sure where he ran off to.

"Well, whatever," Tatsuji whispered to himself.

His memories of the previous day were fuzzy, but there were things he specifically remembered. That black door only appeared once every seven days. While the restaurant was full of all sorts of dangerous types, fighting was off limits, lest they be banned from entering the place forever. He also remembered that the master of the joint accepted human currency, so if you could pay, it didn't matter if you were an ogre or a monster. You would be served food and drink...and that food and drink would be positively delicious.

"Six days till the next time, eh?"

"Ayup."

While his brain was still adrift, Tatsuji sighed. They had to go again. It wasn't as if they had any other uses for the money they'd accumulated over the years.

The ogre couple cradled their pained heads as they returned home, determined to make their way back to the Restaurant to Another World.

CHAPTER 31

Crêpes

I N THE LARGELY UNTOUCHED wilderness of the Eastern Continent was a small nation called the Land of Flowers. It was a small nation, a tiny field of flowers which boasted a spring that lasted year-round in a part of the world known for its long winters and short summers.

Perhaps because of that very spring, some hundred years prior, both the federation of human knights and the demons led by the great skeleton king attempted to invade the Land of Flowers during the great demon war. While the great skeleton king was in fact a demon, it had dedicated itself to the pursuit of knowledge, resulting in its reincarnation as a lich possessing terrifyingly evil magic powers. Both the demon and human forces wanted a base from which to build up their armies, so they settled upon the flower fields of the Land of Flowers. This proved to be a fatal mistake, however, as the moment both armies set foot upon the land, the citizens of its nation attacked, robbing both sides of about half of their forces as they retreated in shame.

Indeed, this land of eternally blossoming flowers had been the home of the small, winged faeries for over one thousand years.

Faeries were small beings capable of fitting in the palm of a human hand. They had butterfly-like wings that allowed them to hover in the air and magical powers that equaled the elves. Because of these powers, they were nowhere close to being regarded as weak among the races of the world. In fact, they were occasionally feared by human adventurers as monsters themselves. Despite this strength, they were respectful beings who didn't invade other lands, though they were brave enough to defend their homeland should anyone try to step foot within their domain.

It was this very bravery that allowed the faerie queen of that era, Silvia Silvario XIII, to lead a squad of magic users into battle against the invading humans and demons, fending them off with her tremendous power. Since that time, the humans and demons knew that those who set foot in that field of flowers would meet their end. And so, peace came to the Land of Flowers, its citizens given no reason to wield their awe-inspiring magical powers.

However, approximately half a year ago, cracks began to appear in that peace.

"Your Highness! We have a problem!"

It was around noon when the panicked voice of a faerie echoed throughout the castle, which was decorated in flowers and greenery of all sorts.

"Calm yourself. I can feel it." The current queen of the Land of Flowers, Tiana Silvario XVI, responded to the elderly mage captain with a tired edge to her voice.

Queen Tiana Silvario XVI's skin was white as snow, her eyes and hair a beautiful pale green, and her wings rainbow colored amidst blackish green lines. It had only been two years since she had ascended to the throne as queen of the Land of Flowers after her mother passed away due to illness.

The elderly mage captain seemed stunned. "Your Highness, you've noticed?"

In response, Tiana heavily nodded her head.

"But of course. This is like my backyard. I notice any and all changes to it. Especially when they happen right in front of my castle."

Since the day had begun, Tiana had yet to set one foot outside of the throne room. And yet, due to her talents as the most able mage in the entire country, she could sense the change in her home immediately.

Generally speaking, faeries made up in magical ability what they lacked in physical strength; they didn't engage in battle with swords or bows like the humans did. Instead, they either used their magic directly or utilized golems born from their magic. This meant that those selected to rule over the country were those talented in the magical arts, regardless of gender. Tiana, their queen, was enormously powerful.

"We cannot let this lie. First, we must observe it."

Tiana stood up from her throne with conviction, as if she had been waiting for this report all day.

"Regardless of what it might be, if it dares bring misfortune to our great country, we shall show it no mercy. Onward, follow me!"

The guards that had been quietly waiting for orders immediately assembled around their queen.

Indeed, this was the Land of Flowers, a nation that forgave no one who dared sully its beautiful flowers. It was a land of proud faeries. In response to the queen's words, the knights and ministers gathered behind her in silence. The group walked to the center of the small castle where the disturbance had appeared.

"Is this a door?" Tiana mumbled to herself, a crowd of citizens having gathered nearby.

The object looked to be human-sized. The queen knew full well that there was no door like this in her country. On the front of the black door was a golden handle and an illustration of some sort of animal.

"It appears to be some sort of teleportation magic."

Tiana came to a decision. "All right. We will enter the door. Mage squads will choose those who shall remain to guard the country. The rest will come with me."

The longer the identity of this door remained a mystery, the more unrest would settle upon the Land of Flower's citizens. Tiana was quick and decisive.

"What?! Your Highness, that's too dangerous!" the mage captain said.

"Fear not," Tiana said calmly, reasoning with the panicked captain. "I am this country's queen. It is my responsibility to protect the people. Don't worry, I'll make sure this place is guarded properly before I depart."

Tiana decided to make use of the Land of Flower's secret weapon.

"O Guardian, hear my call. Come forth before me!"

Tiana pulled from a small bag a single seed and dropped it to the ground, beginning the spell's incantation. This seed could only be harvested once a year, and it came from a flower said to have been born during the Age of the Old Wyrms, long before the elves had taken over the land. This unique flower was grown in a special garden protected by the castle's magic. Only past rulers and royal gardeners could tend to it.

Through the spell, passed down from ruler to ruler, was the Land of Flower's most powerful guardian born.

From deep within the ground, a voice could be heard as the seed began soaking up the resources from its surroundings, growing rapidly. Thick green vines grew out from the seed, wrapping around one another and creating the form of a green giant. The vines had settled like massive muscles, and pink flowers blossomed from the spots where its eyes and nose should be. It was about three times larger than the average human.

The court ooohed.

"Now, Guardian. Obey my command."

Ooooooooh.

The giant responded to the queen's orders with a low roar, confirming its allegiance to its master.

Tiana nodded, satisfied. "Excellent. Citizens, step away from the door!"

Leaving the giant behind, Tiana and the others backed away from the black structure. All they knew was that it was magical by nature, which meant they had no way of knowing how truly dangerous it might be. Tiana wanted to play it safe.

"Guardian, open the door!"

The giant obeyed its master's orders and bent over. It wrapped two of its thick, branch-like fingers around the handle and gently turned it.

Ring ring!

The ringing of bells signified the activation of magic as the door opened.

"Huh... It's some sort of teleportation device then."

The other side of the door was hidden by a thin layer of mist, but Tiana could still make out several humanoid figures in a bright room.

"What shall we do, Your Highness?" the captain asked.

"Well, first..."

Tiana surveyed her surroundings, eventually stopping on her elite mages.

"Let us first find out the motives of those on the other side. I'll take command on this. Understood?"

Once that had been decided, a plan quickly formed in her head. Tiana delivered her orders.

"B-but that's far too dangerous! We don't even know what lies beyond the door yet! And the Guardian won't be able to come with us due to its size!"

Tiana refused to listen to her mage captain's words. "You needn't worry. We'll be more than prepared. I'll have you remain here. Prepare a series of magical escape circles. If the need arises, be prepared to activate them immediately."

She was not only the queen of her nation, but also the strongest mage in the land. The queens of the Land of Flowers had long since maintained independence from the rest of the world, protecting their lands. Rather than sit in the back and give orders, they were far more inclined to bravely stand on the frontline. Tiana was no different from her forebears in that regard.

"Clearly they're inviting us in," she said. "Why not see where the door goes?"

It had been some hundred years since the foolish humans and demons dared trespass on the faeries' land. This little bit of excitement stirred something within the young queen, even if she did not realize it herself. Indeed, things had been so peaceful that the queen had yet to find the opportunity to flex her own knowledge and strength. Now was the time to show her people what their queen was made of.

"I am the leader of this great nation and its people. It is my duty to talk to the one in charge on the other side."

Even if that meant putting herself in danger, Tiana refused to back down.

She flew through the door.

❧

The moment she came out on the other side, the thin layer of mist vanished, allowing Tiana to see everything with great clarity.

"Wh-what is this place?!" One of the mages accompanying the queen raised her voice in stunned shock. She could hardly be blamed, however, given the nature of what she was looking at.

"Calm yourself," Tiana snapped.

Humans. Demons. Demi-Humans. Monsters. All of them were gathered together in a single room, but not a single one was engaged in combat. Instead, they all appeared to be preoccupied with eating.

But really, what is this place?

It went without saying, but Tiana herself had no idea where she was. She lacked information. The young queen took a moment to focus, using her powerful energies to look at the flow of magical power in the room.

"That half-elf over there is a mage."

Tiana singled out one particular individual. She was a silver-haired half-elf wearing a simple yet beautiful blue dress. Judging by the mythril staff sitting next to her, she was most certainly a magic user. Given the powerful flow of magic energies around her, as well as how in control of them she seemed to be, the mage likely had abilities comparable to Tiana's. It was highly likely she trained under someone with incredible talents.

Perhaps she might be able to tell me what this place is.

The queen left her team behind and approached the half-elf.

"Excuse me. You are a mage, are you not? I am Tiana Silvario XVI, queen of the Land of Flowers. If it's not too much trouble, could you explain to me what this place is?"

The half-elf mage stopped eating her yellow, slime-like food and turned to answer the newcomer.

"My name is Victoria Samanook, princess of the Samanook Duchy. Queen Tiana, ruler of the Land of Flowers, it is an honor to make your acquaintance. This is 'Nekoya,' the Restaurant to Another World. That door over there connects this place to ours."

"The Restaurant to Another World?" Tiana echoed. "You're telling me this is an eatery?"

"Exactly. In exchange for human currency, the master offers us fine cuisine...er, all manner of foods that have been prepared and run over fire. This place has a great deal of rare foods unavailable to us in our world. Many kinds of customers come here in search of those meals, me included."

Tiana took a moment to mull over Victoria's general explanation.

"A place that offers food run over fire? I seem to recall that humans and elves liked that sort of thing."

When Tiana was a young child, one of her teachers had traveled the human world. That teacher had taught her all sorts of things about human society, including that their appetites were different from faeries, who ate fruits and honey as is from the flowers and fields. Instead, they used fire or hot water to prepare warm food before eating it. So this Restaurant to Another World was a place that also prepared food before serving it then?

"But does the food really taste any good like that?" asked Tiana. "According to an acquaintance of mine who traveled the human world, nothing was quite as tasty as the honey found in the Land of Flowers."

"It's delicious," replied Victoria with a firm nod.

Eight years had gone by since Victoria first started frequenting the Restaurant to Another World, and even now there were no signs of her ever growing tired of its many great meals.

"I see. Well, no time like the present, correct? Lady

Victoria, would you mind picking something out that you think we might enjoy?"

Victoria's firm answer ignited the flames of curiosity within Tiana. If the food here really was as good as the half-elf proclaimed, she should at least give it a shot.

"Of course. Let's see, something you all might like..." Victoria quietly thought to herself.

Clearly the right answer here was some sort of dessert. Faeries primarily feasted upon fruits and honey. In other words, sweet foods.

A parfait might be good, but the glass would be a problem.

Victoria glanced at the other princess enjoying her parfait with a massive smile on her face. Nope, that wasn't going to work. The sort of glass that parfaits came in were deep and heavy. It'd be far too much trouble for a faerie-sized being to reach into.

There's always pudding a là mode... But wait, faeries don't like bitter foods. Guess that's a no.

She looked down at her own plate with disappointment in her eyes. She couldn't possibly recommend pudding without its caramel topping.

Something fruity would be perfect. Oh, and it should also be something that takes little preparation, since faeries are constantly eating things as is. That leaves us with...

Victoria finally arrived at the one and only answer.

"A fruit crêpe would be my recommendation," she said.

"I see. Then that I shall have," the queen responded resolutely.

"All right. Master, could I get one fruit crêpe? It'd be lovely if you could cut it into small pieces like the pancakes."

"A-aye, you got it."

The master was ever-so-briefly shocked at the sight of the winged faeries in his restaurant. It was like something out of an old bedtime story. As usual, however, he quickly collected himself and returned to the kitchen. Soon after, a blonde-haired demon girl came out holding a plate with something on top of it.

"S-sorry for the wait. Here's your fruit crêpe!"

The young lady's hands were trembling. Perhaps she was unused to dealing with royalty like Tiana, or maybe the cautious group of faeries made her nervous. Either way, she set down the plate on top of the table. In front of the small creatures of legend was a thin, cloth-like object, with light yellow and brown patches all over it. This cloth wrapped itself around some sort of white, soft-looking stuff and a host of colorful fruits. It almost looked like a bouquet of flowers.

So this is a crêpe? Humans think of the most fascinating things, Tiana thought to herself.

Red, orange, and green. The beautifully patterned "cloth" and the white filling wrapped themselves around the colorful fruits like a gentle embrace. Judging by appearance alone, this "crêpe" was quite the meal.

"Let me just cut this right up for you."

The demon girl used a glistening, silver knife to cut the crêpe into small chunks, which would be easier for the tiny people in front of her to handle and eat. She was careful to do just as the master had instructed her. It was important that each piece be equal, every small chunk containing fruit so there weren't any lesser parts.

"Please take your time and enjoy!"

The demon girl finished cutting the crêpe and let out a sigh, finally relaxing around the faeries. She then left them to enjoy the meal.

"I shall be the first to give it a try," Tiana declared to the squad on the table.

"What?!" a mage exclaimed. "Absolutely not! What if it's poisoned?!"

"That's why I need to be first," Tiana calmly responded. "The blessings of my magic arts mean that I am unaffected by almost all poisons. Which means it's safest for me to try first."

While Tiana did intend to calm her subjects, that was just a front. Her real objective was her pure curiosity for this bizarre food. What did it taste like?

First... Hm? This doesn't taste like anything.

She took a bite from the corner of the cloth-like food and tilted her head. It barely had a flavor to call its own.

Faeries liked sweet things, so if this was what Tiana could expect from the rest of the dish, this was a swing and a miss.

Next, let's see about this white stuff. Huh?!

With her expectations lowered, Tiana licked the white creamy substance and widened her eyes. It was meltingly sweet and soft. But not only was it sweet, it had the flavor of fresh milk.

Amazing! And this level of sweetness is...?!

Tiana continued eating the piece of crêpe but was once again stunned into near silence. The orange-colored fruit was both sweet and incredibly moist. Tiana suspected it would probably taste incredible as is.

Did the master enhance the sweetness with some sort of sweet liquid?!

Tiana of all people knew her sweets, and yet here was this fruit, sweeter than any she had ever encountered before. Even crazier was the sweet honey that dressed the fruit! It made them so sweet she feared they might melt.

Tiana was in a trance.

How could this be so scrumptious? Perhaps...

After experiencing the flavor for herself, Tiana leaned

in to look at the crêpe, one step closer to the truth. Inside it was a host of other fruits sandwiched together.

I knew it!

After taking another bite, Tiana concluded that each of the fruits had been prepared in a different fashion.

The red berries had been boiled together with a great deal of sugar, giving them a sweet flavor and melty texture. The green berries were likely frozen with some sort of magic, lending them a crunchy but cold feeling.

Last but not least were the yellow fruits unknown to Tiana. She imagined they were likely originally sour, but they, like the orange fruits, had sweet honey mixed into them.

I see. So that's why they're all wrapped like this.

The more Tiana ate, the more she noticed. The cloth-like wrap that she had previously dismissed as tasteless was actually well thought out. This neutral base supported the sweet white cream and the variety of fruits. By not adding further flavor to the whole package, it created balance so it wasn't overly sweet. Indeed, without the wrapping, this could not be a crêpe.

Curses, this crêpe thing really did turn out to be poison.

Tiana chewed on the piece of crêpe, her eyes having been opened to the truth. While her stomach was satisfied with each bite, she could not stop eating.

This must be some sort of deadly poison designed to captivate my stomach.

The combination of sweet and sour fruits, and the sweet white stuff that was delicious beyond words... What else could this pairing be if not poison for the soul? It was as if there were some magic spell cast upon it, robbing Tiana of her ability to resist overeating. Until her stomach was full, she would be incapable of stopping.

The queen ate as much of the crêpe as she possibly could before letting out a cute sound and stopping. She let out a sweet sigh and turned to her followers.

"How was it, Your Highness?"

One of the mages swallowed their saliva in anticipation as Tiana wiped some cream away from her lips and replied simply and directly:

"There appears to be no poison. You may eat."

The moment Tiana's words left her mouth, the faeries began swarming the crêpe. It had been more than a little difficult watching the queen deliciously indulge in the crêpe in front of their very eyes. The faeries let out their own stunned, bliss-filled cries of joy as they dug in.

"Victoria, you have my gratitude. This is a token of my appreciation."

While watching her people enjoy themselves, Tiana

handed Victoria a prize worthy of any royalty: the Land of Flower's secret treasure.

"This is a flower seed from my country. I'm sure someone as knowledgeable as you understands what that means."

Victoria widened her eyes in surprise. "Are you sure?"

At first glance, it looked like an old brown seed. But for one as attuned to the magical arts as Victoria, it was clear as day that the small object had an incredible amount of magical power lurking within it.

Long, long ago, in the time of the old Kingdom, it was said that the king had sought this mythical seed to prolong his own life. Simply brewing and drinking it was enough to restore a person's youth. The seed was a catalyst for immense magical power but could only be grown and harvested in areas brimming with magical energy, like the Land of the Flowers. The Duchy happened to have a single seed of its own, locked away in a safe protected by all manner of magic. It was, in fact, a secret treasure.

"Of course I am. I've long heard that humans valued these seeds above all else, but we faeries have easy access to them," Tiana replied, a beautiful smile across her face.

"...Understood. Then in return, I promise to handle your payment for any and all dishes you and your people eat here, from now on."

Victoria was more than aware of just how valuable the gift she received was. In order to try and pay back even some of that, she formed a pact with her new friend. She could pay for these faeries until the day she died, and it still wouldn't be enough to match the value of the gift she received, but that was all she could think of.

"You would do that for us? You have my gratitude."

Tiana accepted the princess's kindness. Because the Land of Flowers had cut itself off from human society, it was not easy for them to get their hands on human currency. While she had yet to voice it aloud, Tiana had been concerned about how she and her people would be able to pay for the crêpe moving forward. She was genuinely happy that the problem was now behind her.

And just like that, visiting the Restaurant to Another World once every seven days became a thing set in stone for Tiana. She doubted the others would object.

About a hundred of her followers had already devoured the crêpe and were on the verge of ordering another. Tiana just couldn't imagine a world in which they would disagree with returning here.

And so, half a year passed. Today was the ever-important day of the "Door Countermeasure Meeting."

"We should be ordering the chocolate banana! Are you telling me you can't see how scrumptious its bitterness is?!"

"Nonsense! You know full well that the sweet flavor of strawberry jam pairs fabulously with the sourness of cream cheese!"

"If we're talking sweetness, how could you foolish fools possibly ignore custard?! We need to be focusing on a dish that utilizes custard!"

"Wrong, wrong, wrong! How could you possibly recommend custard while ignoring heavy cream and its gentle fluffiness?! It is a simple fact of this world that heavy cream is more delicious than custard!"

"Um, I've actually heard that there are crêpes that aren't sweet."

"REJECTED. An unsweet crêpe is no crêpe at all!" shouted the voices in unison.

The theme of the meeting was simple: "Other than the fruit, which type of crêpe should we order?" Unfortunately, they couldn't reach a consensus.

The mage captain slipped into the frantic meeting and delivered their report to Tiana. "Your Highness! The citizens chosen for today's visit have already gathered at the plaza of Nekoya's door! If we don't leave immediately, we may be dealing with a riot on our hands!"

"Understood." Tiana stood from her seat and addressed the committee. "Let us be on our way. It's unfortunate we could not reach a decision, but we can just think about it on the other side."

Thus the great Queen Tiana made her way to the plaza where her citizens were waiting.

Since that fateful first visit, Tiana and her subjects came to one simple conclusion regarding Nekoya. Despite how large the dining hall was, partially as it was designed for humans, bringing the thousands of citizens of the Land of Flowers to dine all at once would cause trouble for the master. It was decided that once every seven days they would hold a lottery, unrelated to age, power, or status, where only the chosen two hundred citizens and Tiana would be allowed to visit Nekoya on that specific day.

"I apologize for the wait! My people, let us go beyond the door! To the Restaurant to Another World!" Tiana spoke to her people, many of them holding baskets made of vines with which to hold treats from the other world.

They raised their voices in joy and began gathering in front of the door.

"Come, Golem! Open the door to another world!"

At this point, the once-guardian of the Land of Flowers had essentially been reassigned to door-opening duty. As usual, it turned the handle of the large, black structure and opened it. As the sound of bells rang out, countless faeries made their way through the entrance.

"Ah! Welcome!" The demon waitress greeted them, clearly having grown used to their patronage.

"Thank you. Take us to a table, if you will. We would also like a menu." Tiana nodded to the waitress and delivered her orders, marking the beginning of yet another sweet and delicious party.

CHAPTER 32
Tanmen

I T WAS ALREADY nine at night.

"Now then. What to do, what do..."

The master was lost in thought in front of the kitchen table. He had left Aletta alone to finish cleaning the dining room. Another special business day at the Restaurant to Another World had ended, and the place was mostly cleaned up. There was just one big problem: it was late and they still hadn't eaten dinner yet.

Today they made a killing.

Too much of a killing, even.

Nekoya found itself on the receiving end of ten halflings, those bare-footed little people with seemingly endless stomachs. As far as the master could tell, it was an entire family of them.

According to Aletta, halflings were a different race than the humans, but the master really couldn't tell the difference between them and children.

Ten halflings. Just ten. That's all it took.

A single halfling could eat an entire family's worth of food. Now imagine an entire group of them coming together. The master always found himself impossibly busy on days like that, which was especially rough when the halflings in question were bigger foodies than the usual.

It certainly didn't help that halflings could often only visit the restaurant once every few months. Halflings didn't really understand the concepts of "planning" or "saving," so they typically spent all the money they had on food. This had a bizarre trickle-down effect on the rest of the customers, who would then go on to order significantly more than usual.

And so, the Restaurant to Another World's placid Saturday would eventually come to resemble the battlefield that was a weekday lunch rush, and the master and Aletta's dinner would be delayed until well into the night. Unfortunately, that wasn't the only issue.

"We don't even have any pasta left? Geez," he muttered.

Nekoya was all out of its primary stock dishes. This too was part of the halfling's aftermath. As mentioned previously, halflings didn't seem to understand the concept of "self-restraint." Long ago, there had once been a rat-faced halfling who tried to dine and dash. He failed and rumor of his fate seemingly spread across the entire other world, because not a single halfling ever tried to repeat his behavior.

Oddly enough, there were quite a few halflings who emptied out their wallets long before they filled their stomachs. Fortunately for them, they still managed to fill up on refills of bread, rice, and soup.

Nekoya offered free refills on all three foods. No matter how much a customer ate, the price never changed. Which of course meant that the halflings would keep ordering refills in the hopes of satisfying their hunger. Miso soup and rice. Normal soup and bread. The halflings freely explored every possible combination. They'd even take the various seasonings and sauces on the table and mix and match them.

It appeared as though they took something away from the pork soup with butter served on Meat Day, because the halflings had started to save the butter they received with their bread, instead using it on the steaming hot rice and pouring soy sauce atop the whole shebang. The master never gave them a single hint, and yet here they were, discovering new ways to eat on their own.

Needless to say, the rice, bread, and soup were all gone.

He had already been low on pasta and flour to begin with, so there wasn't even enough left for one person. Fortunately, the master still had meat and vegetables left, but as a citizen of Japan, a meal without the core food was rough on the stomach.

"If I start making something now, it's gonna get real dang late. But I can't *not* feed her..."

If he were on his own, the master could always just sleep on an empty stomach. But since it was Saturday, it meant he had one final customer: Aletta. Now that he thought about it, the day had been so busy that the staff lunch wasn't anything special to speak of. That wasn't good.

"C'mon, there's gotta be something... Oh, I know!" The master quickly formulated his thoughts. "I'm pretty sure I had a reserve of instant noodles left up on the third floor."

Every now and then the master had a craving for instant salt ramen, so he had bought a five-pack a few weeks back. He'd only actually used one pack to boot.

"Which means today we're eating tanmen."

The master gently rubbed his hand across his slightly protruding belly. He had recently made it a point to start eating more vegetables.

With the evening's menu decided, he got to work. After running them through hot oil, he'd cook up some meat and veggies and toss them on top of some tanmen. As of late, whenever the master felt the urge for instant ramen, this was his go-to dish.

"Right. Guess I'll get started!"

He had about ten minutes until Aletta finished cleaning the dining room. That was more than enough time to wrap things up on his end. He shuffled off to the elevator and headed to his home storage space on the third floor of the building.

Meanwhile, as the master was proceeding with his dinner plans, Aletta had just wrapped up cleaning the restaurant.

"Great! All done!"

In her right hand was a mop, in her left a tablecloth. She surveyed her work with a satisfied expression on her face. The wooden tables were sparklingly clean, and there wasn't a single crumb to be found on the floor.

"Now then, I better go wash my hands before letting the master know I'm finished," Aletta whispered to herself and put away her tools before trotting off to wash her hands. First, she wet her hands using the mysterious magical device that ran water just by waving one's hand underneath it. She then took some of the green stuff used for cleaning hands and let the suds build as she rubbed her hands together. Aletta made sure to do just as the master instructed her so many months ago, cleaning under her nails and in the spaces between her fingers.

"That just about does it. All clean!"

With her hands glistening clean, the only job left was to clean the kitchen after she and the master ate dinner.

"I wonder what's for dinner today..."

Just the thought alone was enough to trigger strange sounds from her stomach. For lunch she had eaten three sandwiches, leftovers from the halflings. Each one of them was differently flavored, but they were as delicious as usual. The only problem was that they simply weren't enough to fill her. Aletta was still a growing young woman after all. While she certainly couldn't pack it down as hard as the halflings could, she was still quite the eater.

Aletta made her way to the kitchen.

"Master! I'm finished cleaning the dining room!" She alerted the older man who seemed to be in the middle of making their food.

"Aye, good work. I'm just about done here."

Just as the master anticipated, he was right on time. Two large, deep bowls were filled with a pale yellow soup. The master then took two servings of freshly boiled noodles and split them up evenly between the bowls. He then topped the noodles with cooked vegetables, meat, and small shrimp that he'd sautéed alongside the rest of the ingredients.

"Perfect. My special tanmen is done!"

The kitchen was filled with the warm aroma of the slightly spicy soup.

Aletta had to stop herself from drooling. "Oh, gosh."

The scent was enough to once again trigger her stomach's voice, making Aletta's face turn bright red. The master chuckled.

"Looks like you're hungry, so how 'bout we dig in?"

"O-okay!"

The pair made their way to one of the tables in the dining room.

"Thanks for the food," the master said.

"Yes. Thank you, oh god of demons, for this, my daily bread. I offer you my gratitude."

As per the usual, both the master and Aletta offered up their respective pre-meal "prayers" and began digging in. The former took a big sip of the soup using the soup spoon and nodded in satisfaction at the flavor.

"Yup. If you're gonna eat instant ramen, this is the way to do it!"

It was a flavor from the master's childhood. Of course, he'd gotten significantly better at cooking since then, and he obviously enjoyed proper ramen. But at the end of the day, there was something special about tanmen.

Or maybe I'm just a fan because I grew up with it. Well, it's not like I didn't use proper ingredients for everything else.

The master slurped down some noodles and grabbed a bite of the cooked vegetables, which had absorbed the flavors of the pork and shrimp. A long time ago, back when he'd worked part-time at a Chinese restaurant, he learned one of his boss's special techniques for stir-frying vegetables. Even now, the master knew it was key to make sure that all the ingredients passed through the fire equally. He also remembered to pass them through hot oil as well.

It wasn't long before the ramen disappeared from his bowl.

On the other hand, Aletta was still carefully exploring her tanmen. She began by taking a bite of the stir-fried vegetables atop the noodles.

Ah, this is delightful!

Each batch of stir-fried veggies she grabbed with her fork left her surprised. Every single bite was delicious. They had absorbed the rich flavors of the pork, broth, and shrimp, creating something truly brilliant. The ingredients included a light-yellow vegetable that felt delightful to bite into, as well as a black, slightly translucent food of some kind. There were also the dark green, bitter vegetables she'd grown used to seeing and eating at this point.

Additionally, Aletta spotted some light green veggies that had been carefully run through flames, as well as a thin, white, translucent root of some kind. The young girl also noticed that the dish featured karoots and oranie that had been cooked to the perfect level of softness.

Despite all the vegetables being properly cooked over fire, they still maintained their moisture and texture. Each bite was satisfyingly crunchy, while also bringing out the vegetable juices that had fused with the fat of the pork and the savoriness of the shrimp to create an incredible ensemble of flavor. Aletta felt herself utterly charmed by the dish.

And these noodles, too!

Indeed. The noodles hiding below the rest of the ingredients were not to be underestimated.

They were quite different from the "pasta" and "spaghetti" that Nekoya usually served. They were thinner and wavy. After wrapping her fork with some of them and taking a bite, Aletta found that these noodles paired wonderfully with the slightly seasoned, salty soup.

Speaking of which, even the broth was different from what Nekoya usually served. That said, the balance between the spices and savory flavor was as perfect as always. The ingredients, the noodles, and the soup: these three elements morphed into one whole known as tanmen.

If Aletta had a single complaint...

Ah, it's all gone.

The bowl emptied out in no time at all. Even though Aletta had literally devoured an entire bowl's worth of the stuff, it still wasn't enough. It certainly didn't help that she'd worked all day long with barely a break.

"Would you like seconds?" the master asked Aletta after watching her stare sadly at her empty bowl.

She looked up. "Huh?! Can I?"

"Aye, of course. I know you didn't get to eat much today. I happen to have two more packs of noodles, and well, I was thinking of just finishing them all off. I could use a partner in crime."

"Gladly!" Aletta nodded not once, but twice at her boss. She was still far from being full at this point, so as far as she was concerned, she could fit at least another whole bowl's worth in. She was all but sure of it.

"Excellent. Let's see about getting some eggs up in here."

The master stood up and began cooking the day's second serving of tanmen.

Thus a long and profitable day came to a close with a quiet evening of noodles.

*Restaurant to
Another World*

CHAPTER 33
Hors d'Oeuvres

TEDD, THE HALFLING ADVENTURER, waited impatiently for the ethereal food.

"C'mon, c'mon."

He kicked his legs back and forth, resisting the urge to listen to his empty stomach and order something else.

When Tedd last visited the restaurant seven days ago, he was shocked to find a great deal of his kind present. He got swept up in the excitement and spent far too much money on that visit, resulting in his current conundrum. Tedd's stomach was empty, and his wallet was in a similar condition. He had borrowed just enough money from a friend to be able to pay for "that" and some drinks, but absolutely nothing else.

Seven days ago, Tedd ordered what was considered to be a legendary dish among the halflings. A single plate was the most expensive item on the Restaurant to Another World's menu, but it also provided the most food. Not only was it not ordinarily listed on the menu, it took a great deal of work to prepare, so it was impossible to eat on the day it was ordered. Instead, one would come by seven days later to pick up the order.

Truth be told, it didn't actually take a full seven days to prepare. If a customer made an order two days before they intended to eat, the master could have it ready. But because the residents of the other world only had access to Nekoya once every seven days, there wasn't much anyone could do about it.

As halflings were rarely able to stay in one place, due to their immense curiosity for the world, most spent their entire lives hearing about the legendary dish from other customers.

Fortunately for Tedd, his predecessors were the wisest of foodies.

Halflings rarely gathered together in large groups, but these specific ones not only did so, but did immense research and mapping. Over one hundred halflings ultimately came together to plot a course between two doors that was exactly seven days' travel by foot. By using the path between those doors, even halflings had a way to access the legendary dish that so many spoke of.

Fortunately for them, the food was so delicious that it was absolutely worth all the hard work the halflings put into trying to eat it. It satisfied both their stomachs and curiosity.

That was how the halflings of the Eastern Continent began traveling the path between the two doors just so they could grab a bite of the dish in question. Tedd was indeed one of those very people. While adventuring with his comrades, he discovered they would be passing along the path, and so, seven days prior, he made his order.

"Thanks for waiting. Here's your number two hors d'oeuvre set."

"Wahoo!" Tedd cheered. "It's finally here!"

Hors d'oeuvre, a plate filled with both the flavors of the mountains and ocean. Tedd needed to use the fingers on both his hands to count the quantity of dishes sitting in front of him. Truly a legendary meal.

"Oh me, oh my. This is incredible."

The master had set down a strange plate that was neither metal, wood, or ceramic. It carefully divided the different foods from each other, making sure they didn't mix. Tedd delicately caressed the container.

It was still hot; the master must have just finished preparing it. Tedd looked through the translucent cover at the various delicious colors, tempted to immediately start digging in. But he wanted to go ahead and enjoy the beer he bought with it.

He nodded to the master. "I'll be on my way then. Cheers!"

"Thank you! We'll be looking forward to your next visit."

Tedd somehow managed to hold himself back, thanking the master and exiting the restaurant.

"Righty-o! I better hurry home before this gets cold!"

The halfling man began dashing, careful not to spill the contents of the strange dish he was given. In order to get his hands on the hors d'oeuvre plate, he had to borrow money from his friend. He hurried to them to fulfill the promise he'd made when he first took their money.

The group of adventurers had just finished preparing for the evening at their campsite, erecting a rain-resistant tent that stood tall on the grounds. The adventurers were waiting for the return of their comrade, who had gone off in search of food.

"Geez. Where the hell did Tedd get off to? That dummy." Galius angrily stomped his stubby feet on the ground. He was a dwarf warrior clad in metal armor, and he was clearly operating on an empty stomach.

"Now, now. Have some patience," said Albert, the leader of this merry band of adventurers. "It's all thanks to Tedd that this journey has gone so well in the first place. I'm sure he's thought of something."

Albert came from a family of knights. His body was clad in leather armor, with metal plates covering his vitals. At his waist was a magic sword that he had been given when he left his home to begin his journey.

"Hmph, I can't imagine he's got anything lofty going through that head of his."

Galius snorted and went quiet, one of his habits. It wasn't as though he didn't recognize Tedd's achievements and talents. The tiny man recommended they take this "Hors d'oeuvre Road," popular among his kind. As it turned out, it was an incredible shortcut. While they had to navigate their way through several dangerous dens of monsters and beasts, it took them less than two weeks to travel across an area that would normally take a month or more.

Zack, a skilled fighter, leaned forward. "Well, we do have Tedd to thank for this nice and relaxing journey of ours, no? I mean, I knew Tedd was on the up and up when it came to travel routes and the like, but I didn't think he had something like this up his sleeve."

The demon warrior's body was covered in hard, red lizard scales. He was more than aware that halflings, Tedd included, were all tremendously skilled with their hands and with the various foibles of travel, but this was well beyond what he expected.

"But I wonder why Tedd specifically wanted us to set up camp here? Is there something around these parts?"

Rydia surveyed her surroundings as she spoke up. She was a half-elf from the forest capital and was a talented swordswoman and magic-user. Over her normal clothes she wore a thin mantle infused with magic, and at her waist was a mythril rapier. As far as she could tell, there were no dangerous monsters in the area. There was, however, a source of water nearby. All things considered, this was a great spot for camping out. The only problem was that by the time they settled here, the sun had yet to begin its trek westward. If they hurried, they should've been able to reach the nearest town with little effort.

And yet Tedd had insisted on camping in this specific spot. Since so much of this journey's success was thanks to Tedd's guidance, they decided to let him have his way, but that didn't make the whole thing any less confusing.

"Beats me," Sash chimed in. "All I know is that before he ran off, he came and borrowed six silver coins from me. He was all, 'I'll treat you all to a feast beyond your wildest imaginations, so please lend me some cash!' Weird, right?"

Sasha was a priestess of the Lord of Water and wore his silver seal. She had thick, straight black hair fitting of someone from the Western Continent. She wore a strange set of clothes made by a diviner there.

Sasha couldn't imagine that there'd be anywhere to spend money in a place like this, but she could tell by the look in Tedd's eyes that he was serious.

"A feast?" the other four adventurers had replied in unison. There were no settlements even remotely nearby. How could he treat them to a feast?

Albert gave it some thought before voicing his opinion. "Maybe there's some sort of delicious food that can only be harvested around here?"

"But then that doesn't explain the coins," said Rydia.

"Hrm, good point."

Rydia's interjection easily derailed Albert's hypothesis. If there were a food like that around these parts, they'd have heard the rumors.

Zack decided to change the topic. They could theorize all they wanted, but they wouldn't get a proper answer until Tedd returned. "A feast, eh? What do y'all think of when you hear that word?"

"Ain't it obvious? Since the beginning of time that's meant meat and booze!"

Galius stated his opinion as if it were fact. Fatty meat

and booze. It didn't matter the time or the place, so long as you had those two things, you had yourself a feast. And then there was that new whiskey stuff that had the dwarf world talking. It was supposedly delicious and strong as hell. One of the dwarves he met not too long ago on the road shared a cup of the stuff with him, and it was indeed incredible. He'd love some of that right about now.

"You're so boring! This is why dwarves are so frustrating... I'd personally love some fresh vegetables. Oh, and young elf beans would be delightful around this time of the year."

Rydia dismissed Galius's answer and went on to suggest her own idea of a feast. Despite both of her parents being full elves, she was a half-elf changeling. Compared to the other elves who lived in the capital, not only were her magical powers weaker, but she had a shorter lifespan as well. It didn't take long for it to become difficult for her to stay in her homeland, so she eventually left. Nearly ten years had passed since then, which meant she'd had ample time to grow used to eating meat and fish. She still wasn't terribly fond of them, however, and often found herself reminiscing about the taste of her homeland.

Unfortunately, there were barely any people in the human world who grew elf beans.

Sasha recalled the scent of the ocean from the

fishermen's village she called her home as she stared off into the distance. "I'm all about that fresh fish from the sea! Oh, and shripe are delicious as well."

The only way to get one's hands on fresh and fatty fish that were light on bones was to live in a town near the ocean. Sasha's favorite dish, a red-hot soup made from boiled shripe and chili pepels, was increasingly rare outside of the small island she called home in the Ocean Nation. Much time had passed since she'd left for the Eastern Continent for her training, but she had only stumbled upon the dish a handful of times.

"A feast, eh…? Actually, when I was a kid, I always used to look forward to the sweets I got to eat on days of celebration and the like." Albert recalled a distant memory from his childhood.

The treat from his memories was made of wheat, milk, and eggs baked together with a plentiful amount of honey. It then had a dash of sugar sprinkled atop. Albert remembered it being so sweet he thought his teeth would melt. As the third son of a noble family, he rarely got the chance to eat it himself. This made days of celebration that much more exciting for him.

"I'm all about eggs. When I was just a brat, I would drop by this stand in the imperial capital that sold croquettes. Those were the best!"

Zack was the last one to give his thoughts on what he felt a feast was. He merrily spoke of the food he enjoyed when he lived in the imperial capital, a city in one of the very few nations that allowed the presence of demons: an egg dish that was only made on special days, and croquettes, a delicious food made from mashing cobbler's tubers into round balls and frying them in wheat crumbs. Even as an adult, Zack struggled to forget these two great flavors.

"...Haha, not even one of us mentioned the same food. How 'bout that?" Albert was amused by how the five of them each had their own idea of what a "feast" was.

Sasha nodded in response to the group's leader. "We all hail from different places after all."

They'd worked together as a team of adventurers for five years now. The group had seen some members come and go, with Tedd being the sixth person they'd welcomed into their ranks. Every single adventurer on the team had a unique history, so of course their concepts of what a feast constituted would be different.

The group shared a laugh over this.

"I'm back! Sorry about the wait! I hope y'all are ready for one helluva feast!"

And so Tedd finally returned from his little side quest, his voice bright and energetic, a far cry from the nostalgic tone of his team's previous conversation.

This marked the beginning of their party.

The five adventurers locked their eyes on the plate. They had no idea how, but Tedd had gotten his hands on a proper feast. The halfling set it down atop a rock for all to see.

"Whoa, whoa, hey now. Am I dreamin' or something? Tedd, what the hell kinda magic did you use to get your hands on this?" Galius asked the question the rest of the team had on the tip of their tongues.

"Mm, I can't give you the details, but if I had to describe it in a few words...teleportation magic?"

Tedd delivered his answer with bizarre levity. If word of this location ever got out, some jerk would inevitably try to take control of it. Then nobody would ever have access to hors d'oeuvres ever again. It was imperative that the halflings kept the "Hors d'oeuvre Door" a secret. This was a rule shared among his people, and Tedd had no intention of breaking it.

Rydia asked, "So what is this stuff? It's all pretty weird looking."

She looked at the strange plate in front of her. It was oddly thin, made from some sort of material she'd never seen before. All manner of food was piled atop it.

"Oh, well, it's called hors d'oeuvres. It's got meat, fish, vegetables, and all kinds of other different foods. Apparently, it's used primarily for big parties," Tedd explained with a smile, almost as though he'd been waiting for the opportunity to explain his find to his friends.

"And this stuff here is called beer. It's a type of ale. Lemme tell you, it's cold and delicious. Ah, and I got you some whiskey, Galius."

Tedd took out his trusty knife and used it to pop open the brown glass bottle of ale. He then proceeded to pour its contents out into each of his teammate's mugs. Finally, Tedd handed Galius a small bottle the size of his hand filled with brown alcohol.

"Now c'mon, folks, let's dig in! Hors d'oeuvres are best hot!"

With the drinks out of the way, Tedd passed out paper plates and white forks made of some unknown material to his friends. He opened the translucent cover of the meal plate.

And just like that, the party found themselves in the center of an amazing aroma.

It was impossible to tell who had just gulped, but it was clear that every single one of them wanted to dig in immediately.

"Th-then I suppose we should just go for it, yeah?"

Albert spoke up as the representative of his party, and the five adventurers each reached out toward the plate.

Galius took a sip of the alcohol that Tedd had handed him and happily cried out, "By my axe! Th-this is that new-fangled whiskey, ain't it?!"

As the liquid spread through his mouth, he found it was just as strong and uniquely aromatic as the liquor the traveling dwarf shared with him on that fateful day. If anything, its flavor appeared to be even higher in quality.

"Ain't nothing better than meat and booze!" he said.

Tremendously grateful for this chance encounter with the delicious drink in his hands, Galius reached for some meat off the plate. He grabbed a ball of chicken meat fried in oil and some sort of fried food with minced meat and oranie stuffed inside of it. He brought them both to his mouth.

The skin of the fatty and gingery chicken meat crumpled into pieces with each chew, leaving behind the delicious meat juices in its wake. Meanwhile, the fried minced meat tasted of pork and slightly sweet oranie. These two flavors fused with that of the aromatic skin and spread throughout the dwarf's mouth. As the meat juices made their way across his tongue, he took a swig of his whiskey, washing out the flavor of meat from his mouth. It was scrumptious. No matter how many times he tried this combination out, he showed no signs of growing tired of it.

"Ah, Galius. If you're gonna be digging into the fried chicken and the mince pork cutlet, you should try putting on some of that juice from that yellow thing over there. Oh, and the pork cutlet goes amazing with that black sauce."

"Mm. Mmmm?!"

Galius did as his friend instructed and poured some of the yellow juice on top of the fried chicken before taking another bite.

He was rendered speechless (not that he could speak with his mouth full). The juice added an unspeakably fresh, sour bite to the chicken. Meanwhile, the black sauce transformed what Tedd called as mince pork cutlet dish into something else entirely. Both toppings had completely changed the flavor profiles of their respective foods.

"This be unbelievable!"

The dwarf man downed some more whiskey and continued shoveling food into his mouth. He wouldn't stop until there was nothing more to eat.

Meanwhile, Sasha focused entirely on eating the fish in front of her.

This is tremendously good, but what sort of fish is it?

She couldn't recall having ever tasted a fish like this. It was fatty like tuna, but it was also like tilapia in that it lacked a strong scent. The meat itself was uniquely pinkish, tasting as though the red and white fish had been fused together to create a single new flavor.

It paired amazingly with the milky-white, sour sauce.

Where could this fish have come from...?

Sasha continued munching on her food as she pondered the origins of Tedd's feast. It was then that she heard his voice.

"Whoa now! This is shripe?! Dang, so not only can you fry 'em and make a gratin out of 'em, but they even go great with spicy seasoning!"

Did he say shripe?!

Sasha instinctively reacted to the word and reached over to grab some of what Tedd was eating. It was a square surrounded by some sort of fried wrapping. At first glance, it didn't appear to be anything special. Sasha stabbed her fork into it and brought it up to her mouth.

"...Oh my gosh, this really is gosh dang shripe, ain't it?! E-er...pardon me."

In her excitement, Sasha briefly slipped into the same verbiage she used when she used to live in her small fishing village. Her face turned bright red as she tried to focus on enjoying the food in her mouth.

And boy, was that food something else. It was undoubtedly the flavor of fresh shripe, and it had soaked up the hot seasoning of the chili pepel as well. This meant that every bite allowed her to experience the flavor of the crunchy skin as well as the spice. Sasha felt as though she had returned to her hometown for the first time in years.

"I can't believe this..." she said. "It's so delicious. It truly is incredible!"

Sasha was unable to hold back tears. This was the nostalgic flavor of her homeland, a taste she had yet to experience since leaving on her adventure so many moons ago. She refused to let anyone else indulge in the food in front of her.

Elf beans. These were undoubtedly elf beans boiled in salt.

I never thought I'd run into these out here of all places.

Rydia kept her surprise to herself as she reached over and grabbed elf bean after elf bean, dumping them into her mouth. These were young elf beans with just the right amount of salt, and they went harmoniously with the ale Tedd had poured for her and her companions.

There wasn't much of a drinking culture in the forest capital, which meant ale was hard to come by. On the other hand, boiled elf beans were pretty much impossible to find outside of the forest capital or woods with elven communities. Needless to say, the combination of ale and elf bean was entirely unknown to Rydia until this very moment, so she was genuinely stunned by how well they went together.

I could eat this forever, she thought.

There was only one, huge, problem. The plate of food Tedd brought back simply didn't have that many beans on it. It didn't take long before Rydia had nearly made her way through all of them.

I guess that's it for tonight's dinner then. Too bad.

Rydia couldn't get herself in the mood to eat meat or fish after indulging in her people's food. While it pained her to admit it, her part in this feast was over.

...Or so she thought.

"Mm, kucumber and miso is the way to go, no doubt."

Rydia's sharp ears twitched as they caught Tedd speaking to himself.

Miso?

The half-elf looked toward Tedd upon hearing the

strange word. Her eyes settled on the halfling man and the food he was merrily chewing. It was a green kucumber with some sort of brown paste topping on it. Seeing Tedd eat any kind of vegetable was odd, considering he wasn't much of a fan of the stuff.

He said "miso," right? Is that this paste?

Rydia replicated Tedd's actions, taking a fresh piece of kucumber and topping it with the brown paste.

It has a strong scent, but the adventurer confirmed there was no sign of meat or fish in the "miso," and took a bite. With a satisfying crunch, the fresh kucumber shifted around inside her mouth...

"What is this stuff?! It's delish!" she exclaimed.

Rydia was the next of her party to raise her voice in stunned surprise. The mysterious miso substance was intensely salty but also incredibly delicious. She could sense the tang of fermented vegetables mixed in with the taste of the elf beans. It hit her like a ton of bricks.

The combination of the salty miso paste with the refreshingly light, watery flavor of the kucumber made for a feast in and of itself. It was only further amplified by pairing it with the rich flavor of the ale. This was by far the most delicious feast Rydia had ever had in her life, and that included her time spent in the forest capital.

Rydia shoveled kucumber after kucumber into her

mouth in silence. She had to hurry; if any of her companions discovered this ultimate combo like she had, they'd start taking from her portion of the plate.

Huh, this has a slight sweetness to it. Oh, and this sausage is delightful as well.

The first thing Albert reached for was a mysterious, light brown food on a skewer. It was pork sausage of some kind, wrapped in a fried blanket of soft dough made from eggs and milk. The surface was thin and crunchy, a pleasant contrast to the soft and slightly sweet insides and carefully cooked juicy sausage. The sausage itself was well prepared, with a variety of spices that mixed well with its fatty flavor. As it turned out, this wonderfully complemented the faintly sweet dough. By applying some sauces—one red and sour, the other yellow and spicy—the entire flavor profile of the food shifted. This new combo went elegantly with the ale Tedd brought Albert and his companions.

There's no doubt about it, Albert thought approvingly. *This is the good stuff.*

Albert reached for a second skewer, then a third. It didn't take many bites for him to finish the small portion and wash it all down with some ale. He greatly enjoyed the faint sweetness to it all.

Then he overheard something.

"Ah, these are rum raisin sandwiches, eh? Yeah, they're dang sweet. Mmph, and they go real well with alcohol."

Tedd's words reached Albert's ears.

Did he say "sweet"?

The leader of the adventurers glanced over at what Tedd was munching on and found it on the main plate. Sandwiched between two pieces of brown, tough, baked treats were dried blackberries and some sort of white cream. Tedd had been eating them with his bare hands, so Albert did the same.

Albert's eyes widened. *Wh-whoa! It's so sweet! My word, this is scrumptious!*

The dried blackberries were both sweet and bitter, while the white cream tasted of sweet milk. The baked treat that surrounded these flavors was only lightly sweetened but nonetheless tasted of wheat. It worked wonders to bring out the alcohol-tinged flavor of the berries.

This is better than any of the sweets I had when I was younger. Let me see, just one more...

Satisfied with the flavor of the first sandwich, Albert began reaching for even more baked goods.

"Aaah! These eggs are top class!"

The first thing Zack reached for was some sort of fried egg. It was bright yellow and cut into portions just large enough for a single bite. It wasn't just made of eggs however. Mixed inside of it was diced cheese, light pink meat, and thick green vegetables. They fused with the gentle flavor of the egg to produce something truly magnificent.

Zack took a moment to express his thoughts after taking a sip of his ale. "This is damn good."

Where exactly did Tedd find a feast like this? Everyone, including Zack, was currently head over heels for the platter of food, leaving them with little energy to focus on anything else.

Let's see, next up is...

"Ooh, Zack!" Tedd called. "Those are imperial-style croquettes! I recommend trying them with ketchup."

"What? There are even croquettes?!"

Upon receiving confirmation from Tedd, Zack immediately began his search for the croquettes. He stabbed his fork into one of the round and light brown balls, then topped it with the red sauce as instructed.

"The hell is this?! It's definitely a croquette, but the flavor is outta this damn world!"

Zack raised his voice in shock at the somewhat familiar yet wholly new flavor of the croquette. The red and sour sauce fused majestically with the steaming hot food. Unlike the usual ones Zack was familiar with, it appeared to have had milk and cheese mixed into it, lending it a smooth texture.

At the center of the croquette, and mixed into the core of the cobbler's tubers, was a great deal of cheese.

"The hell is this, Tedd? Where did you find all this stuff?!" Zack's voice was a mix of joy and surprise as he shouted out to Tedd, who was blazing a path of destruction through his share of the food.

Zack was filled with gratitude for this day and for this meal. The five adventurers couldn't possibly have been more satisfied by the feast of hors d'oeuvres he bought for them. Their little party was filled with smiles.

A brief period passed before the joyous occasion turned into a vicious hellscape.

"Yo, wait! I've only touched the eggs and croquettes!"

Zack was the first one to notice. After finishing with the eggs and croquettes, he had decided to finally try something else on the plate. That's when he realized everything else was nearly gone.

"Huh? But I only got to eat the shripe and fish!" said Sasha. "Wait, Zack! You ate all the croquette, ya gosh dang...er, you jerk!"

"Excuuuuse me? You're telling me there was some kinda fried food with sausage and everything?! Why're you the only one who got to eat 'em?!"

"I-I'm sorry... Wait, Galius! What about you?! You pretty much annihilated all of the meat dishes!"

"Now, now, everyone," said Rydia. "Let's calm... HEY! Take your hands off my kucumbers!"

As one might expect, the entire party only thought to try the rest of the foods on the plate when they found themselves satisfied by their first picks. And so, by the time they decided to move on, all that remained were a few pieces of each type of food.

A black wind howled through the campgrounds.

They ate my portion!

That was the only thing running through the adventurers' minds.

Just like that, cracks appeared in the once strong bonds that held the group of adventurers together for so long. They were on the verge of drifting away from one another.

"Oh, c'mon!" said Tedd. "We just got to enjoy something super delicious, didn't we? We shouldn't be fighting!"

The relaxed halfling was the first one to try and break the awkward silence building between them all.

"Say what you will, Tedd, but... Wait a second."

Just as Albert was about to respond to his halfling friend, he noticed something strange.

Tedd was the biggest foodie in their party, capable of eating far more than any of them could individually, and yet he wasn't participating in their brawl. That made no sense. He should've been the loudest of them all.

Just as Albert arrived at the answer, so, too, did the other four. All five adventurers turned their sights toward Tedd.

"TEDD?!" they yelled in unison.

"Mm, mm. Delicious, right? I can totally see why it costs three whole silver coins." Tedd nodded to himself in satisfaction, having enjoyed an entire plate of hors d'oeuvres all by himself. "The best part is that there are over ten different foods, and all of them are great. Hell, I should've bought another plate!"

The halfling continued nodding to himself, shoveling more food into his mouth. Tedd was quite satisfied with the variety of the hors d'oeuvres and his delicious beer...

In fact, he was so satisfied that he didn't notice the cold stares his party was aiming at him. By the time about half the plate had disappeared into Tedd's stomach, the remaining five adventurers' hearts had come together as one.

The halfling looked up and tilted his head in confusion at his comrades.

"Eh? Wha? What's wrong, everyone? Y'all got such scary looks on your faces! H-hey, wait a sec?! Why are you reaching for my food?! No, back! Back I say! This is all mine! No! Noooooo!"

Tedd's mortified screams rang out from the campground that night.

Restaurant to Another World

CHAPTER 34

Melon Soda Floats

O N THAT DAY, the siblings found themselves walking side by side in a corner of the Sand Nation.

"Brother, I think you're being far too shy," said the young woman wearing a magic-infused coat to shield her skin from the sun's scorching heat.

She was Renner, princess of the Sand Nation and younger sister of the man next to her, Shareef.

"I-I know, but...we're talking about a princess of the Eastern Continent! It's going to take many preparations to get her to leave her home and come all the way here as my bride. That's why I decided to start things off by sending an envoy over to the Empire to request an alliance and trade," Shareef attempted to explain himself to one of the very few people in the nation who spoke straight with him on topics such as these.

Renner shook her head. "That's not what I'm talking about. I'm specifically talking about *you*, Brother. I just don't feel like you're really trying to win her heart. It's all well and good that you're trying to deepen the ties between our nations. I even think taking her as your bride to prove those ties are real is a logical idea. It's certainly not a bad deal for the Empire when you think of it as a chance to strengthen their ties to our royal line. It's not as though you'll be able to wed her until she's recovered from her illness anyway. But here's the problem, Brother: As I'm sure you're more than aware, our nation is just another prominent one here on the Western Continent, while the Empire is top dog on the Eastern Continent. The difference between our power and influence is massive. If the princess personally turned down your offer, that would be enough to axe this whole thing. That's why you should try and get close to her now, before she recovers."

Unlike other noblewomen her age, or even the servants of the inner palace, Renner's brother was knowledgeable in all manner of things, making him fun to talk to. She enjoyed this time with him, even as she tried to guide his hand.

When it came to marriage between royalty, especially in the case of a prince and a princess, the benefits to both nations were a top priority. How either party personally felt didn't even factor into the equation. Yet at the same time, if their feelings were viewed too lightly, the marriage would be naught but misfortune for both. That was why it was so important that both parties worked hard to love one another. This was Shareef's biggest problem. While all number of women had approached him over the years, he had personally never chased after a partner himself. Renner was more than aware of this.

Unlike Shareef, who was born from proper royalty, Renner's mother was the court mage who had worked in the palace, and she eventually won the affection of the king, becoming one of his concubines. The Sand Nation was a place where, with enough talent in the ways of the magical arts, one could rise to glory and honor regardless of birthright or gender. Renner's mother was born as a low-class noble but had learned the ways of magic directly from her great-grandmother, who was a changeling. As a result, her magical talent and wealth of knowledge outdistanced those around her and led to her appointment as the court mage. It was there she won the heart of the king and ultimately gave birth to Renner, accomplishing what some would refer to as true social success.

As the court mage, she had also taught both Renner

and Shareef magic. The two had grown up together learning under the same teacher, and they were as close as could be.

"Ah, we've arrived," said Renner.

Their destination was a black door with a cat illustration on it, suspiciously sitting out in the middle of the desert, almost like some sort of mirage caused by the burning sun up above.

"Shall we?"

"Let's. It's far too hot out here during the day."

The pair opened the door and were greeted with the familiar ringing of bells and a cool blast of air.

"This place is always so nice and cool!" Renner said joyfully, as she followed her brother through the door.

"Welcome!" said the master.

"Greetings!" replied Renner. "Thank you kindly in advance."

Beyond the door was a room as cool as the evening itself. As expected of someone of her status, Renner switched to a slightly more feminine, dignified tone in response to the master.

She was more than aware her generously proportioned feminine body and facial features were best received when she acted this way. She wasn't ignorant of how the world worked.

Renner stopped her brother just as he attempted to relocate to a table far in the corner, instead pointing at one near the spot his beloved princess usually chose. "Now then, it looks like that table is open, Brother."

"A-ah, that it is," Shareef stammered.

"Excuse me, pardon."

And so, the princess and her brother made their way through the other populated tables and reached their seats.

"Welcome! Here's our menu."

"Many thanks," said Renner to the demon waitress wearing an otherworldly outfit that showed off her slim legs.

The royal siblings took a pair of menus and gladly received the cups of ice water the young lady brought them. After the waitress parted ways with their table, Renner switched her tone back to her usual one and spoke to her brother, her eyes not once leaving the menu in front of her.

"...Hmm, looks like your beloved princess isn't here yet."

"Yeah, you're right," Shareef replied calmly, flipping to the drink tab of the menu. "Do you know what you're getting, Renner?"

"Wait just a moment. Hrm..."

Shareef was ready to order the usual, while his little

sister battled with her own indecisiveness. That said, she still had a general idea of what she wanted. It was a drink she could only find here.

Hrm, what kind of soda float should I have today?

Soda floats were a dessert as well as Renner's absolute favorite drink. It was also the source of much frustration every time she visited Nekoya.

The carbonated drinks are ginger ale, cola, orange, grape... No, melon is the only right choice here!

Renner ran her finger across the plethora of carbonated drinks on the menu, each capable of sending a unique shock down her throat. When ordering a soda float at Nekoya, one could choose whatever combination of drink and ice cream one wanted. The problem was that there were so many options, and almost all of them were great.

Today... Hrm. Let's go with vanilla soft cream.

After a bit of puzzling, Renner settled on melon soda and soft serve. Among the various potential item combos, this was one of her favorites.

"I'm ready, Brother."

"Excellent. Pardon us! We'd like to order!" Shareef called out to the waitress.

"Okaaay! What would you like?" Aletta asked.

"I'll have a coffee float with ice cream. Make the cafa extra sweet, please."

"I would like a melon soda float with vanilla soft serve, thank you."

"No problem! They'll be right out!" The waitress nodded her head and disappeared into the back to let the master know. It wasn't long before she returned with the drinks in hand.

"Sorry for the wait! Here's your coffee float and melon soda float."

She placed the beautiful glass cups on the table with a light thud.

It's gorgeous, Renner thought.

The insides of the transparent glass reminded Renner of the palace garden. The juxtaposition of the lush green drink and white soft cream atop it was nothing if not stunning.

"Please enjoy!"

The waitress gave her usual line and disappeared to help the other customers. Upon seeing her leave, Renner immediately grabbed the spoon sticking out of the soda float.

First thing's first...a bite of the soft cream.

Renner had an order to things, so she started with taking a bite of the frosty, white treat at the very top of the glass. She pierced the soft, slippery mountain of cream with her spoon and brought it to her mouth.

Mm. This soft serve stuff really is delightful.

Renner's smile deepened as the frosty flavor and aroma filled her mouth. The so-called "ice cream" that Shareef brought her some time ago was delicious and varied, but soft cream was far superior as far as she was concerned.

Unlike ice cream, soft cream was both soft and smooth, just as the name implied. It didn't take much for it to start melting. Even when paired with the otherworldly ice that didn't leave behind water once it vanished, soft cream couldn't survive a trip home. In other words, it could only be eaten at this restaurant. And since ice cream could be ordered as takeout, Renner made it a point to choose soft cream to go with her melon soda float every time.

Mm, mm. Next is the soda.

After taking a bite of the soft cream, Renner turned her attention to the straw sticking out of the cup. She sipped on it lightly, drawing out the green liquid from within the glass. Her mouth was overwhelmed by the refreshing sweetness of the soda. Unlike the soft cream, the melon soda's flavor reminded her of fruit, as its intense sweetness danced across her tongue.

Aaah... It's as amazing as always. Brother's missing out by not trying some for himself.

Renner let the melon soda splash back and forth in her mouth while she eyed her brother sipping his coffee float next to her. Shareef wasn't particularly fond of carbonated drinks. According to him, he just couldn't grow to like the shocking flavor that came with them. After he ordered it the one time, he never ordered it a second. In fact, the first time Renner visited the Restaurant to Another World, he actively prevented her from ordering a cream soda just out of initial curiosity.

If anything, it's the combination of sweetness and bitterness in cafa that I find questionable.

On the other hand, Renner was not a fan of cafa, the Sand Nation's most popular beverage. She just couldn't make it past the drink's bitterness. The "coffee" served at the Restaurant to Another World was the same sort of beverage, so she had never ordered the coffee float that her brother so adored.

Now then, it's about time to dig in.

Only after experiencing both the soft cream and the melon soda on their own terms did Renner truly begin digging into the soda float the way it was meant to be enjoyed. She took a bite of soft cream and immediately followed that up with a sip of melon soda. The soft cream's smooth sweetness and the melon soda's more shocking sweetness fused together in perfect harmony.

Yeah, that's the stuff.

This combination of flavors was the true appeal of the

soda float. Renner took a moment to treasure it before going for the final piece of the puzzle.

Gotta save the best for last.

This final item was key to completing the drink known as the soda float. Just above the melon soda was a thin layer of crushed ice that served as a platform for the soft cream to float atop of. Renner used her spoon to scoop some of it out from under the icy confines of the soft cream and took a bite. The bits of ice tasted like a mix between the soft cream and the melon soda, while also maintaining its icy texture. It was chaos of the best kind.

The soda float experience is only complete after all three flavors have been tasted properly!

Tremendously satisfied by the fusion of flavors, Renner finished her melon soda float and placed her spoon down.

At that very moment, the door to the restaurant opened, announcing the arrival of a new guest. Shareef's body locked up. It was clear to Renner who the guest was.

"Welcome!" the waitress called.

"Why, hello, Aletta!"

The young lady had an elegant presence to her yet was still graceful and kind even when addressing those who were technically "below" her. She was the object of Shareef's affections; the imperial princess herself, Adelheid.

"Renner!" she said. "My friend, it's been quite some time!"

Adelheid greeted the Sand Nation princess, one of the very few friends she had her age, with a big smile.

"Indeed it has!" Renner answered, then elbowed her brother. "Come now, Brother."

"Y-yeah, um. Well, I'm glad you look well."

The fact he was able to deliver a single line was progress, all things considered.

Renner asked, "Would you care to sit with us? I'd love to hear all about the Empire."

"Oh, it would be my pleasure! Pardon me."

Adelheid's expression brightened at the invitation by one of the friends she had made in the Restaurant to Another World, and she naturally sat down next to her. This placed her directly across from Shareef, whose expression grew even more anxious.

"I absolutely must order a chocolate parfait today."

"Then I'll have a cola float. Is that okay with you, Brother?"

"C-certainly. Have what you want. I'm feeling a bit chilly, so I'll take a Vienna coffee."

Geez, Renner thought. *If he was even half as dignified as usual right now, he'd have no trouble winning Adelheid's heart.*

She silently laughed at her older brother.

Well, I suppose it's a minor miracle that he can even exchange words with her now. That's progress.

Renner continued thinking to herself, exchanging words with Adelheid, the young woman who could potentially become her future sister-in-law.

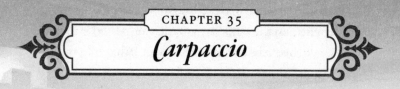

CHAPTER 35

Carpaccio

IN THE GREAT BLUE DEEP that separated the Eastern and Western Continents was the Continental Passage, the singular naval route that connected the two different land masses. Despite its frequent use, it was a dangerous area that all sorts of monsters called home. Ultimately, it wasn't nearly as dangerous as the Dragon God Sea, demon territory to the south ruled by the Blue Emperor. Nonetheless, every year upward of ten or so ships would vanish into the deep, never to reach the mainland.

The sirens who called the Continental Passage their home had wings upon their backs, bird feet, and faces that resembled beautiful young girls. Their powerful songs were laced with magic capable of charming anyone who heard them. They were a race of monsters feared specifically by seamen for their ability to sink entire ships into the ocean.

It was a hot summer day when one such siren, a young boy named Arius, decided to settle on Chimera Killer Island to make his new nest.

It all started when his friend, a siren girl named Iris who had hatched on the same day as Arius, suggested it to him.

"Hey, Arius! About our new nests... What d'ya say we check out Chimera Killer Island?"

Arius looked away after hearing Iris utter the name of the island where a legendary, dangerous creature lived. "Are you serious? Grandma always told us that place was super dangerous!"

Grandma was an elder siren who had lived the longest among their kind, nested in countless locations, and had the knowledge to prove it. She had told them all about Chimera Killer Island.

The Chimera Killer was a being that defeated the former master of the island, an impossibly powerful chimera, by itself. Although technically human, they had managed to become the one true ruler of an island filled with all manner of dangerous beasts. Given how sirens were perceived by humanity, there was little doubt that, should they encounter the Chimera Killer, they would likely meet their end.

The relationship between humans and sirens could hardly be called "good." While they weren't actively enemies, humans, especially those who made a living on the open seas, felt that sirens were dangerous, bothersome creatures.

Sirens were feared as monsters that charmed and ate humans with their songs, sunk boats, and took the form of beautiful young girls, but that wasn't at all the truth of the matter. While it was true their songs were capable of charming humans and other creatures, they had slim bodies designed for flying, with little difference between males and females. No doubt this was the source of the humans' confusion over their appearance. While it was true a siren could use its powers to defend itself against a human who came at them, they would never eat them. They wouldn't even think to.

That rumor likely came to fruition because of the fact sirens loved eating fresh, raw fish. Or at least that's what Grandma theorized. According to her, humans felt that eating raw fish was something only beasts did. And so, sirens went hundreds of years with barely any human interaction. Iris's suggestion to visit Chimera Killer Island was in direct violation of this way of life.

"Aw, c'mon!" she said. "Don't worry. I mean, think about it. The Chimera Killer appeared way before we were born, right?" Iris began explaining her reasoning to her friend.

"Well, yeah, but..."

"Which means no matter how big and strong the Chimera Killer used to be, they've gotta be way older now, right? And weaker! Plus, they may've already died from illness or something! It won't kill us to just fly overhead and check things out, right? If tough monsters like chimeras make it their home, that island must be something special!"

Iris piled on the logic, sensing her friend's resolve weaken. She said, "We'll check things out from above, and if it looks dangerous, we can just fly away. The Chimera Killer is a human, right? That means they can't fly!"

"Y-yeah, I guess you're right," said Arius.

"Awesome! It's settled then! Let's go!"

And so Iris dragged Arius into the air with her. Their destination? Chimera Killer Island. What they didn't know was that its master had left it months ago, rendering it a deserted island...

The sun had risen to the very top of the sky by the time the pair landed on Chimera Killer Island.

Iris looked around. "Wow, so this is it, huh? It looks pretty swell!"

"It looks like the Chimera Killer isn't anywhere to be found either," said Arius. "Thank goodness."

The pair of sirens had circled the island multiple times

in search of humanoid creatures. Once they confirmed there were none to be found, they made their way to the front of a cave. It was the single place on the island that appeared to show signs of human presence.

"So this is where the Chimera Killer lived?"

"I'm sure of it."

The nest had been modified by human hands to make it more livable.

Underneath a hole for light was a large container meant for catching rainwater. Clumsily constructed wooden shelves lined the stone walls, and in the corner of the cave was some sort of bedding made of dried vines. Next to that was a wooden box, likely brought in from outside the island. There was a series of lines carved into the walls, signifying how many days had passed since the Chimera Killer came to the island. The lines were so plentiful that they covered almost the entire cave. The sirens could feel in their bodies just how long the Chimera Killer lived there.

Hm? There's something strange about the way these lines are scratched...

Arius inspected the carvings carefully. There were six vertical lines, and a single horizontal one running through them, almost erasing the others.

"Huh? What's this?"

Meanwhile, Iris was peeking into the large box. She raised her voice upon discovering something and immediately brought her findings over to her friend.

"Hey, Arius. Do you know what these are?"

She showed her companion the insides of the bag she pulled from the chest. The bag was filled with shining flat rocks of some sort. There were tons of silver ones and even a handful of gold ones, too.

"Ah, these are gold and silver coins. Humans trade them for all sorts of stuff." Arius had a wealth of knowledge about the humans thanks to Grandma's teachings.

"Oh, and this looks like a letter written in human language."

Deeper inside the bag was a new-looking piece of parchment that had been rolled up.

"Let's see."

Arius began reading the letter out loud so Iris could understand as well.

I leave this behind for anyone who visits this island after me. To the unlucky, pitiable castaway who arrives on this island: do not give up hope. Live on. I lived here for twenty years. This money is my gift to you. Use it when you pass through the door on the top of the hill on the Day of Satur, on every seventh day. I wish you good fortune.

Alphonse Flugel

"The Day of Satur?"

Arius tilted his head in response to the words he'd never seen before. Was it some sort of legend passed down between humans? Supposedly it came at the end of every seven days.

"There wasn't anything at the top of the hill when we flew over, right?"

Iris was also puzzled. They'd circled the island to check for the Chimera Killer before landing, so they both knew exactly what hill the letter referred to. The problem was that there had been no such door when they passed overhead earlier.

"Hrm. I'm guessing that Alphonse is the Chimera Killer, but..." With the mysterious letter in hand, Arius began thinking about their next move.

"So? Whatcha wanna do? It doesn't look the Chimera Killer or any other dangerous monsters are here."

"Right? I think we can stick around for a while," Arius gave his siren companion his verdict.

Iris nodded happily in response. "Sounds good to me! I was just looking for a new place to make a nest, and this island looks perfect!"

And so, the pair set out to make sure everything on the island was in order. They confirmed locations for drinking water, checked to make sure the fish in the area were edible, and kept an eye out for any dangerous monsters. After finally finishing prep to set up their nests, the so-called "Day of Satur" arrived.

A black door suddenly appeared at the top of the hill. Iris and Arius noticed it during their third morning on the island.

"What's this thing doing here? It definitely wasn't here yesterday," Iris remarked and tilted her head in confusion, rushing to check things out after Arius mentioned it to her.

Up until yesterday, this mysterious black door with its golden handle and cat illustration didn't exist.

"Today's probably the 'Day of Satur' mentioned in that letter, which means this is the same door Alphonse mentioned," said Arius.

It must be some sort of magic. Unfortunately, the letter left behind didn't explain what existed beyond the door itself.

"Let's go in!" Iris said. "Seems like fun!"

"Hrm... Well, I guess it'll probably be fine," Arius said.

Arius thought on Iris's plan for a moment before quickly deciding to check things out. If the information in the letter was to be trusted, there was something wonderful on the other side of the door. He couldn't bring himself to believe that the letter was a trap.

"All right, I'm opening it up."

Arius put his hand on the golden handle and turned it, opening the door.

The sounds of ringing bells greeted them, along with a brightly lit room.

"Ah, good morning! You're quite early! Welcome to Western Cuisine Nekoya!"

A young lady with two small horns growing out of her head stopped wiping one of the many tables in the empty room, looking up and greeting the siren pair with a big smile. Her face showed no signs of fear or surprise in response to the monsters in front of her. Instead, it seemed like she was truly glad that they had come.

"Y-yeah, um...what is this place?" Arius asked nervously.

"Oh, it's a place where we serve food to visitors. We even have plenty of monster-kind customers like yourselves," Aletta replied confidently.

While sirens were monsters, she had grown used to dealing with everything from ogres to lamia, faeries, and even lizardmen. Given how everyone was welcome at Nekoya, what was there for her to be surprised by?

"So what do you say?" she asked. "Would you care to grab a bite?"

Arius and Iris glanced at each other and nodded.

"Well, since we're here and all..." Iris said. "What kind of food do you serve?"

"All kinds, really," Aletta responded, a somewhat troubled expression on her face.

Nekoya served so many dishes that she'd only really memorized about half of them. There were still plenty of menu items that she had difficulty explaining by herself even now. The fact that the two sirens in front of her had never visited before only made this situation all the more difficult.

Arius asked, "What do you mean by that?"

"U-um, uh, oh, I know! If you tell me what kind of food you like, I can get the master to recommend something!"

Questioned into a corner, Aletta finally came up with an idea. The master knew everything there was to know about Nekoya. Heck, he would even make dishes not on the menu sometimes. Aletta was confident he'd be able to come up with something for the pair.

"Um, then..."

"I want fresh fish! Raw, please!" Before Arius could even assemble words, Iris blurted out her request.

"Huh?! You can eat fish raw?! Ah, n-no, I mean, let me go ask the master!"

Surprised for a moment by the request, Aletta quickly regained her composure and nodded her head. She went to the back to talk to the master, who was likely still preparing for the lunchtime rush.

"What are you thinking, Iris? You know humans don't eat raw fish," Arius hissed.

"Huh? Really? That's so weird! Raw fish is great." Iris couldn't wrap her head around Arius's explanation. All she did was order her favorite food.

"Geez."

It wasn't worth getting frustrated over. It's not like they were going to actually serve raw fish. Arius let out a sigh. He knew full well that humans didn't make dishes like that. What he didn't realize was that he was only thinking within his own world's "common sense."

After a brief period, Aletta returned to the pair. "Um, he says we have a raw fish dish called 'carpaccio.' Would you like to try that?"

"What? Really?" Arius raised his voice in shock. Not once did he actually think the restaurant would have anything to serve them.

"Yeah! Hurry and bring it to us!" Iris, on the other hand, immediately requested the dish before her companion could snap back out of his shock.

Aletta smiled with relief at Iris's response. "Understood! Please wait a moment. I just finished wiping down those seats over there, so feel free to make yourself at home."

She vanished into the back to deliver the order.

"I can't believe they serve raw fish," Arius said.

Iris nodded. "Right? It's awesome!"

The siren pair shared the sentiment. Arius's eyes were open in surprise, while Iris had a huge smile on her face at the thought of eating something tasty.

"Maybe because this is another world?"

"Maybe! But isn't it great that we found out humans eat raw fish, too?" Iris was clearly pleased by this new discovery.

Before long, a human man, likely the master of the restaurant, appeared before the pair and set down something on the table.

"Sorry for the wait," he said.

Before the two sirens was a plate of thin, red slices of fresh fish topped with oranie.

"This is tuna carpaccio. Take your time and enjoy yourselves," the master said, then left them to it.

Arius's and Iris's eyes were glued to the plate in front of them. This strange fish dish looked incredibly appetizing.

The pair began digging in the moment the master left. They used the pointed human utensil known as a fork to dig into the slices of fish meat and lift them up. It would have been truly unfortunate if the fish were on the verge of going bad, but, as luck would have it, it was as fresh as fresh could be. The red color of the fish meat was reflected in their eyes, causing them to inadvertently gulp. The young pair took their first bites.

"It's delicious?!" they shouted simultaneously in surprise.

An incredible amount of savoriness was contained within the fish, and each bite helped draw it out. That savoriness fused with the unique saltiness of the seasoned marinade in their mouths. But it wasn't just that the fish was fresh: the blood had been carefully drained from the fish, and the meat itself was cut very deliberately. It was clear the master hadn't just arbitrarily taken a knife to the creature. The cutting style on its own was enough to turn this into a brand-new dish.

Neither siren was capable of uttering words at this point. They simply dug into their servings. The fish's savoriness, the oranie's spiciness, and the sourness of the juice that rested atop the entire dish... These three sensations made it certain that Arius's and Iris's hands wouldn't stop moving anytime soon.

Before long, their plate emptied out.

"Excuse me, would you like another serving?" Aletta asked.

"Absolutely!"

"Pretty please!"

They nodded not once, but twice.

"Wonderful. Then I'll be right back."

"Whew."

"Whoa."

By the time their hands had stopped moving, Arius's and Iris's stomachs were filled to the brim with fish.

So the Chimera Killer was talking about this place in his letter.

All the pieces fell into place for Arius. He finally understood why the Chimera Killer left behind all those silver and gold coins. The young siren glanced at Iris across the table. She, too, looked satisfied.

And so Arius came to a decision: he would make this island their new nest from here on out. After all, there was no way Iris would say no at this point. He was sure of it.

*Restaurant to
Another World*

CHAPTER 36
Hot Dogs

THE MASSIVE TREE Touichirou used to play on as a child stood tall, unchanged from its appearance eight years ago.

"Oooh! So today's the Day of Satur!"

Touichirou had been visiting the tree daily over the last few days. On this specific occasion, however, he noticed a familiar black door sitting on top of the massive natural structure. He raised his voice in pleasure. The last time he and Aya had used the door together was some eight years ago...

He had long since forgotten what day the Day of Satur was, so he made it a point to visit every day. Today told him that his efforts weren't for nothing; he was finally reunited with the door.

"Now then, shall we? Let's go, Aya..."

He reached for Aya's hand like he always did, only to remember that he was alone.

"...Yes, that's right. I'm alone now," he muttered sadly to himself before starting his climb up the tree.

When he was but a child, his arms were lanky and he was significantly shorter than Aya. This caused all sorts of trouble when it came to trying to climb the massive tree. However, as an adult, Touichirou had the trained body of a swordsman. A tree such as this was nothing to him. In no time at all, he made his way to the very top, where several thick branches sat, capable of holding the weight of multiple adults at once.

"Now this is a sight for sore eyes," he said.

From atop the giant tree, Touichirou looked back at the green mountains that stretched into the horizon underneath the blue sky filled with white, fluffy clouds. It was all just as he remembered it, and he took a moment to burn the view into his eyes once more.

"...I suppose I should get going."

Disappointed he couldn't share this unchanging vista with Aya, Touichirou decided to move on and accomplish his actual goal. Attached to the large tree trunk was a mysterious black door with a cat illustration on it. The swordsman placed his hand on its golden handle and turned it slowly.

The familiar sound of bells filled the air.

"Aye, welcome... Wait, is that you, Touichirou?" said the master.

Touichirou nodded. "It's been quite some time. Sorry to rush you, but could I get a hot dog and a cola, please?"

While he didn't say it aloud, he was relieved to find a familiar face.

"Of course. Will you be dining alone today?"

"Yes, I've come alone. Hence, I only need one serving. If you could prepare three to go, I'd be grateful."

The master repeated the order, and Touichirou nodded his head to confirm it all. Indeed, he had come alone on this day... Aya was not with him.

"Understood," the master said. "Sit tight."

Rather than pressing the subject, the master simply returned to the kitchen in silence.

"Hmph, this place hasn't changed a bit."

Touichirou found a seat and surveyed the restaurant. Reflected in his eyes were a handful of new faces alongside the usual batch of regulars who had been around for years. The demographic was as varied and chaotic as always: men, women, beings that weren't remotely human... Everyone came here to enjoy the good food and company.

Now that I look back on it, this restaurant was the start of it all. I would've never realized how vast the world truly is if I hadn't come here first.

Indeed, through Nekoya and the other world, Touichirou would go on to learn about just how mysterious and wonderful his own world was. As someone who grew up in a tiny town, this led to him becoming fascinated with the outside world, eventually causing him to leave his home on a journey of training and self-discovery. He wasn't alone in that, either; Touichirou had left the village with Aya, a priestess of the Lord of Earth and the daughter of a senior priest.

A lot's happened since then.

As part of his training journey, he and Aya crossed over to the Eastern Continent and went on to see a great deal of things. There were times when they nearly perished in battles with dangerous monsters. They got their hands on precious treasures and shared their joy with their companions. They shed tears over the loss of friends. Five long years had passed since Touichirou left home, but everything that happened in that period helped to shape him into the mighty warrior he'd become.

But that's all over now...

Touichirou's reveries were interrupted by a trio of voices.

"So, what's the plan when we go? Are we gonna start with goblin hunting?"

"Definitely not. We don't have any real combat experience, so any kind of hunting job is way too dangerous. We should try and see if we can tag along on some bodyguard gigs with merchants. It'll be easier to get to bigger cities that way, so we can kill two birds with one stone."

"I'd love to go to the royal capital in that case. Dad told me the most talented mage in all the Kingdom lives there."

Elsewhere in the restaurant were a group of three boys. They must've been about the same age as Aya and Touichirou when they first decided to set off on their journey. The three boys were enjoying colas with their meals while they discussed the details of their trip. They appeared to be from the Eastern Continent.

Touichirou thought back on his own experiences. A few months ago, he'd returned to his hometown after realizing he was no longer capable of continuing his own journey.

Despite essentially running away from home and abandoning his status as the family heir, he was welcomed back with open arms. Touichirou's father had cut ties with him, but he had long since passed away. The swordsman's younger brother had since inherited the family, and he was just happy to find that his older brother was safe and sound. The days that followed were so peaceful that it almost felt like all those years of adventuring had been nothing but a lie.

On the one hand, it was tremendously boring, but on the other, he no longer had to fear the next day and the vicious battles to the death that might've come with it. He was still unused to that sensation, but in time it would grow on him. If nothing else, Touichirou recognized that this was what normality felt like. That this was what his world and life used to be, once upon a time.

"Sorry for the wait! Here's your hot dog and cola!"

Touichirou was still lost in his own thoughts when a young demon waitress brought his food to him.

He was unfamiliar with the young lady who was wearing garments of the other world. The last time he visited the restaurant, the master was working alone in the kitchen. He must have hired her after Touichirou left town.

I see. Some things do change, then.

"Thank you, young lady," he replied.

"I'll bring over the rest of your food when you're ready to go. Take your time and enjoy yourself!"

The young lady placed down his food and drink with grace and then left to help another customer.

"Well then. I suppose I should dig in."

After watching the waitress leave, Touichirou set his eyes on the meal in front of him.

A hot dog. It was an otherworldly dish that he and Aya had loved since their youth.

The hot dog currently sitting atop the white plate in front of him was still steaming hot. The pork sausage was sandwiched within a baked bun, topped with a bitter red sauce and a spicy yellow one. It was a remarkably simple food, but it was also only available at the Restaurant to Another World.

The swordsman first grabbed the hot dog with his bare hands. This dish was much like rice balls, as it could be eaten without chopsticks or Eastern-Continent-styled utensils.

First...

Touichirou lifted the hot dog and took a single bite. In that very moment, his mouth was filled with its amazing flavors.

The first thing he felt was the taste of the toasted bun. The outer crust was crunchy, but the insides were fluffy, white, and sweet.

Looking back on it, we used to think this was the norm.

In the Mountain Nation, having rice with meals was customary. As such, its citizens knew little of bread and

327

its many forms. On the flip side, the Eastern Continent rarely engaged in rice dishes, focusing primarily on bread instead. This led Touichirou and Aya to expect great things, but they were instead faced with disappointment when they realized the bread there was nothing like what they ate at the Restaurant to Another World.

The next wave of flavor that washed over the swordsman was that of the pork sausage that sat snugly within the bun. Its surface had been cooked well, making for a pleasant initial crunch when he bit into it. The faint spiciness of the yellow sauce and the sour red sauce proved to be the perfect seasoning for the pork sausage, as its meaty flavor filled his mouth. Each bite into the meat saw it burst with juices that covered his tongue. The incredibly savory meat paired impossibly well with the blanket-like bun.

That being said, the real experience was only just beginning.

Mmph, the oranie and cabbage are delightful.

As Touichirou continued eating, he made his way beneath the sausage to a place that was filled with thinly-sliced, fried oranie and fresh, crunchy cabbage. Both vegetables acted from the shadows to support the main element of the dish.

Mm, mm. This really is the absolute best.

It had been quite some time since Touichirou last got to enjoy a hot dog, but it was as satisfying as ever. He'd traveled all across the land, adventuring in many dangerous places. The swordsman ate all manner of foods during his time away, but there was nothing quite like the hot dog.

I would have loved for Aya to have one fresh out of the kitchen.

The taste of the hot dog reminded Touichirou of the person who wasn't here: his beloved Aya. If she were next to him, surely this would have tasted even better.

And so he chugged down the last of the remaining ice-cold cola, letting the sweet liquid wash away the remaining hot dog aftertaste in his mouth.

"Master, that was delightful. I'm ready to pay."

"Aye, you got it. Your takeout is also ready."

"Fantastic. Thank you for everything."

Touichirou handed the master the money for the food and took the strange bag from him. The faint scent of hot dogs made its way to his nostrils, making him feel like he was hungry all over again.

"I'll be back."

"We'll be waiting!"

Touichirou exited the restaurant and collected himself.

"Now then, I should hurry."

The swordsman carefully made his way down the tree and hurried toward town.

He had a reason to rush: He had to get home before the hot dogs he was carrying grew cold.

"Just you wait, Aya. I'm gonna make sure you get your fill of hot dogs!"

Touichirou had to make sure that his beloved wife Aya got to eat her fill. After all, she couldn't leave the house because she was too busy taking care of their newborn child.

CHAPTER 37
Sweet Potato Tarts

THE MASTER AND PÂTISSIER of the "Flying Puppy," the cake shop on the floor above Nekoya, came down to the basement with order in hand early that morning, while the restaurant was still being prepared to open its doors.

"Yo. Hard at work as always, I see?"

"Yo-ho."

"Ah! Good morning, Master!"

Nekoya's master and Aletta both greeted the man as he strolled in with his wagon covered in cakes.

"G'morning to you, too, little lady. I've come bearing the gift cakes! I got the usual set aaand one special addition."

The Flying Puppy's pâtissier began unloading the usual suspects like pound cake and pudding, and then took out "today's special cake."

"Wow, those look amazing!"

Aletta couldn't help but voice her impressions. The surface was a reddish purple, but its insides were a rich, golden yellow. They looked unbelievably delicious. Just a glance at them told her they were packed with sweet amazingness.

"Don't they! I actually used stuff from this season's first harvest, you know?"

The pâtissier couldn't help but crack a smile. Every year, from the end of summer on "Vegetable Day" to the end of the year, this particular item was a staple of the Flying Puppy's fall menu. Regulars had been asking him to make it a normal addition to the menu for years, but he made it a point to limit it to this specific period. It was part of why it was so popular.

"It's sweet potato tart season around these parts now, you see."

The pâtissier grabbed a tart off of his wagon and handed it to Aletta.

"His treat. Give it a try."

"Huh?! Really?!" Aletta instantly turned to her boss.

"...Just the one."

"O-okay. H-here I go..." Aletta gulped and took a bite of the tart.

Ah. This is...

The baked treat crumbled and melted away, spreading its sweet flavor throughout her mouth. It had a fruity sweetness to it stronger than anything sold at Nekoya but also completely different from the cream available here. It was mysterious.

The baked dessert slowly made its way to the bottom of her stomach. The texture of the cake disappeared from Aletta's mouth, prompting her to take another bite. It only took a paltry five bites before the tart had vanished.

"How was it?" the pâtissier asked, his eyes narrowed and focused on the young lady.

"Delish!" responded Aletta with an instantaneous nod of her head.

"Well, I'm dang glad to hear it!"

The pâtissier, relieved by her words, turned to the master. "So I'm gonna be selling these starting today. You'll help a pal out, right? If I remember correctly, you got some sweet potato tart fans on that side, right?"

Not too long ago, the master had told his friend about the regular who only showed up when sweet potato tarts went on sale every year.

"Aye. In fact, I'm kinda getting the feeling they're gonna pop up today."

Nekoya had a regular who only showed up during

the fall months, their eyes keenly locked on to the sweet potato tarts and little else. It was about time for them to show their face. Or at least, that's what the master's honed instincts were saying.

It was the Day of Satur, and the remaining snow in the town at the foot of the mountain had finally melted, signaling the arrival of spring.

"Mm, today seems about right." Antonio, a priest of the Lord of Gold, ruler of the skies, nodded to himself. "I'm going to train for a bit. I'll be back by this evening."

Antonio briefly informed his wife and children of his business and set off to his training space.

"Hrm."

It was a location that had long been used for that purpose. Antonio looked up at the sheer cliff in front of him, impossible for any normal human to climb. It was so high up that its very top was covered in snow and nearly invisible. Fortunately, this was hardly a problem for Antonio. He was one of the most talented priests among those who worshiped the Lord of Gold.

"It's time for me to be on my way," Antonio whispered to himself and began preparations with great haste. He took off his simple top and wrapped it around his waist, revealing his well-built body and dark brown skin. The priest quietly closed his eyes and brought his hands together in prayer toward the master of the skies and lightning, the Lord of Gold. This great deity was one of the Ancient Six, legendary beings who took the form of the most powerful creature in all the land, the dragon. In order to have some of that power shared with himself, Antonio focused all his energy toward his prayer.

"Nrnn!"

The powers activated the moment he shouted into the air. Through his prayer, he was able to grow two golden wings out of his back, not unlike the ones the Lord of Gold had.

"Hrm."

The priest took a moment to practice moving his wings, mostly to help his body become acclimated with the new limbs it just sprouted. Once he was sure everything was in order, Antonio looked up into the sky and took flight. The ground below him grew smaller and smaller, the cliff of stone in front of him zooming by.

Near the very top was his objective. It was a small area jutting out from the cliff with only the narrowest of standing room. It was there that he found the suspicious black door stuck to the wall of stone.

"I hope he has them in already." Antonio put his top back on and opened the door.

The sound of bells filled the air.

"Master, I have arrived. Hrm?"

"Ah, welcome!"

The overwhelming presence of the Lord of Red immediately washed over Antonio the moment he stepped through the door. He turned and curiously tilted his head in response to the young waitress who hadn't been there when he last visited during the fall.

"Hm. Woman, who are you?"

"Oh! My name is Aletta, and I work here part-time as a waitress! It's a pleasure to meet you!"

Judging by the goat horns atop her head, Antonio deduced she was likely a follower of the old god of chaos, the same deity who had been cast to the great beyond by the Ancient Six. Most citizens of the north would be taken aback by Antonio's appearance, but there wasn't even a hint of fear in the young girl's eyes as she introduced herself. The priest concluded that she must've been hired during the winter, which would explain why she was used to dealing with all manner of customers. After all, this place was more than happy to serve even monster folk.

"My name is Antonio, and the pleasure is mine. By the way, are sweet potato tarts available for purchase yet?" He wasted no time.

"Absolutely! We just started selling them today in fact! Would you like to place an order?" Aletta answered his question with a beaming smile, and Antonio immediately nodded.

"Indeed. Can I get...five orders for now and some milk?"

"Understood! That'll be right out!"

After watching Aletta return to the kitchen, Antonio sat himself down at one of the tables.

Citizens of the north don't believe in the dragon gods, and yet here she is in the Lord of Red's holy territory. Fascinating.

It'd been about half a year since Antonio last dropped by the restaurant, so he took a look around to see what, if anything, had changed. He could sense the energies of the gods flowing throughout the room. This really was a bizarre place.

As per the usual, Nekoya was overflowing with the energies of the Lord of Red, one of the Ancient Six and master of the flame. When Antonio was just a young lad, he set out on a journey across the continent, partially so he could acquire his wings. On that journey, he learned all sorts of things and saw all manner of places, one of them being a temple built out of the Lord of Red's shed carcass from 500 years in the past. He recalled the deity's presence being overwhelmingly strong even then.

There's no doubt in my mind that the Lord of Red herself must be a patron of this place.

If the Lord of Red truly was frequenting this land, that would be the only possible explanation as to why. The implication, then, was that Nekoya's food was fit for even the gods.

Which I suppose explains the citizens of the north.

Antonio turned his attention to the customers who were already seated. Sure, there were beasts who worshiped the Lord of Green, and even lamia, followers of the Lord of Red. But for the most part, the customers here all lived in completely different cultures than Antonio. They were the citizens of the north, those who lived in a godless land.

He first heard of their kind some three years ago. It all began with a young man who claimed to be a treasure hunter. A bizarre job description to be sure. Apparently, he had been sent flying to Antonio's continent by the powers of an old ruin left behind by the long-eared invaders of yore. According to the man, who was searching for a way home, there was a continent beyond the "Sea of the Lord of Blue" to the north. He claimed that a great deal of people lived there, and his suggestion was that the land Antonio and his people lived on should be referred to as the "Southern Continent."

The people of Antonio's town found the man's story to be curious, but not the priest. If anything, it helped fill in the blanks. As someone who had long since been visiting this strange little restaurant, he now knew for sure that the people he saw here were citizens of the north.

Antonio rarely saw people from the Southern Continent at Nekoya. It was more than likely that most of the doors on the continent had simply not been discovered yet. Despite this, there was still a small but growing population of southerners appearing at Nekoya.

"Um, sorry for the wait! Here are your sweet potato tarts and milk!"

Just as Antonio found himself lost in thought, the woman from before returned with food in hand.

"Ooh! It's here!"

The priest immediately cut his thoughts short as his expression brightened. Sitting atop the dessert dish was a delicious golden kumaala, the sweet potato goodness he hadn't had the chance to eat in roughly half a year. Six years ago, it was this very dessert that had charmed Antonio.

"Take your time and enjoy!"

Antonio watched as the girl politely exchanged words with him and left, leaving him to immediately begin his assault on the sweet potato. He lifted the plate, small enough to fit in his hands, and bit into the potato.

The sweet, moist flavor of crushed and baked kumaala filled his mouth and melted away into his stomach.

Ah! Spring has finally arrived.

It wasn't until Antonio was eating a sweet potato tart that he felt like spring was truly here. Kumaala were easy to raise and store, so it was common to see them on the dinner table throughout the year. However, Antonio was never much of a fan. Boiling or running fresh kumaala over flames typically sucked the moisture out of them, leaving one with a dry mouth.

That's what made these sweet potatoes so different. They were sweet, moist, and melted away in Antonio's mouth. As far as he could tell, the master likely used milk or butter to make up for the missing moisture.

The way the sweet potatoes were mashed and reformed allowed for them to release their true sweetness.

If I could eat sweet potatoes like this over on my side, I would've never had any issues with kumaala.

But there was no use crying over what he didn't have. Instead, Antonio decided to enjoy the food available to him in this holy land and continued dumping sweet potato after sweet potato into his mouth, occasionally breaking to take a swig of some cold milk. It only took two bites for an entire sweet potato tart to vanish into thin air. Soon after, his entire plate was empty.

"Woman, I'd like another serving."

"Okaaay! Hold on just one moment!"

And so, the feasting resumed.

This is the perfect springtime food.

Antonio felt the arrival of spring as he filled his stomach with sweet potato tarts. This was his yearly tradition.

Antonio paid for his food and enjoyed a cup of "coffee," a bitter, black tea-like beverage. The beverage was effective at washing away the taste of the kumaala.

With his business taken care of, the priest returned to the cliff from whence he came.

"Hiyah!"

Antonio took his top off, and, with a yell, sprouted wings from his back and flew into the air.

"Another seven days to go."

The winged man hovered in place, all the while eyeing the spot where the door was. It wasn't a long period of time to wait, and yet it still felt like an eternity. Antonio flew away, vowing that he would return.

This was the one thing Antonio looked forward to every year. For him, spring had only just begun.

CHAPTER 38

Mushroom Spaghetti

THERE WAS A SMALL, nameless village in the middle of a forest. On its outskirts lived a healer named Alisa. She had been quietly waiting for the morning of the seventh day with excitement, and, as usual, smiled with relief when she spotted the black door.

"Thank goodness."

In the garden of her house in the woods, Alisa had a crowded little medicinal garden in which she planted difficult to handle herbs and the like. Three years ago, the black door first appeared there. Since then, she'd looked forward to visiting the Restaurant to Another World on the other side.

"I'd better hurry and get ready!"

And so, Alisa began prepping herself to go out for the day. She put on the homemade makeup she created from flowers and herbs she found in the forest and fields, then put on her best dress. Alisa was an orphan but had the good fortune of being picked up and raised by a kind healer who would go on to become her master. This same healer sewed her that very dress years ago. Lastly, Alisa took just a handful of coins from the money she earned selling medicine.

"All right, perfect. I can't wait!"

Despite her thoughts being set firmly on the joyous occasion that only came once every seven days, Alisa still found it in herself to make medicine until it was actually time to head out. In her excitement, she ended up botching a handful of things, but she was able to let it go because of the happy mood she was in.

It was around the time that the sun had settled directly overhead. Alisa made her way through the black door, right on schedule.

Her ears were met with the sound of bells as the door closed behind her, only to almost immediately reopen.

"Hey ho! Hiya, Alisa! Doing well?"

"Hiya, Meimei! I'm doing awesome."

The person who entered behind Alisa was a young lady with a big smile, brown skin, and large, white goat horns poking out from under her deep black hair.

"Awesome! That's what I like to hear! Now let's get to sitting!"

"Yup..."

She must be busy, since it's around lunch time.

Alisa's attention drifted toward the waitress collecting and bringing out orders to the customers. After a moment, she turned back to her friend and nodded her head enthusiastically. The pair sat down at one of the empty tables.

"Welcome." At about the same time, the master of the restaurant appeared with water in hand, having just brought out another customer's meal. "Will you be having the usual?"

Since first arriving at Nekoya a few years ago, the pair almost always ordered the same thing.

"Yes. I'll be having the Japanese-style mushroom spaghetti, please."

"And I'll be getting the cream mushroom spaghetti! Oh, and can you bring some choppy chopsticks, too?"

"You got it," replied the master with a nod, returning to the kitchen from whence he came.

"So? How've things been going for you over there?"

"Oh, same as usual. Just tending to the goats and all. What about you?"

"Same old, same old. I check on the herbs and flowers, collect mashruums in the forest, make herbal medicines... Oh, but recently a customer came by and..."

The pair of friends continued chatting with one another. Their conversation wasn't particularly deep or unique; just two friends enjoying their time together. For someone like Alisa who had been living alone ever since her master passed away due to illness, this shared time together was incredibly important.

"Hey, what's up? You've been looking over at the waitress girl for a while now!"

"N-no, it's nothing," replied Alisa, a smile on her face.

The healer thought this restaurant was rather comfy. If nothing else, her hometown would never allow a demon to work as a waitress. It would just never happen. Alisa's master was an incredibly talented healer, someone who was kind enough to look after an orphaned girl who had no blood relation to her. Yet even someone as good and decent as her had to hide her eyes and scales by wearing bandages and a hood to mask her face. Nobody cared about the demons.

"Yo! Booze! Three more bottles of that shochu stuff!"

"Roast chicken and fried rice balls if you please!"

"Then I'll be gettin' an order of scotch eggs!"

"Seconds on the carpaccio, please!"

"Lemme get that with smoked salmon next!"

"Mm. Another order. Omelet rice."

...At this point, little surprised Alisa about this

restaurant where ogres, lamia, lizardmen, and all sorts of monster folk could politely enjoy a hot meal together.

"Sorry for the wait. Here's your Japanese-style mushroom spaghetti and cream mushroom spaghetti."

Alisa had her thoughts interrupted by the arrival of the master with their food.

"Now this is what I'm talking about! Geez, it looks as delish as ever, Master!"

"It certainly does. Shall we dig in?"

The pair began eating their respective meals as the master left them to their devices. Alisa took her fork in hand and began burying it into the brown, Japanese-style spaghetti. Across from her, Meimei had chopsticks in hand as she waged a full-frontal attack on the white cream spaghetti.

It's amazing how she can eat with those sticks.

Alisa watched as Meimei skillfully scooped up the cream mushroom spaghetti doused in white knight sauce and ate. Her own stomach could be patient no longer, so she looked down to her own plate of food and began digging in. Mixed into her spaghetti were all manner of meats, dark green vegetables (Meimei explained that these were apparently "spinach"), oranie that had been fried to sweetness, and mashruums. The pasta itself had two different types of mashruums in it, both of which had completely different flavors and textures to them. The plentiful mashruums were what drew Alisa to the dish.

Gotta start with the mashruums.

Alisa used her fork to grab some mashruums along with spaghetti. Both mashruums were visually distinct from one another despite being dyed brown by the Japanese sauce covering the dish. One of them had been thinly sliced, while the other still had its full, black head intact. She brought them to her mouth alongside the noodles with their distinct buttery and salty flavor.

Mm. The stars of this plate are definitely the mashruums.

It went without saying that both mashruums were perfect in their deliciousness. Not only did they maintain the tastiness inherent in them, but they had also absorbed the flavors and juices of all the other ingredients. They were truly glorious.

There was the stir fried oranie's distinct sweetness, the savory flavor of the fatty meat, the buttery aroma of the noodles, and perhaps more important than all else, the Japanese sauce used to bring flavor to the entire dish.

With each bite into the mashruums, her mouth was filled with its savory juices. According to the master, the mashruums he used in the dish were the "shimeji" mashruum and the "mushroom." Alisa believed herself to be fairly knowledgeable in all manner of herbs and the like, but she'd never heard of these otherworldly mashruums before. Nonetheless, they were both tremendously delicious. The spinach included in the meal had an appetizing savoriness all its own, but it didn't stand a chance against the mashruums. Alisa's smile widened as she continued eating.

"Whew."

After making some progress in her meal, Alisa put her fork down for a moment. Meimei followed in kind.

"Then as usual..."

"Let's trade."

The pair washed out their mouths by sipping down some ice water before trading plates of the remaining spaghetti with one another. As young women living alone, they didn't exactly have deep pockets. So, when Meimei came up with an idea for them to be able to experience two flavors for the price of one, Alisa was all over it.

Yeah, this is super good, too.

The cream mushroom spaghetti she got from her friend was undeniably tasty. It wasn't particularly different from the pasta dish she ate before in the sense that they both included the same basic set of ingredients. The main difference came in the form of the way they were seasoned, so to speak.

The "cream" part of the dish's name referred to knight sauce. It was a rich sauce made using milk, butter, and wheat flour. Compared to the Japanese sauce of the other dish, it had a sweeter smell to it, on top of being significantly more buttery. Their combined sweetness melded well with the other ingredients. In fact, it was much more delicious than the standard knight sauce made for use during festivals and the like.

In Alisa's hometown, knight sauce was served during special days like festivals, but where Meimei was from, it was apparently still relatively unknown.

The first time the healer discovered it at the restaurant, she ended up shedding tears over how incredible it was. Meimei got a good laugh out of that.

It really is fascinating. Even though we live in the same world, what we eat couldn't be more different.

Alisa thought back on all the stories she had been told and giggled to herself.

According to Meimei, her hometown had a sauce that was similar in flavor to Japanese sauce. It was made by letting salted fish ferment, and it was something that made the rounds in her homeland, the Ocean Nation.

Being a resident of the Eastern Continent, Alisa knew what knight sauce was but hadn't the slightest clue about Japanese sauce.

This all served as a reminder that their cultures were altogether very different.

It really is fascinating.

There was no way Alisa, a healer who lived in the woods just outside her hometown, would ever come to meet someone like Meimei. She took a moment to express her gratitude to God as she continued eating the creamy pasta in front of her.

The pair finished eating at just about the same time and paid the master before heading to the exit together.

"Then I'll see you in seven days!"

"Yup! That's a promise."

Alisa stepped through the door somewhat sadly after exchanging promises with her friend. She once again stood in her familiar herb garden, but there was nobody next to her. Meimei must've come out the other side of the door from where she entered it, most likely the farm where she was taking care of goats.

"It's really too bad..."

Alisa sighed as she watched the black door behind her vanish into thin air after having fulfilled its primary objective. Meimei was a dear friend, but she could only spend time with her once every seven days, and only at the Restaurant to Another World.

It didn't matter if she was human and her friend a demon. It was nonetheless tremendously sad that she could only see her friend once in a blue moon. With those thoughts running through her mind, Alisa returned to her medicinal herb duties, quietly longing for the next time she'd be able to enjoy a delicious meal alongside her best friend.

CHAPTER 39
Seafood Pilaf

ALFRED WALKED THROUGH the city district of the imperial capital with his beautiful young mistress. While she was a noble from the Western Continent, Alfred himself was originally from the Empire.

"...And you're sure about this?" asked Aisha, the young noblewomen who hailed from the Desert Nation, her long black hair flowing over her light brown skin.

"Yes, quite sure in fact." Alfred nodded his head in response.

He had a secret plan in place to make his mistress happy. She already longed to return home, and he felt this to be the perfect remedy to that problem.

The imperial capital was still quite young. In fact, it had only begun to prosper when the great Wilhelm first came to call this country the "Empire." A paltry fifty years had passed since then. Progress took time.

There was once another nation that called itself the Empire. While it wasn't quite as massive as the Kingdom on the Eastern Continent, and didn't have the historical connections to the old kingdom said to be the first nation of man that the Duchy had, it was still apparently a prosperous country. But one day, the old Empire met its end. It was simply a matter of bad luck.

In the final stages of the great war, after humans and demons had engaged one another in countless battles, the area around the old Empire had become the final battleground. This battle was as fierce as it was terrible, ultimately engulfing many cities and towns in the flames of war. It was then that Altina, a demon general with incredible power and hundreds of demonic beasts at her beck and call, decided that she wanted the human city for herself. Leading her army of beasts and demon warriors who chose to serve at her side, she waged an assault on the imperial capital.

Needless to say, it was a slaughter. The demons of that era were ferociously powerful creatures, each a more than capable warrior in their own right. It didn't take long for the old capital to fall. Outside of a branch princess and her young son who were saved by the four legendary heroes, the entire royal family was murdered.

As luck would turn out, the branch princess who survived was none other than Lady Adelheid herself, with the prince in question being the boy who would eventually become the great Emperor Wilhelm. That would prove to be the beginning of the Empire as the world knew it.

All was not necessarily well from the outset: The Empire was quite the poor nation for some time. The citizens were left to survive off what few resources they had to their name. This all changed when Wilhelm discovered cobbler's tubers and spread them throughout the nation. This was precisely why the imperial capital still lacked in high-class shops and restaurants; there simply weren't enough people of great wealth in the nation.

And because it was located smack dab in the center of the Eastern Continent, the ocean was far, far away. It was a land that lacked the fine dishes that Aisha so desired.

"Honestly, I can hardly believe it. You're telling me there's a restaurant here that serves rice dishes with seafood?"

Aisha was born in the Desert Nation on the Western Continent. Rice was the most common of crops there, and seafood was fairly easy to come by in the port city she lived in. Both foods were woefully difficult to acquire in the Empire on the Eastern Continent. And when it came to the specifics meals that Aisha wanted, regardless of price, unless she borrowed the magical abilities of a mage and had them bring it specifically to her, there was no way she'd get to eat what she desired. So when Alfred proclaimed to know a restaurant that had what she was looking for, she couldn't believe his words.

"There are barely any shops around here. My word..."

The fact that the area Alfred led her to was barely populated only led credence to her belief that he was full of it. They were currently walking through a section of the city lined with mansions that wealthy noblemen and women from abroad used. These sorts typically had merchants directly bring them the things they wanted. Common sense dictated that there wouldn't be any restaurants around here.

"Well you see, I discovered that there is in fact one. It only recently appeared."

Alfred chuckled as he answered his mistress. Seven days ago, he spotted a halfling in this very area. What business could a halfling have in a noble district? Out of pure curiosity, he asked the small person what their business was, which led Alfred to make a startling discovery: the one place in the imperial capital that the "restaurant" appeared.

"See? We've arrived." Alfred pointed to an alleyway between two different mansions.

"...And pray tell, why is there a door there?"

Normally, nobody would even think to look for one in a place like this to begin with. Yet the fact remained that in the thin alleyway was a sturdy, black door. Aisha tilted her head.

"Um, well, that's just how it works, apparently."

Alfred couldn't help but chuckle as his mistress responded the exact same way he did seven days ago. He went on to describe what the halfling told him.

"It's the door to a restaurant that only opens once every seven days. The door to the Restaurant to Another World." He silently recalled the taste of the very dish Aisha so desired, the same amazing taste he experienced seven days ago.

The ringing of bells signified the opening of the door.

"Welcome to Western Cuisine Nekoya!" A waitress in a short skirt immediately turned around in response to the sound and greeted the two visitors.

"...A demon waitress? Just what sort of institution is this?"

After seeing the small horns growing out from the waitress's head, Aisha turned to Alfred more puzzled than ever. While there were many demons who called the imperial capital their home, you would never find them working in establishments meant for nobility.

"So it would seem. But I must stress, Lady Aisha, you mustn't let this surprise you. There does not appear to be any present today, but this restaurant even has monster customers." Alfred attempted to prepare his mistress for the most surprising of scenarios.

"Monsters?! Surely you jest."

The ringing of bells suddenly announced the arrival of a new visitor.

"Mm. In the way. Move."

"Eeeeee?!"

Aisha turned around only to be faced with a massive lizardman covered in ripped muscles. She let out a tiny cry of fear.

"M-my apologies, we'll be right out of your way."

"Mm."

Aisha was frozen rock solid with fear. Alfred grabbed his mistress and pulled her out of the way of the lizard-man, who simply nodded once before sitting himself down at an empty table and ordering a meal. The waitress seemed altogether unmoved by all of this as she simply smiled and took his order.

"Wh-wh-wh-what's wrong with this place?!"

Aisha's eyes were beginning to fill with tears in response to all the sudden horrors she was being forced to come face to face with.

"Quite frankly, even I'm a bit stunned. When I last came here, it was evening so I didn't really notice, but..."

The door to the restaurant opened again, this time welcoming a group of small faeries. Alfred chuckled once more. When he first came to Nekoya, he assumed all the stories he was told about it were naught but tall tales and fiction. It certainly didn't help that halflings loved all manner of jokes.

"In any case, shall we sit down? Um...are these spots open?"

Alfred walked up to one of the open tables next to some seats occupied by a beautiful imperial girl he swore he'd seen before and another woman who appeared to be a noble from Aisha's home country. The two of them were happily conversing with each other, lost in their own world. Alfred spoke to the man next to them, who wasn't involved in their conversation.

"...Yes. Do as you please." The man nodded with little to no interest.

Judging by his light brown skin, carefully treated shiny, black hair, and all the gold threads used on his attire, he was likely some sort of nobility from the Sand Nation.

"Is that so? Wonderful. Thank you very much. Come now, Lady Aisha. Over here." Alfred, relieved that he received permission to sit down, gestured to his mistress to come forward.

"Are you sure this place is really okay?"

Aisha was already exhausted from all the surprises. At the same time, she kept trying to convince herself that it was merely happenstance that the "siblings" seated next to them looked familiar to her. They couldn't possibly be who she suspected they were.

"Excuse me! We're ready to order."

Once he confirmed Aisha had taken a seat, Alfred called over to the waitress.

"Excellent! What will you be having?"

"Um, can we get two plates of seafood pilaf, please? Oh, and two cafas, er, coffees for after the meal?"

Alfred quickly placed their orders, the same things he ordered the last time he came in. This was the dish Aisha had longed for: "a rice dish with seafood."

"Of course! Thank you for your order. Your food will be out momentarily!"

The waitress returned to the master to deliver their order.

Sometime later...

"Sorry for the wait! Here are your orders of seafood pilaf."

The middle-aged master of the restaurant came out

himself, two large plates of food in hand, and set them down in front of the pair.

On each plate was a pile of beautiful rice mixed with thinly sliced vegetables, curled red shrimp, shucked shellfish, and white krakeen that had been skinned and cut into a grid with a kitchen knife. The pleasant, mouthwatering aroma of butter found its way into Aisha's nose.

"Please take your time."

Leaving those words behind, the master returned from whence he came.

"...I suppose it looks fine," Aisha remarked with a composed expression despite her watering mouth.

It was at that precise moment that her stomach also decided to respond in kind, letting out a noise that immediately turned her face bright red.

"Now, now. Let's eat before it gets cold!" Alfred did a remarkably elegant job of pretending he didn't hear a thing.

"F-fine!"

Still somewhat flustered, Aisha reached for a silver spoon and scooped up some of the rice and seafood from the plate.

...She took a bite.

Ah, this is lovely...

This was more than she could have ever hoped for. The moment Aisha began chewing, she was overwhelmed with a feeling of nostalgia so strong that it actually brought tears to her eyes.

The faint aroma of butter lingered over the soft rice, with all manner of spices (many of which were rather priceless in the Empire) used to season the dish. The rice absorbed the savory juices of the seafood, spreading them throughout Aisha's mouth with each bite. The base rice grain was so high quality that every time she swallowed, it invited her to eat more.

The various seafoods atop the rice were equally as wonderful. Everything was so fresh that it was hard to believe it had all come from the ocean. There was no foul smell to speak of, the elasticity of the small shripe was just right, and the krakeen had been cut in such a way as to make it easier to consume. The delicious soup was filled with some sort of shellfish that Aisha had never seen before, and even the sliced vegetables were surprising in their own way, with bright orange, yellow, and green ones mixed throughout the dish.

And because the rice absorbed the soup exuding out of said vegetables, its own flavor was elevated that much higher.

It didn't take long before the seafood pilaf had disappeared from Aisha's plate. All that remained was a sense of satisfaction in her stomach.

She let out a sigh, almost as if she were releasing the cozy warmth that had built up inside her.

"How was it, Lady Aisha? Was it to your liking?"

"Well, I suppose it was all right."

Aisha noticed Alfred's smile and immediately tried composing herself, a rice grain sitting just below her lips.

"Absolutely wonderful. I'm pleased as punch that you enjoyed your meal."

After confirming his mistress was more than satisfied, he began digging into his own plate of food. As expected, it was delicious.

I'm glad I was able to bring her here.

The food here was to his foreign mistress's liking, fortunately. She normally had quite the small appetite, but she laid waste to the seafood pilaf with incredible speed.

Hrm?

But as Alfred continued eating, he noticed something: Aisha was staring directly at his dish.

"Um, excuse me. Could I get another order of seafood pilaf, please?" Alfred signaled to the waitress.

"Of course! Coming right up."

"Huh...?! I-I didn't ask for more! I'm fine with just one plate!" Aisha immediately objected to the additional order.

"Yes, I'm quite aware of that. But as you know, I am an adult man, so one plate simply isn't enough to satisfy my hunger. However, this is quite the conundrum for me. I couldn't possibly finish a whole other serving on my own. Do you think you could provide me with assistance, Lady Aisha?"

His mistress was adorably flustered as he offered her an olive branch to take hold of.

"F-fine, I guess I have no choice but to help out!"

Aisha nodded her head, a smile incidentally slipping out.

What a troublesome mistress I have. Though I suppose that's part of her charm.

The moment they exited the restaurant, the door magically vanished into thin air.

"What a strange place."

"Well, it is another world after all."

The two exchanged words as they left the small alley behind them.

"Would you care to join me again some time, Lady Aisha?" Alfred presented his mistress with an offer he knew she couldn't refuse.

"I suppose I could take precious time out of my busy schedule to accompany you once every three days or so."

Aisha did her best to hide the pure joy slipping out from beneath the cracks of her calm demeanor.

"Ah, about that. The door to Nekoya only appears once every seven days."

"Huh?! Really?!"

Alfred watched as Aisha's expression darkened with sorrow.

We'll definitely have to come back in seven days.

He quietly planned out their next trip.

Restaurant to
Another World

CHAPTER 40

Katsudon

THIS IS A TALE from some twenty years ago, when the previous master of the Restaurant to Another World ran things.

※

"Now, now. Don't ya worry yourself. Ya got special permissions, ya see? Ya can use that weapon of yours just like ya always have."

It was the first day of his battle to the death. The old, one-eyed demon attendant, likely a survivor of the great demon war, looked at Lionel with his one eye.

"But the Demon King sure is kind! For just 10,000 gold coins, you can buy your way to freedom! The same amount they paid for ya. And since you're the fresh rookie everyone's so excited about, your reward for winning's gonna be that much bigger, ya hear me? If ya win today, you're gonna be earning 100 gold coins in one go. I'm damn jealous!"

Hmph, like hell you are.

Lionel could see in the old man's eye that he was looking at someone who was ready to head to his own death, and it pissed Lionel off big time.

"Well, good luck, pal! Your match is around noon. Try not to get yerself killed!"

And with that, the man exited the waiting room, leaving only Lionel and silence.

Why did it come to this?

How many times had Lionel asked himself that very question? Alone in the small room, surrounded by the faint scent of dried blood, he felt the uncomfortable texture of metal around his neck.

Just half a month ago, Lionel was leading a fulfilling life.

It was a life any demon of old would have enjoyed.

Yet now here he was, a magical collar wrapped around his neck to prevent him from fleeing, and all he could do was wait for death's cold embrace.

Lionel was born with a blessing so strong that had he been born one hundred years—no, even just fifty years earlier, it was said he could have been a demon king's right-hand man. His entire body was covered in steel-like muscles and fur, while his face had a distinguished, lion-like mane. His roar was enough to kill small animals on the spot, and he was capable of lifting stones larger than himself with no effort. His tail could smash a giant tree to pieces with one swipe, and, despite his size, he was as fast as any beast.

"Just make something tough enough that it won't bend or break due to my dumb power."

Lionel didn't request the dwarf blacksmith to make a sharp sword, but rather a large, blunt object that he could wield. The weapon he got back barely had a blade attached to it, but if swung with Lionel's strength, it could pierce iron and split a man in two with no problem.

Lionel was a man born to fight, which was why he left his village behind and threw himself into battle. When there was a fight to be had, he lived life as a mercenary with the ability to completely change the course of any given battle. When the fighting stopped, he continued to swing his blunt sword as a feared mountain bandit. It was said that any who came into contact with him would never be seen again. Lionel raised money fighting back the knights who were sent on missions to dispose of him and even served multiple large-bosomed witches. He lived life as a first-rate monster of sorts, with both humans and demons jealous of his incredible strength.

But eventually, those days came to an end.

"Heheh, whaddya think? One hell of an attack, right? I bet you can't even move! You see, I'm confident in my sword skills. Not just the one in my hand, but the one between these here legs, too. Heheheh."

Despite the disgusting things being said, the voice speaking to Lionel as he was stuck on the ground was beautiful.

Lionel didn't understand. What he knew for sure was that he was unable to get a single strike in. Instead, he found himself on the receiving end of but one attack from his enemy's thin sword. That attack was enough to make everything from the neck down crumble to the ground like a weighted stone.

"Fear not. You won't die. That's how this attack of mine works! In three days or so, you'll be able to move just fine. Same with those underlings of yours. That's how I stabbed 'em after all."

There was no longer anyone else on the battlefield who could move. The man continued speaking to Lionel.

"You see, according to the contract with my boss, I'm supposed to get 30% of the cash he makes from selling you and your belongings. It'd be a real big problem for me and my wallet if you just upped and died on me now. Sorry, pal. Today's your unlucky day."

Lionel just barely managed to get movement in his neck back, so he looked up at his chatty assailant. They at least appeared to be a half-elf but had the power of a monster.

"It sure is a good thing you were born in this era though. You're just as powerful as all the rumors said. Hell, if you were born at least fifty years earlier, you probably could've become the demon king. Then you would've been put down by Yomi, of course."

The half-elf's appearance was that of a boy too young to be called a man, or perhaps a young girl who had yet to blossom into a lady. Deep within his eyes was the innocent, desperate light of a child mixed with the light of a cold, sleazy old man.

"Feel free to brag about it later. 'I fought the legendary Alexander and lived to tell the tale!' I suppose you should probably do that while you're still alive, but hey, your call. It's probably less impressive if you're already dead."

The monster standing over Lionel introduced himself as one of the "legendary four heroes" who traveled the world, slayed the demon kings, and even killed the dark lord himself. The creature gave the signal to the carriers he brought with him who had been watching the one-sided battle unfold with stunned looks on their faces. They moved in to pick up Lionel.

"Y-you damn monster."

The words Lionel managed to squeeze out from his throat were laced with true fear. For the first time in his entire life, Lionel was scared. He had met a being who had been fighting on battlefields for over a hundred years. Someone who had perfected the way of the sword. Someone completely and utterly terrifying.

"Hahah, me? A monster?" The creature laughed lightly in response to Lionel's words and cast his eyes down at the warrior. "Sorry, but I don't qualify for the role. I'd have to be about as strong as Yomi if I wanted to be considered a true 'monster.'"

The creature then turned and made his way toward Lionel's bed. That was where he kept all the treasures he'd acquired up until now. Eventually, he was placed in a horse carriage with multiple others.

This was the beginning of Lionel's life undergoing a massive change. In the demon capital, he and his comrades would be sold as slaves to the highest bidder, with Lionel bringing in a hefty 10,000 gold coins alone. His buyer? Altina's child and ruler of the demon capital. This meant they were the tribe of the demon king.

Needless to say, those in said tribe didn't earn this status for themselves. They merely had the good fortune of sharing the same blood as the demon king who survived the war and the four legendary heroes. They had no real combat experience to call their own. That said, when the war ended and a new, young country called the Empire rose to power, they chose the path of least resistance that would result in the demons acquiring land with which to live on. They were one of the very few, truly high-class noble families who lived in the Empire.

As those who chose to lead the demons not through raw power, but through knowledge, law, and bloodline, they decided to make an example of Lionel. He was a creature who committed heinous acts within their territory and a remnant of a time when demons prized pure strength over all else. He was sent to the slave colosseum to provide bloody entertainment to the masses.

Of course, if that were all that was, Lionel had the confidence to survive. He would never lose to a human or a demon. The problem was that the other side was more than aware of this.

A manticore, eh?

His opponent in battle was a high-level monster that had been a sticky thorn in adventurer parties and small knight squads during the war. It took incredibly powerful magic (that of a demon king) to force it into submission.

Rationally speaking, even someone as powerful as Lionel had close to no chance of defeating the beast on his own.

Can I win? I couldn't even beat that gangly bastard before...

The experience of his singular, brutal loss colored all of Lionel's confidence. There was once a time when he believed himself to be strong, that he could defeat anyone.

Even one of the four heroes.

But reality was unkind. Lionel couldn't afford to have such reckless confidence. He had no chance against Alexander, a hero who, like Lionel, did not use any magic. In fact, his loss was so one-sided that he even found himself thinking he was glad he wasn't born during an era in which the four heroes were traveling the land together as a party.

This was an unforgivable personal defeat and more than enough to prompt Lionel to abandon his trust and confidence in himself. He clasped his hands together in the hopes of throwing away his fear of losing, of dying.

Psh, I'm bored...

Lionel looked like a prisoner on his way to the gallows as he stood up, trusty blunt sword in hand. He still wasn't sure how to spend the rest of his time alive.

That was when it happened.

"The hell's this?"

Behind his beloved blunt sword was a door. What was a black, wooden door doing in a room made of stone? Lionel stared directly at the illustration on its surface.

"Why in the blue hell is there a door here?"

Lionel turned around and looked at the door the old man from earlier had left through. It was made out of iron. In order to keep battle slaves like him from fleeing, the walls were made almost exclusively of stone and the doors made of steel. This thing was clearly out of place.

"Well, whatever. It's not like I've got long to live anyway."

Lionel sighed once before putting his hand on the golden handle and turning it.

The lion man's ears were met with the sound of bells singing.

"Oh, welcome."

Lionel suddenly closed his eyes, unused to the brightness of the room.

"Well, this is rare. Two new customers in one day?"

The demon opened his eyes in response to the voice speaking to him.

"Hey, old man. What is this place?"

Standing in front of him was an older, human man. He had short hair up top and a well-kept white beard. Despite his age, he was clearly in good shape.

"Well, ain't that a way to greet someone!" The old man laughed in response to Lionel's "greeting."

"This is Western Cuisine Nekoya. A restaurant, get me? From your point of view, it's a restaurant in another world. My name's Yamagata, and I'm the master of this fine culinary establishment."

Yamagata explained things like he always did.

"This is a restaurant...?"

Lionel looked around the inside of the room, his expression screaming, "Why the hell is this place in a colosseum?"

The place was fairly quiet. The only customers present were an older mage sipping on a glass of booze and eating some kind of brown food, and a middle-aged man who was viciously devouring what looked to be brown-colored mud of some kind.

"...Looks like you got a popularity problem, pal."

"Right?"

Yamagata simply laughed in response to Lionel's straight shooting.

"Not much I can do about it, to be honest. Doesn't look like there are too many entrances on the other side yet. I started serving folks like you some ten-ish years ago, when my grandson was just about to start elementary school. He's a high schooler now, and we still don't really get many customers of your kind around these parts."

"Entrances? You mean that black door?"

Lionel turned around to look at the very one he came through moments earlier. This time, however, he noticed the little bell attached to the top of it. That was likely what connected this restaurant and the colosseum where he came from.

"So, hows about it? Care to grab a bite? If you don't got no cash on you, I can just put it on your tab," Yamagata asked in a friendly voice.

"Well... You know what, why not? I'll eat something. I don't have any money though."

Lionel decided to accept the master's kind offer. He realized he hadn't really had anything proper to eat ever since losing that horrible battle, which caused his stomach to remember that it was, in fact, extremely hungry.

"So, what's good here anyway?"

The once proud warrior knew this could very well be his final meal, and if that were going to be the case, he at least wanted something delicious. If he could get a meat dish of some kind, that'd be perfect.

"Well, you're in luck, buddy. We got anything and everything, and it's all damn good. That being the case, if there's something specific you wanna eat, just lay it on me. It's a little tough trying to explain the menu to folks from your world." Yamagata chuckled.

"I see."

Lionel glanced at the customer devouring the brown mud-like stuff at the other table.

"Master! Another plate of this curry rice stuff!"

With amazing timing, the man had cleared out his plate and immediately requested another serving of "curry rice."

It was a dish of white stuff topped with brown stuff, and Lionel couldn't even imagine what it might taste like.

"Aye, you got it. Just give me a hot second. I wanna take this guy's order first."

The master responded to the other customer, paying no mind to the fact that Lionel was not only a demon but an intimidating-looking one at that. He may be human, but the man running the restaurant was clearly good-natured. Lionel decided to make his order.

"I guess for now, I'd just like some meat. Oh, and..." Lionel gulped. "Something to help me win... No, never mind."

Lionel stopped himself before he voiced his own weakness.

"Aye, you got it," Yamagata replied with a big smile and a nod of his head.

"You have something like that?"

"Just you wait and see!" Yamagata replied to the surprised lion man.

"Right then. Just hold on, and I'll get you all set up once I get that man his curry," said the master before happily trotting to the back where the kitchen probably was.

"...Just what is this place?"

Lionel was left to himself, a puzzled look on his face.

It's so bizarre.

He took a moment to survey his surroundings. The space was a clean, well-kept dining room. Each table and chair were lined up neatly, their surfaces sparklingly clean. There wasn't even a single crumb to be found on the floor. While there were no windows, there was a gentle light coming down from the ceiling. It felt like the middle of the day.

"Here you go, pal."

As Lionel glanced around the dining room, the master returned with tray in hand. First, he placed down a bowl filled with brown soup and sliced yellow vegetables. Next to that he set down a ceramic bowl with blue and white horizontal stripes running across it. On top of it was a lid with the very same pattern, preventing Lionel from seeing what was inside.

"What is this?"

"Well, you see, it's called 'katsudon.'"

The master responded with a word that Lionel had never heard before.

"Katsudon?"

"Yup. Katsudon."

Yamagata voiced the word once more and then went on to explain its meaning.

"You see, in the country I'm from, the word 'katsu' means 'to win' or 'victory.' The dish itself is packed with meat, eggs, and rice, so it's full of nutrients. It's the perfect meal for a fighting man, you get me?"

He finally lifted the lid off the bowl.

"Oh..."

A sweet aroma filled the air around Lionel, who couldn't help but let out a sound. Underneath the ceramic lid was a smattering of light brown, the yellow of the eggs, and some sort of white substance all mixed together into one colorful food.

Lionel's stomach let out a ferocious growl. He hadn't eaten anything remotely good since becoming a slave.

"Take your time and enjoy!"

And with that, the man called Yamagata cleared the table of any extraneous dishes and returned to the back.

"All right, let's see what this tastes like."

Lionel gulped and picked up the fork next to the bowl.

"I'll start with this."

The large man took his small fork and gently stabbed it into a piece of meat. As he lifted it closer to his mouth, the scent of the "katsudon" grew stronger.

"Here goes nothing."

He took a bite of the meat covered in some sort of breading and eggs...and nearly roared.

It was delicious. More delicious than anything he had ever tasted.

The first thing to hit Lionel was the sweetness of the seasoned eggs and the underlying flavor of the oranie. The two great tastes mixed with the juices dripping from the breading of the meat and sweetly spread across his tongue. Immediately following that was the meat itself. Despite having absorbed all manner of juices, the meat still had a tenderness to it. It was clearly some sort of high-quality pork, and each bite caused it to gently fall apart in Lionel's mouth.

It overflowed with meat juice and fat, which, when combined with the breading, made for an unbeatable fusion of flavors.

"Hm? What's this at the bottom?"

More than satisfied by the meat alone, Lionel noticed something as he reached for the next piece. There was something beneath the layer of meat.

"What is this?"

It was a food he'd never seen before. More than half of the bowl was filled with small white grains of some kind that had been stained light brown by the juices of the meat.

"Oh, this must be that 'rice' stuff the old man mentioned."

Lionel brought his fork down into the sea of white grains and lifted some from the bowl. The otherworldly, magical light of the restaurant made it easy to see how the white rice had mixed with the brown juices of the layer of meat.

He took a bite.

I see. Not bad.

The large man inspected the flavor with every chew and confirmed that the rice itself didn't appear to have much of a taste at all. Fortunately, it absorbed the juices of the meat, so in that sense it was still good. But something was missing.

I guess it's meant to be padding? Wait a second...

Lionel realized something and immediately looked at one of the other customers.

It was the middle-aged man furiously eating the so-called "curry rice." His clothes were in complete tatters, almost as if he had been in a storm. But judging by what his attire once looked like, he had to have been some kind of nobleman. Additionally, he was quite fit, which led Lionel to guess that he was also a skilled knight. The curry stuff he was devouring also had the "rice" stuff in it.

Watching him deliciously down the white rice and brown topping gave Lionel an idea.

What if he were to eat the layer of meat and the layer of rice below together in a single bite? He immediately brought the food up to his mouth to test his theory.

"OoooOOOHHHH!!!" Lionel roared out into the air.

This was it. By eating them together, the flavors of the meat and rice intertwined, almost as if they were destined for one another.

What is this stuff? It's unbelievable!

He hadn't noticed it before, but the meat by itself had a rich, thick flavor, while the rice was far lighter.

But when he combined the two into one bite, the dish reached its maximum potential. Lionel was convinced. He didn't care how uncouth it was, he lifted the bowl and directly placed his mouth on it, using his fork to shovel the food in as much as possible.

It's incredibleeeeeee!

Lionel's mouth was assaulted by a wild tidal wave of meat and rice. In fact, he barely had any time to chew on the food, the sounds of munching filling the air around him as the katsudon made its way to his stomach.

The sweet and warm katsudon satisfied his insides on a level of which Lionel had never experienced before. All his worries, his concerns about the upcoming battle, had disappeared that very instant. It wasn't just the katsudon, it was the fact that he was alive to experience it for himself. It felt like the happiest time of his life.

But all good things must eventually come to an end.

"…Wow."

Lionel finished up the salty vegetables, drank the rest of the soup, and let out a long sigh.

"I could still go for more."

A single bowl of katsudon simply wasn't enough to satisfy someone with such a large frame. Lionel had completely cleared out his serving, leaving not even a single grain of rice in the ceramic bowl. While he was certainly fuller than he was before he entered the restaurant, it just wasn't enough.

"Damn it all! If only I had money." Lionel muttered to himself, frustrated.

The day he became a slave warrior, he had all of his treasures taken from him. Lionel had no money to his name, and he likely wouldn't live past tomorrow. He would never again be able to experience this incredible food.

…If this were a different time, a different place, he could have easily intimidated a single chef into doing his bidding with no trouble at all, but Lionel didn't want to. Despite being a human, the master named Yamagata had treated him like a prized customer. There was no fear in his eyes. Doing harm to someone like that didn't feel right, and Lionel simply didn't want to do it.

"I guess that's it then..."

Just as Lionel was about to stand up...

"Aye, here you go, pal. A second bowl of katsudon."

The master gently placed another bowl on the table in front of Lionel.

"...Well, you know. After seeing how you downed that first bowl, I figured one wouldn't be enough to satisfy the likes of someone like you! If you don't want any more, I can just have it for lunch, so don't worry about it."

"I'll eat it!" Lionel nodded his head rapidly and lowered himself back into his chair.

"Great. You want another bowl after this? You can just pay me whenever you get the money. No worries."

"Absolutely! You have my thanks, old man!"

Once again extremely grateful for Yamagata's kindness, Lionel took fork in hand, ultimately devouring a grand total of five bowls before finally taking his leave of Nekoya.

Lionel stepped through the door, once again returning to the room that smelled of dry blood.

"Hrm, he did me a real solid."

The demon rubbed his stomach, now filled with kat-sudon. He couldn't even remember the last time he ate so well. It went without saying that the quality was beyond anything he'd ever experienced.

"Now then, I guess it's time to go make some money. Gotta pay for all that katsudon after all."

Lionel casually grabbed his giant sword and exited the waiting room with a bounce to his stroll. He no longer feared defeat. It didn't matter if he was facing a manticore or some other legendary beast, he'd just swing his sword as hard as he could and kill them till they were well and dead. Just like he always had.

The proud warrior made his way to the colosseum hav-ing come to that most simple of conclusions. There was no doubt in his step. He knew he would never lose again.

As soon as he entered the battlefield, the spectators burst into cheers, drunk off the smell of blood and death. It was their way of greeting the poor souls who would be forced to battle to the death. In return, Lionel let out a ferocious roar that could pierce the heavens itself. This was his declaration of war against the assholes who thought they could put him in the dirt.

...But Lionel couldn't have known.

He couldn't have known that after effortlessly defeat-ing the manticore with three strikes and without ever getting hit a single time, he would go on to defeat count-less dangerous enemies. He couldn't have known that in a single year he would earn enough to buy his own freedom.

He couldn't have known that this was the beginning of twenty years at the top of the colosseum as the stron-gest warrior in all its history.

He couldn't have known that this was the debut fight of the man who would eventually come to be known as the "Lion King."

Steamed Potatoes with Butter

I REMEMBER IT like it was just yesterday.

A full season had passed since I had started working at the Restaurant to Another World. That was around the time when I first ate "it."

I typically work from early in the morning before Nekoya opens its doors, all the way until after the last customers leave.

The first thing I do when I come in is clean myself under the warm water. I use this lovely scented oil that completely washes away all the dirt and filth on me. It's amazing! When I run the soft cloth in the "shower room" over my skin, it gets all sudsy and everything! Apparently, the oil I use is called "body soap," while the stuff for washing my hair is called "shampoo." Crazy, huh?

The master of the restaurant always tells me to make sure that I'm nice and clean before I start working. According to him, a place that serves food to customers always has to be clean, and that includes the employees!

To be honest, I always feel a little reluctant about using his stuff to clean myself. It feels like I'm wasting his precious belongings. But I guess since he wants me to, it's not too big a deal.

At the end of the day, I can't afford to lose this job.

So anyway, after I wash myself, I'm always shocked by just how nice I look! Not a speck of grime or dirt on my slightly tanned skin, and I end up smelling really wonderful!

After that, I put on the comfortable undergarments that hug my body perfectly and slip into my otherworldly waitress uniform. It's a tiny bit embarrassing because you can see so much of my legs, but it's a lovingly crafted uniform!

After eating a delicious breakfast with the master, I clean the dining room and help him out with all sorts of chores before the customers arrive.

"Hrm, just the meat and potatoes aren't gonna be enough at this rate. I'm gonna go grab some stuff, so can you come with me?"

"Of course!"

That particular day, the master apparently didn't have everything he needed to make a dish, so he took me with him to go get the rest of the ingredients.

I follow him through a silver door and into a small room in the back of the kitchen. After the master presses the second protruding square from the top, the room starts to shake a little, and we exit into a completely new place.

This is the room where the master keeps all the food he uses for cooking. There are all kinds of brown boxes, strange see-through bags filled with packaged food, and all sorts of other things!

"All right. I'm gonna grab the meat, so you get this, Aletta. Just take it straight to the kitchen. It may be a little heavy for a girl your size, so be careful."

The master then heads to the cold room in the back where the food is stored, leaving me to carry a small box.

"No problem!"

It's a little heavy, but it's no trouble for me! I grab the box and enter the moving room, pressing the second protrusion on the wall. After putting the box in the kitchen, it isn't long before the master returns with a large piece of meat in hand.

"Perfect. Time to get this party started!"

He puts the meat down and opens the box I brought down for him.

"Ah, are these cobbler's tubers?"

I'm very familiar with the foodstuffs the master takes out from the box. They're lumpy cobbler's tubers still covered in dirt. Oh! Apparently in his world, they're called "potatoes."

The other world's vegetables are sometimes super strange! For example, the karoots over there are pointy, and peeled oranie are white on the inside. But tubers are different. They look exactly like the ones from my world.

"Ah, I guess potatoes are the only ones that look and taste about the same in both our worlds, eh?"

The master examines the cobbler's tubers and comments, almost as if he's responding to my inner thoughts. I bet he must feel weird when he sees how different our vegetables are compared to the ones he's used to!

"Hm? What's up, Aletta?"

After inspecting the goods for a bit, the master places them in the cleaning space and calls out to me, a worried expression on his face. He's probably concerned because I was staring at the tubers for so long.

"Oh, no, I'm fine. It's just...I don't have many good memories when it comes to tubers."

I try my best to smile.

"I didn't realize you weren't a fan."

I shake my head in response. "It's not that. All the dishes you make with tubers are really delicious. I love them! But when I use them to cook, it never turns out very good..."

I tell him the truth, even if it does make me a little sad.

I honestly don't hate tubers at all. In fact, I think they're pretty tasty when warmed up. But when I look at uncooked tubers, they just remind me of my life before the master took me in. It brings me back to when I was eating cold tubers all alone.

Day after day, they were all I could afford to eat. At some point, I stopped seeing them as a food; they were just a means with which to keep myself alive. Before I found my way to Nekoya, filling my stomach was priority number one. I didn't have the luxury of worrying about taste or anything else.

And unlike the master, I can't really cook. I spent so many of my days making vegetable and tuber soup or just boiling tubers on their own. That's about the extent of my cooking abilities.

"I see... That's right, you did say something about not being able to cook."

The master stops for a moment and then smiles.

"All right, how about I teach you how to make a simple but delicious potato dish?"

"Huh? You mean me? Cooking?"

I blink in surprise at the master's sudden offer.

"Aye. I remember Gramps telling me a while back that you folks over there don't really steam foods. Truth be told, steaming potatoes is really, really easy. I figure you can pick up how to do it pretty quickly. Of course, this'll be after we close for the day." The master points to the tubers. "In the meantime, could you wash those for me, Aletta? You just have to get the dirt off," he says before splitting the meat and beginning to prep for cooking.

"Yes, of course!"

I'm super curious as to what this "steamed" food is, but I decide to focus on doing the job asked of me first. I use the mysterious magic tool that produces water just by turning a handle on it to wash the tubers, and eventually it's time for the customers to start showing up.

So begins my day of work.

It's nighttime. After seeing off the last customer, carrying her large pot of stew home, the master emerges from the kitchen with some sort of tool in his hands. He places it on the table.

"Um, Master? What is that?"

"Ah, this here is a steamer. This is what we're gonna use to steam those potatoes. That said, as long as you don't let them get moist from the steam, you can also use a strainer."

The master takes the lid off the "steamer" and quickly washes out its insides. He then tosses in some of the potatoes, each one with a plus mark carved into them. The master then grabs a shallow pot just large enough for the "steamer" to sit atop of and pours some water into it. He doesn't attempt to fill it up, instead settling for less than half.

"Huh...? Master, is this going to be enough water?"

At this rate, the tubers are going to end up half-cooked! But the master simply laughs in response.

"Yup, this is just right. Too much water and it'll take too long to boil. You see, steaming isn't about boiling the food. You know how if you heat water in a pot long enough, it'll start to give off steam? We're gonna use that steam to cook the food."

The master places the pot on top of the magical tool for producing fire and lights the flames. It's not long before white steam begins exiting the top of the "steamer."

"I had two cooking teachers growing up. One of them was Gramps, the other was a man who specialized in things like dumplings and steamed foods. He had me making fried rice and these kinds of foods over and over again for practice. Making shumai and manju takes quite a bit of work, but steaming potatoes ain't so tough."

The master seemed to enjoy himself as he watched the white steam rise out of the pot. He always looks like he he's having so much fun when he cooks.

"Wow..."

I also can't help but stare as the white steam billows out of the "steamer." I can sense something delicious in the air.

"...All right, that about does it." The master whispers to himself, stops the flames, lifts the "steamer" off of the pot, and opens it up.

"Wooow..."

I can't help but raise my voice when I see the cobbler's tubers inside.

The meat of the tubers visible from the plus-shaped cuts in them is golden brown. They smell so good I can hear my own stomach growl!

"You can tell whether it's been cooked properly or not by jamming this into one of them. Give it a try."

"O-okay. Ah."

Just as the master says, I take the thin, pointy stick from his hands and stab it into the tuber. It takes almost no effort to pierce, gently sliding right into the food.

"Just like that. If it goes straight through with no trouble, you're all done. All that's left is to season it how you like."

The master disappears into the kitchen and returns with all manner of seasoning in hand.

"Salt, cheese, miso, soy sauce, ketchup, mayo... Topping steamed potatoes with something salty seems to be a thing folks do, but as far as I'm concerned, this is the one true answer."

The master drops a single square-shaped something or other right on top of the tuber and hands it to me on a plate with a fork.

"A steamed potato with butter. The absolute basic of basics."

Sitting on top of the plate is a piping hot cobbler's tuber topped with melting butter that slowly starts making its way across its surface.

The scent of melted butter mixes with the hot tuber's aroma, melding into one irresistible scent.

Meanwhile, the master prepares a tuber for himself, also using butter as a topping.

"Thank you, oh god of demons, for this, my daily bread. I offer you my gratitude."

I watch the master as he cuts a small piece off the tuber with his fork and deliciously eats it. I say a quick prayer and immediately start my own food journey, incapable of holding out any longer.

I copy the master's technique, cutting out a small piece before blowing on it to cool it down.

As I bite down into it, my mouth is filled with the sweet flavor of the cobbler's tuber and the slight saltiness of the butter.

It's wonderful!

Instead of words, hot air escapes my mouth as I attempt to eat without burning myself. The cobbler's tuber is still piping hot, and each time I open my mouth a little to release the heat, I can feel it further crumble atop my tongue.

But because of the melted butter, it's easy to eat and comfortably goes down the throat despite its temperature.

Its richer-than-usual flavor must be because of the unusual way in which the master cooked it. It's delicious!

I've never had a cobbler's tuber that tasted this amazing in my whole life, and before I know it, all that remains is the skin.

"You see, the thing about steamed potatoes is that they're delicious all on their own. You can pretty much season them however you want. Ah, would you like another?"

I immediately nodded my head to the master's offer. He's always so kind and thoughtful. Right now, I feel like I could eat a million of these!

I wonder if I'll really be able to cook them, too.

Sarah has a pot and a strainer at her house, which means I have everything I need to give it a shot.

It'll probably take tons of practice before I'm able to do it like the master, but even so... Before the master saved me, I had eaten nothing but boiled cobbler's tubers every single day. If there's a chance I can make something way tastier than those all on my own, I can't afford to be scared of messing up.

First thing's first. Once I get home, I'll give it a try.

I poured a little bit of mayo on my tuber while thinking to myself.

It was in this very moment that I finally understood that cobbler's tubers weren't just a thing I ate to keep myself alive, but a delicious food in their own right.

TO BE CONTINUED IN
Restaurant to Another World Vol. 3